A DREAM
OF KINSHIP

Richard Cowper

A TIMESCAPE BOOK
PUBLISHED BY POCKET BOOKS NEW YORK

Another *Original* publication of TIMESCAPE BOOKS

A Timescape Book published by
POCKET BOOKS, a Simon & Schuster division of
GULF & WESTERN CORPORATION
1230 Avenue of the Americas, New York, N.Y. 10020

ISBN: 0-671-43304-0

First Timescape Books printing August, 1981

10 9 8 7 6 5 4 3 2 1

POCKET and colophon are trademarks of Simon & Schuster.

Use of the TIMESCAPE trademark under exclusive license
from trademark owner.

Printed in the U.S.A.

CONTENTS

The Seven Kingdoms
circa A.D. 3000

PART
OF 6th KINGDOM
(DYFEDD'S)

SEVERN
REACH

■ New Bristol

(PART
OF 4th
KINGDOM)

BRITTANY

Corlay

MENDIP ISLE

EXMOOR
(PART
OF 1st
KINGDOM)

QUANTOCK
ISLE

Tallon's

Taunton Reach

SOMERSEA

Chardport

Broadbury

BLACK-
DOWN

NORTH DORSET
(PART OF 2nd
KINGDOM)

Sidbury

FRENCH CHANNEL

PART I

CORLAY

Chapter One

January 3rd, A.D. 3019. Dawn of a cold hard day. A low, flat millstone of a sky remorselessly grinding out the thin, gray flour of a winter's daybreak against the rocky coast of Brittany. Out to sea the Breton trading schooner *Sans Pareil*, swinging listlessly at anchor, awaited the breeze that would nudge her the few remaining kilometers southeast into the harbor of St. Brieuc. The slow deep swells of the Atlantic, rolling ponderously up the French Channel, lifted and lowered the schooner as if weighing it thoughtfully before moving on to other things. The ship's timbers sighed resignedly: a new block high up in the rigging squeaked in protest: moisture trickling down a halyard gathered at a splice and wept quietly into the scuppers. By slow degrees the riding light at the masthead grew paler and paler until it was scarcely visible at all.

A man emerged from the cabin into the still-shadowed well, muttered a word of greeting to the dozing watchman at the helm and made his way forward. Grasping a dew-damp stay in his right hand he leaned out over the ship's side, fumbled with the buttons of his leather breech-flap and then urinated powerfully into the gray, indifferent waters below him. A long arching mane of steam wavered like a ghostly pennant in the cold, still air and was lost in the mist. The man yawned, fastened up his flap, spat explosively, then thrust back the scuttle of his patched, leather cape and scratched vigorously at his short grizzled hair and beard. That done he cupped his hands, blew into them and rubbed them briskly together. And all the while his alert blue eyes scanned the rocky coastline which was slowly beginning to emerge from the thinning mist.

This man was not a member of the crew, though like so many inhabitants of the Seven Kingdoms he was no stranger to the sea. By profession (to use a term which he himself would surely have scorned) he was a furniture

13

maker, but his true calling was itinerant Jack-of-all-Trades.
Tinker, chairmaker, clock-mender, water-diviner, the Magpie traveled the Kingdoms of the West and his caravan
was known from Edinboro' to Lyon. Formally speaking
he owed fealty to Earl Robert, Lord of the First Kingdom,
having been born on the Isle of Blackdown fifty-three
years before, but in practice he was his own master and
he made a fair living from the skill of his nimble fingers
and the sharp wits he had been gifted with.

To look at he was nothing very special. Somewhat less
than average height, broad-shouldered and barrel-chested,
with arms a thought longer than was usual (his fingertips
just reached to his knee-caps), nevertheless he was not the
man you would choose to pick a quarrel with. And in this
you would surely be wise, for the Magpie had already
handed more than one man his final pass into the next
world. He did not boast about it—indeed he hardly ever
spoke of it at all—but the fact that he had done it lent him
a subtle aura of quiet self-confidence that other men detected like a pungent warning scent. It made them pause,
think twice, and more often than not, elect to give him the
benefit of a doubt.

But this man possessed one especial talent which set him
apart from all but a handful of his fellows, while to those
select few it linked him with a tie stronger than any tie of
blood. The Magpie was *huesh*. Translated out of its archaic
Cornish tongue this marked him out as being blessed (or
cursed, he sometimes thought) with the gift of second sight.
It was the *huesh* which had driven him aboard the *Sans
Pareil* in New Bristol and would assuredly drive him
ashore the moment they docked in St. Brieuc, for whatever else the *huesh* might be it was not a command that
could be lightly ignored.

Feeling the first stirrings of a breeze upon his bare neck
he hefted up the hood of his cape and made his way astern
just as two deck hands emerged from the hold, headed
sleepily for the anchor windlass and leaned their weight
against the spokes. The schooner's sails flapped wetly as
she crept forward along her dripping cable, paused on the
slow uplift of a rising swell, hung for a moment, then
dipped into the long decline of the following trough. The
Breton skipper appeared at the companionway, glanced up
at the leaden sky, grunted to the watchman and took over

the wheel. A minute later, festooned with weed, the anchor rose to the surface and thumped against the bow.

Escorted by a raucous squabble of sea birds and helped by a flooding tide the *Sans Pareil* entered the harbor of St. Brieuc just as the cathedral clock commenced its elaborate chiming of the ninth hour. By the time the first quarter had floated out across the town the schooner was tied up alongside the cobbled quay and the sails were coming down. The Magpie shook the Captain by the hand, slung his knapsack across his shoulder, stepped ashore and glanced along the waterfront.

Already the port was astir. Fishing boats were unloading; others preparing to put to sea; iron-shod barrows rattled over the uneven cobbles; voices shouted; blocks and winches squealed: the racket of sawing and hammering echoed back and forth across the narrow water. And permeating everything was the wild shrieking of the gulls as they swirled in a perpetual blizzard around and around the leafless forest of bare masts.

The Magpie sniffed the air like a dog then began picking his way among the net-menders and the heaps of empty fish baskets, heading toward one of the shabby waterside taverns. Scarcely had he entered and thrust back his hood than there came a great shout from the shadows: *"Sacré Oiseau! C'est La Pie!"*

The Magpie grinned and dropped his knapsack on to a vacant settle. "Well met once more, eh, Belle?"

A vast woman, sheathed in a stained apron of unbleached canvas, came sailing out from the back of the tavern like a full-rigged man-of-war. She grappled the Magpie to her enormous bosom and kissed him heartily on both cheeks. "Three years!" she cried, thrusting him out at arm's length. "Do I lie? Where has the rogue been? Whose bed has he been warming, hey?"

"Ah, *ma plus Belle.* Could I ever deceive *you?*"

"The wretch!" she laughed. "He has only come back for my *moules!* Confess now!"

"And your wine, Belle. You're forgetting the wine!"

"Monster!" she roared, gripping the flesh of his cheek between finger and thumb and tweaking it fondly. "Come, old gray dog. In beside the fire and tell me all. Môme! A place here, you offspring of a snail!"

The Magpie allowed the woman to conduct him to the seat of honor—the inglenook settle beside the glowing fire—while the little serving wench scurried up, grinning broadly, and set before him a basket of white bread, a pewter bowl and spoon and two tumblers. Belle vanished into the recesses at the back and returned a moment later carrying a bottle of wine. She poured out two brimming measures then set the bottle down on the table and eased her vast bulk into the opposite seat. She handed one glass to him and raised her own. "So, Ma Pie," she said in an altogether gentler tone. "Tell me what brings you back to St. Brieuc in the teeth of winter?"

"I'm on my way to Corlay."

"Corlay? You?" Her surprise was evident. "Why?"

"I have somebody to meet there."

She screwed up her eyes, regarded him pensively for a moment and then murmured: "We hear things have not been going so well for the Kinsfolk on your side of the water."

The serving maid brought a steaming tureen of shellfish soup to the table and set it down before the Magpie. Belle reached over, scooped deep with the ladle and tipped the fragrant broth into his bowl.

The Magpie tore off a crust of bread, dunked it, and chewed it with unfeigned relish. "Ah, there's none like this anywhere," he said. "You're a marvel, Belle."

Belle nodded complacently and helped herself to another mouthful of the harsh red wine. "You sailed from Black-down?"

"New Bristol."

"And how are things there?"

The Magpie twitched his shoulders. "As always. A bit worse, maybe. The crows . . ." He shrugged again and left his sentence unfinished.

"Ah. Here too," she sighed.

"Is that a fact?"

Belle nodded. "The Queen is old," she murmured. "To-day Duke Alain drives the cart and M'sieu Corbeau is perched at his shoulder. They say Corlay lives on borrowed time." She broke off a piece of bread and dipped it in the tureen. "They mark all who enter and leave the sanctuary. So I have heard."

The Magpie regarded her levelly over his lifted spoon. "Do you know why, Belle?"

"Why? No. There are rumors of course."

"What sort of rumors?"

Belle raised her head and glanced swiftly around to see if they could be overheard. Leaning forward until her lips were close to his ears she whispered: "They speak of a miracle."

The Magpie stared at her for a long moment and then returned his attention to his food. Before she could add anything two men uniformed in the black leather tunics of the Secular Arm entered the tavern and called for soup and wine. Belle heaved herself up, touched the Magpie lightly on the neck and sailed off to attend to her business.

Although it was barely three hours past noon the daylight was already beginning to fade as the Magpie gained the crest of the final hill that lay between him and his destination. Below him, some two kilometers to the east, he could just make out the gray ribbon of the high road to St. Brieuc wriggling back and forth across the floor of the valley. A faint, misty chaplet of lights was all that remained visible of the village from which the castle took its name and where, if Belle's information was correct, the agents of the Secular Arm were keeping watch on any stranger who visited the sanctuary.

Leaning his back against the gnarled trunk of a chestnut tree he unlooped a leather flask from his belt, tilted his head and filled his mouth with brandy. From the shadows all around him came the faint patter of water drops dripping on to the drifts of dead and decaying leaves. He swallowed the spirit a little at a time, savoring it gratefully, conscious of the warmth trickling down into his chilled stomach, while his eyes ranged over the hillside seeking for a path which would not prove too treacherous and would yet allow him cover.

Having found what he sought he allowed his gaze to wander on up to the head of the valley where the distant turrets of Corlay were now sharp silhouettes against the tarnished silver of the western sky. He watched the lights of the castle beginning to prick through the gloom and he saw a plume of smoke waver up from some invisible chimney among the battlements. It rose hesitantly, questing this way and that, and was suddenly shredded and scattered by the freshening wind from the Channel away to the north. A bright vision of the blazing hearth that lay below the column of smoke made him shiver abruptly. He took a final, comforting gulp of brandy, wiped his lips with the back of his hand, then thumped home the stopper and returned the flask to its place on his belt. Taking a firm grip with one hand on the stout ash pole he had selected for a staff he hooked the thumb of his other hand under the strap of his satchel and strode off along the crest of the ridge.

Half an hour later he scrambled up the treacherous bank of a scrub-filled gully, skirted an empty sheep-fold and found himself standing on the ancient slabs of quarried stone that paved the road up to Corlay. Long ago huge oaks and beeches had lined this route, casting a welcome summer shade upon all those who toiled up the steep incline to the château, but few of these giants remained and the leafless saplings which the Kinsfolk had planted to replace them seemed tokens of hope more than of expectation. Stamping his wet boots to restore some feeling in his frozen feet the Magpie set off on the final stage of his long journey.

Directly above the outer gate of the château four carved marble escutcheons had been set side by side into the wall of the gatehouse. Each bore the coat of arms of one of the four royal families who had at one time or another occupied Corlay. Hovering protectively above these, so new that it appeared startlingly white in the thickening gloom, was a spread-winged effigy representing the Bird of Kinship. The sculptor had fashioned his vision in such a way that the airy, soaring, upsweep of the wings combined together with the downward droop of the head to suggest a mingling of aspiration and compassion that was truly unearthly.

As he plodded toward the gatehouse the Magpie noted the avian symbol but experienced no appreciable lifting of the spirit other than the relief normal to a footsore and weary traveler who has at last reached his destination. The outer gates stood open so he walked through and peered about him. Hearing voices behind a door which was set into the gatehouse wall he rapped on it with the butt of his staff and heard a cheery voice cry: *"Entrez! Entrez!"*

He twisted the latch ring, thrust open the door and stepped over the foot-worn threshold to find himself standing in a sort of office. Seated on stools around an iron stove were two men and two women. An oil lamp suspended by a chain from one of the low rafters cast a warm glow over their faces. Between the stove and the doorway where the Magpie stood was a wooden counter, constructed in two sections and bridged by a hinged flap now laid back. Lying upon the counter was an open register.

The Magpie thrust back his hood and nodded to one of the men who had risen to his feet and was now advancing toward him. "The gate stood open," he said by way of explanation. "I saw no bell."

"Those who wish to come, come: those who wish to go, go," said the man, smiling. "That gate is never closed. Welcome in Kinship, friend. You are from across the seas?"

Again the Magpie nodded. "From New Bristol, yes."

"And what draws you to Corlay?"

"I seek a girl," said the Magpie. "One Jane by name. Jane Thomson. She came here last April in the company of a priest called Francis."

He sensed the sudden stir of interest that his words had evoked among the three who were seated around the stove and his sharp ears caught the murmur of "Jehane?"

The man reached up and tilted the lampshade so that the light slanted across the Magpie's weathered face. "You are not Kin, are you?" he asked.

"Does it matter?"

"No," said the man and let the shade down again. "But I must ask you to write your name in the register. It is our custom." He selected a pen from a stone jar, dipped it in a brass inkwell and handed it over.

The Magpie pulled the book toward him, scrawled *"La Pie—Nouvelle Bristol"*—added the date and returned the pen. "Jane is still here then?" he asked.

The man glanced at the entry in the register and nodded. "Yes. She is still here."

"And how do I find her?"

"I am going that way, m'sieur," said one of the women. "I will take you to her. Does she expect you?"

"I doubt it," said the Magpie. "But it's possible."

The woman rose to her feet, picked up a shawl and wrapped it around her shoulders. Then she took down a storm lantern from a shelf, lit its candle at the glowing stove and clapped its window to. She gave the other woman a quick kiss on the cheek then came over to the Magpie and invited him to follow her.

He stood aside to let her pass, nodded to the lodge keeper, and stepped out of the gatehouse, closing the door behind him.

A thin drizzle had begun to fall. The light from the lantern gleamed dully on the worn slabs that paved the roadway between the gatehouse and the main entrance to the château. The woman glanced back to make sure he was following and said: "You have come far today, m'sieur?"

"From St. Brieuc," he said.

"On foot?"

"Yes."

"It is a hard climb that. Especially in the winter."

"You do not have many visitors?" he asked.

"Not now," she said. "In the summer, yes. Some from far away. Even from the Americas."

"And it is"—he sought for a word—"permitted?"

"They come," she said. "In the summer they come. Why should they not? They do no harm to anyone."

"So you feel safe here?"

"Safe?" She repeated the word as if she were unsure whether she had heard him correctly. "But who would wish harm to Corlay, m'sieur?"

"There are plenty of evil men in this world, madame. In the Kingdoms the Kinsfolk are outlawed."

"Ah, so I have heard."

"And I saw many Falcons in St. Brieuc."

"This is not Seven Kingdoms, m'sieur. We are a free people."

"The crows do not trouble you then?"

"No. They keep themselves to themselves. But perhaps down in St. Brieuc it is different." She sighed audibly and clutched her shawl tighter about her shoulders.

They were approaching the wide, vaulted entrance to the château. Huge, blank and impassive the walls and towers loomed up as if they alone were supporting the burden of the weeping skies. This would not be a difficult place to defend, mused the Magpie, provided you were prepared to do it.

The woman gestured with her lantern across the paved and graveled inner courtyard to where two lamps dimly flickered on either side of a balustraded flight of stone steps which led up to a porched doorway. "Jehane lives over there in the Queen's Tower," she said. "Go through that door and climb the stairs which you will find on your left hand. She has the chamber on the first floor where you see the light shining."

"Thank you, madame."

"You are welcome, m'sieur."

She gave him a quick, shy smile, bobbed her shawled head and moved off into the shadows.

The Magpie crossed the courtyard, mounted the steps and tried the outer door. It opened easily. A lick of the damp night air pushed past him as he stepped inside. Within a stone niche the flame of a solitary oil lamp shivered nervously and shadows flapped like black banners across the bare stone walls. He closed the door quietly behind him and dropped the wooden latch back into its slot. Through a corbeled archway he could see the stairs that the woman had spoken of spiraling upward, but before he ventured upon them he walked a little way down the cold, dark hallway and peered curiously about him.

He saw two or three unlit passages and no sign of any living person. The place seemed almost as bare and cheerless as a prison. The only human touch appeared to be a stoneware jar standing on a window ledge into which someone had despairingly stuck some sprays of autumn beech leaves, a few hips and haws, and one or two bleached stalks of dead cowparsley. Dead flowers and cold, dead stones.

Turning on his heel he retraced his own damp footprints to the courtyard door and began to feel his way up the narrow twisting stairs, the butt of his trailing staff tap-tapping against the stone treads. At last he saw a chink of light ahead and, shuffling toward it, discovered a stout oak door on which he rapped briskly with his knuckles. There was a quick pattering of feet from within, the latch clicked, the door swung open inward, and the Magpie found himself gazing into a pair of the bluest eyes he had ever seen. "I'm looking for Jane," he said with a grin. "Am I come to the right place?"

"Who is it, Alison?" inquired a dear and familiar voice.

"It's me, Janie!" he called. "Your old Magpie! Aren't you going to ask him in?"

"Magpie! It can't be! Oh, my dear—my own Magpie!"

She flew into his arms like a bright bird and clung to him hardly able to speak for joy.

"Ah, Janie lass, but it's good to see you again. What's this? Tears? What sort of a welcome for an old friend is this supposed to be, hey?"

"Oh, you're so cold and wet, Magpie. Come over by the fire. You take his cape, Alison. And then run and tell

Francis who's here. No, bring us some wine first. The best one. The *very* best. You know which one. Oh, I can't *believe* it! Magpie! My own dear Magpie!"

She pulled him to the fire, sat him down in a low chair before it and gazed at him as though she would eat him up with her shining eyes. He stretched out his hands to the blazing logs and let out his breath in a long, contented sigh. "Faith, lass, but you're housed a long way from anywhere up here. I've been on the road since ten."

"Have you come in your van?"

"No, I legged it. All the way up from St. Brieuc. A tidy trot." He cocked his head on one side and ran his eye over her. "So how long have we got now, Janie?"

She glanced downward, placed her right hand over her swollen belly and laughed. "A week or two—that is if he isn't late."

"And how's it been with you?"

"All right. They're such kind people, Magpie. And I've always had Francis."

"Aye. So you have. How is he, by the by?"

"Oh, he's fine. You'll see for yourself soon."

The girl with the blue eyes and the barley-bright hair came in carrying a tray on which was a bottle and four earthenware beakers. She set it down by the hearth and said: "Would m'sieur like something to eat?"

"Of course he would," said Jane. "See what you can find in the kitchens on your way back. Take the basket with you."

Alison nodded and a moment later they heard her skipping away down the stairs.

"Who's the golden angel?" asked the Magpie.

"Alison's my best friend," said Jane. "She's lived in Corlay since she was a babe. Her parents are dead. I sometimes think that if it hadn't been for her I'd have run back to Quantock long ago."

"You still miss it then?"

"Oh, Magpie!" She closed her eyes for a moment then drew a deep, gasping breath and shook her head as if to say: "What good does it do?" "Those first two months," she said, "before I could be certain about the babe, I hardly stopped crying at all. And at night I always dreamed about Mum and Dad. Night after night after night. All the time. I even used to wake up crying."

The Magpie reached out and gripped her hand in his. "I did the best I could, Janie. I lay low for a week or two and then slipped across to Tallon and had a word with Rett and Simon. The Grays had cleared out by then and . . . Well, we gave them a fair burial up in the orchard behind the cottage. Under that old cherry tree. Rett cut a headstone and we planted a whole load o' daffs . . ."

Jane gave a slow, sad sigh then ducked down and kissed him. "Bless you for that," she whispered.

"It was the very least I could do for them, love."

She knelt down beside him and laid her head against his knee. "And Thomas?" she whispered. "What of Thomas?"

"Aye," he muttered. "I might have guessed that was coming,"

"Was it the Jaws?"

"It must have been, Janie. There was a great blow from the north in the middle of May. Three days it lasted. The sea wall at Chardport was breached in two places and Lord knows how many fine trees were laid flat. The Quantock combers were out gleaning the wrack when they found him. One Eye told me about it. He guessed it must've been Thomas when he heard tell of a black bolt in the ribs."

"They didn't . . . ?" The words stuck in her throat like a cinder.

"You know the combers, Janie. What was a drowned Kinsman to them?" Suddenly he slapped his hand on his knee and cried: "Hey, I've brought you a present! Something you won't believe till you see it. Sling over my sack."

Knuckling the tears from her cheeks Jane rose to her feet and brought him his leather knapsack. He flipped the toggles undone, delved within and pulled out an oblong packet wrapped up in a piece of faded brown sailcloth. He handed it to her with a grin.

Frowning, Jane unbandaged the wrapping to disclose a pair of pipes, exquisitely fashioned from black wood and yellow bone, and bound together side by side with alternate bands of copper and silver. As she turned them over wonderingly in her hands she saw, etched in flowing script on the back of one of the twin barrels, the words *"Thomas of Norwich—Doncaster 3010."*

The blood drained from her cheeks and her gray eyes

seemed to grow dark and huge. "How . . . how came you by these?" she whispered.

The Magpie leaned forward, poured out two cups of wine, handed one to her and took the other himself. "You mean you can't guess?"

"You *hueshed* it?"

He nodded. "Aye. How else? Last August it was. A place called Stoke Pero, t'other side of Dunkery Beacon. A shrimper found them and I *hueshed* myself there on hand to buy them off him for a silver crown. I cleaned them up and put them aside for young Tom's birth gift."

"His pipes," she murmured, stroking a fingertip over the stops. "His very own pipes. Ah, Magpie, if you knew how much I once longed to hear Thomas play these for me."

"You never heard him pipe?" The Magpie sounded astonished.

"Only that one time in the prison. When Francis came. And . . . and . . ." Her voice faltered to a stop then picked up again. "But Thomas talked so much about it. All that starry night when we sailed over to Blackdown . . ." She heaved another enormous sigh and shook her head.

"Drink up, lass," he said. "This is good wine."

She raised her cup to her lips and took a dutiful sip. "Now I'll tell *you* something, Magpie," she said. "Since then I've not had a single *huesh*. Not one. My last *huesh* was of you finding Thomas up on Windhover Hill. And that was before we fled Quantock."

"Aye, it happens sometimes," he said. "My old mam's often told me how she lost the gift all the while she was carrying me. You'll get it back again."

"I don't *want* it back!" she said fiercely. "What has it ever brought me except pain and heartache? Let the Bird keep it!"

"It brought you Thomas," he said mildly.

"And what kind of gift was that? Given one moment, snatched back the next. Do you think I don't know that Dad and Mum would still be alive today if I had *hueshed* Thomas washed up in the Jaws? None of this would have happened, Magpie. None of it."

He nodded. "I know what you mean, lass. And that's one thing I never did understand. I know Thomas blamed himself for what happened. He believed he should have been drowned out in the Somersea where One Eye found him. He said the pattern had been altered. I never could fathom what he meant."

"He meant Carver," she said leadenly.

"Carver? Who's Carver?"

She lowered herself into the chair opposite and laid the pipes in her lap. "I never really knew who Carver was," she said. "I found him within Thomas when I tried to reach him down in the *Kingdom Come* after Jonsey and Napper brought him into Tallon. All I know is he was from the Old Times before the drowning. It was Carver who kept Thomas alive when he should have drowned out there in the Reach and been washed up in the Jaws. That's what I'd *hueshed*."

"And that's what happened, Janie."

"Not *then*. Not when it should have done. I've thought and thought about it hundreds of times. And you know what I believe? I believe the Bird used Carver to bring Thomas and me together. For this!" She lay back in her chair so that the full, swollen roundness of her pregnancy was displayed. "That's what Carver told me at the end. Just before Thomas died. He said, 'He's in the child. I've done what I had to do.'"

"*Who* said that?"

"Carver did."

"*He* spoke to you?"

"I read him in Thomas."

Totally nonplused the Magpie shook his head and poured himself another cup of wine.

"I think we were used, Magpie," she said flatly. "Simply used. Made *things* of. Thomas and me and Carver too. That's what I believe."

"Aye, well," he said uneasily. "We're none of us free, Janie."

Something in his tone made her sit up and glance across at him sharply. "What are you trying to say?"

"Why, nothing," he replied with a disarming grin. "A *huesh* is a *huesh*, that's all."

She studied his face by the flickering light of the fire and finally she said: "There *is* something. I'm sure of it." Her face suddenly cleared, and pointing a finger directly at him she said: "You didn't just 'come to see me,' did you? You *hueshed* me!"

He shrugged and laughed but would not meet her eyes. "I was coming, Janie," he protested. "Ever since way back. I promised old Mam I'd be in Corlay for the birth. Besides I had that whistle to bring you."

Before she could catechize him further there was a sound of voices on the stairway. A moment later the door was thrust open and into the room bounced Alison, closely followed by a tall, stooping man with thinning hair and dark brown eyes who was wearing a full-length, cassock-like garment clipped in about his waist by a wide leather belt.

The Magpie heaved himself up from the chair and thrust out his right hand in welcome. "Well met, Brother Francis!" he cried. "I'll swear you've not grown thicker by a hairbreadth since I smuggled you aboard the boat in Broadbury."

"Nor you neither, you old sinner," laughed Francis, grasping the proffered hand in both his own and pumping it fiercely up and down. "Welcome to Corlay, dear friend. How goes it with you?"

"I've still my fortune to make," returned the Magpie, "but I manage to keep afloat somehow."

Francis drew up another chair to the fire and nodded fondly toward Jane. "Isn't she the very picture of a madonna? Confess now, Magpie, did you ever see a prettier?"

"Janie? Faith she's just a little scrag-bag full of wind and candle-ends. Never been anything else as I recall it. You mustn't let her fool you with that big belly of hers."

"What does he say?" inquired Alison of Jane.

Jane laughed and did her best to translate it into French but without notable success.

"And what news do you bring us from the Kingdoms?" asked Francis. "Better, I hope."

"Not much. There's a rumor the Grays have had their beaks clipped by the Civil Authority, but like as not that's just hopeful hearsay. There's still a fat price on your head, by the by. Twenty-five crowns was the last billing I saw. But truth to tell, Francis, I hear little of the Kinsfolk these days. They've all been driven underground or back into the Church by the Edict and the September Mass Tax. Your Cardinal Constant's no believer in half measures."

"He'll never win men's souls by fear," said Francis. "That's the oldest error in the world. All Constant is doing is screwing down the lid on the caldron. He'll live to see the whole of Christendom blow apart in his face."

"There's been no move against you here, then?"

Francis flicked a sideways glance at him. "What makes you ask that?"

"Just the odd whisper. Nothing really."

"What sort of whisper?"

The Magpie shrugged. "Someone told me the Falcons were keeping track of all who visited the sanctuary. I took the tip, struck off through the hills and skirted round the village."

"Yes, it's true," admitted Francis. "They began doing it in the summer. Constant must have used his influence on the Vatican. Last May Turin sent an envoy to Duke Alain, the Queen's cousin—he's been at odds with her ever since she embraced Kinship and gave Corlay to the Folk. But Alain wouldn't dare to make a direct move against us."

"No?" said the Magpie in a carefully neutral tone.

"You think different?"

"I think nothing either way," said the Magpie easily. "But this morning I counted close on a score of Falcons in St. Brieuc, and I wasn't looking for them either, believe me."

"Well, they have their headquarters there. Up by the cathedral."

"Oh. Then that explains it."

"He doesn't really think that," said Jane. "Why won't you tell us what brought you here, Magpie?"

Francis, plainly bewildered by her question, gazed at her in astonishment.

The Magpie grinned. "Simple hunger, lass. What's in yonder basket?"

"Oh, forgive me!" cried Jane. "What am I thinking of? Bring the little table over here, Alison."

"I'd best clean myself up a bit first," said the Magpie. "Have you water up here?"

"Indeed we have," said Francis. "Come with me."

He lit a candle at the fire and led the Magpie out on to the stairs and up to a circular wash room high in the tower. "In the day time that throne offers one of the best views in the whole castle," he said. "Many's the contemplative half hour I've spent at stool up here."

The Magpie relieved himself into the dark maw, replaced the wooden cover and rinsed his hands and face at the stone sink.

"The whole room over our heads is a vast water tank," said Francis, gazing upward. "It's fed from the roof. Truly ingenious. Remind me to show you tomorrow."

They returned to Jane's room to find the table had been laid with bread and curd cheese, pickled onions and cucumbers, smoked bacon and red-streaked apples.

"A feast!" exclaimed the Magpie. "What would I have got if I'd warned you I was coming?"

"I steal it just for you, La Pie," said Alison, coloring with pleasure.

"There's a girl after my own heart," he responded, and winked broadly at her.

He attacked his supper while the others nibbled to keep him company and sipped at their wine. During a lull in the conversation he lifted his cup, pointed to it and said to Jane: "If I hadn't known better I'd have sworn that was some of your Dad's handiwork."

"Jehane made that," said Alison proudly. "She is our best potter. It is true, Jehane. Even Georges says so."

"So that's what you've been up to," said the Magpie, spearing an onion on the point of his knife and crunching it with noisy relish. "I might have guessed you wouldn't just be sitting on your bum all day like a broody hen."

"She teaches too," said Alison. "In our school."

"Aye, that follows," he said. "And what do you do, Francis?"

"Francis is the self-appointed midwife," laughed Jane. "Isn't that so, Francis?"

Francis flushed darkly. "Someone has to keep an eye on you," he murmured. "And Thomas laid the trust upon me."

"I was only teasing," she said. "Francis is a marvel, Magpie. Really he is. He teaches Latin and Mathematics in the School *and* he's Chief Clerk to the Sanctuary. He's writing a book too."

"Is that so?" said the Magpie. "What sort of a book?"

"A history of the Boy Thomas," said Francis shyly. "I still have all the notes I made when Constant dispatched me to Cumberland."

"Yes, I heard something about that," said the Magpie. "They say you used a letter from his Lordship to gain you entrance to the fort at Broadbury. Is that why the Grays are after your head?"

"I am an apostate," said Francis simply. "That is a far worse crime than heresy in Constant's eyes. To him I must personify the absolute nadir of spiritual corruption. Compared with me Judas Iscariot was just a naughty child."

"Is the Cardinal mad?" asked the Magpie.

"I no longer know what the word means," said Francis. "Constant believes he has a divine mission to restore the Church to what he sees as being its rightful position of supreme and absolute authority throughout the world. For many years I shared his vision. If he is mad then surely I have been mad too."

"Live and let live is my motto," said the Magpie. "But it has to work both ways. If Constant's buzzards want to stick their beaks into me they'll have to pay for the privilege." So saying he raised his knife and touched the point lightly against his pursed lips.

"But what does that solve in the end?" said Francis. "That is what the Boy taught us. True Kinship is the only answer. It breaks the shackles which bind the soul and frees it from the prison which is fear of death."

"Is that what Constant believes?"

"He believes that Kinship is a terrible threat to the authority of the Church—which it is. What he cannot see is that in each age the Old Truths must be born anew if they are to survive. Wise Old Morfedd knew that and he taught it to Tom, and in Tom the knowledge blossomed into a flower of fire the like of which the world had not seen for three thousand years! The Boy's life began at the instant when Gyre's black arrow pierced his heart."

"You speak in riddles, Francis. How if Constant kills off all the Kinsfolk in Christendom? Will the world wait for another three thousand years?"

"He can kill Kinsfolk, Magpie, but he cannot kill Kinship. It floats on the air like thistledown and seeds in men's hearts. It is a song without end. One day the White Bird will hover over the altars of the world and the image of the murdered man on the cross will be forgotten like a fevered dream."

"And no doubt a sea of innocent blood will have been spilt in the meantime."

"But it will happen," said Francis. "It *will* happen."

The Magpie passed that night on the floor of Jane's room lying wrapped in a blanket before the embers of the dying fire. He did not sleep well. Twice he awoke with a start and each time he snatched instinctively for the knife which lay ready to hand beside his head. On the second occasion he got up, tiptoed across the room and silently unlatched the door to the stairs. He listened with held breath but heard only the thin tooth-whistle of the night wind honing among the cracks and crevices of the ancient stonework; the faint, finger-nail tapping of ivy leaves against the leaded casement. He closed the door again, crept back to the hearth, scratched the glowing embers together and blew upon them. When a flame licked up he laid a handful of dry twigs upon it, then, taking up his knife, he selected a billet of split wood from the log basket and prized off a long, tough splinter. Returning to the door he thrust his improvised wedge between the iron retaining bracket and the latch bar, effectively jamming it down. Then he made his way back to the hearth, gathered the blanket about him and sat staring into the flames.

"Magpie?"

He jerked around and saw the waiflike figure of Jane standing at the curtained doorway to her bedchamber. She had draped a shawl over her shoulders and was clutching it to her throat with one hand. In the other she was holding the pipes he had brought her. Beneath her short white nightgown her legs and feet were bare.

"I'm sorry, lass," he murmured. "I didn't mean to wake you. Get you back to bed."

"You didn't wake me," she said, advancing toward him. "I couldn't sleep either. I heard you moving about. What were you doing?"

He reached out and dragged a chair closer to the fire. "Sit you down before you catch your death, lass. Is Alison awake too?"

"She's sleeping like a stone. She always does. Now tell me what you were doing."

"Making the door fast," he said.

"Why?"

"Because that's the way I am, Janie. Suspicious by nature. Always have been."

"No," she said, "it isn't just that. There's something else. I can feel it, Magpie."

"Oh, yes?" he said. "And just what is it you feel?"

"I'm not sure. Something in you, I think. A sort of shadow. A coldness."

The Magpie gave a grunt which might have meant anything.

"Don't you know what I mean?" she asked.

He was silent for a moment then said: "Aye, I know what you mean."

"Then what is it? Tell me."

"If you must know, it's fear," he said. "Plain, simple fear."

"But why? What is it you're afraid of?"

He stretched out his arm, readjusted a flaming log, then sat back on his heels and muttered: "I'm fearful for you, sweet lass."

Jane stared at him. "Then it *has* to be a *huesh*," she whispered, "for nothing else in the would could make *you* afraid."

He smiled in spite of himself. "Would that were so."

"You know you'll have to tell me sooner or later."

"Aye, that's true," he admitted.

"Then tell me now."

"There's little enough to tell, Janie. You know how it is sometimes. But I got this one twice. The first time I wasn't really sure—not sure it was you, I mean. Then, ten days ago, when I was higgling up in the hills behind New Bristol it came again—so bright and clear I didn't stop to argue. It was like that time I *hueshed* the devils on you in Culmstock Cove. All I knew was I had to get to you quick."

Jane shuddered so violently she all but lost her hold upon the pipes she was clutching. "What was it you saw?" she whispered. "Surely not that again?"

"No," he said. "I saw it snowing. Snowing hard. It was night. And there was something ablaze somewhere—a redness in the sky. And there was a sort of hut or barn, I think."

"And that was all?"

"Aye, that's all. But it was *us*, Janie. You and me both.

I had you held in my arms, lass. It's that that's dragged me all the way down here to your side."

Jane tilted back her head, raised her left hand and pressed the back of it hard against her mouth. A pathetic, half-strangled little cry of utter misery crept from between her lips. "No more," she mourned. "Oh no, no more. Let me be now. Oh please, please, let me be."

Listening to that heartbreaking plea the Magpie was gripped by a fierce, impotent fury against all the mindless malice of a world where the innocent are forever condemned to suffer. "They'll not hurt you again, Janie," he growled. "Not while I'm still alive to prevent it. So set your mind at rest on that score. I'll have a word with Francis tomorrow and see what he thinks."

"It's no good, Magpie," she sighed. "He won't believe you."

"Why shouldn't he?"

"Because some part of him won't want to. Thomas used to be the same. He couldn't ever really trust the *huesh* either. Maybe if you were Kin it would be different."

"What's that got to do with it?"

"Yes, I know, Magpie. I can't explain it. It's something I can't really understand myself. In me the two things are all mixed up."

"Well, I'll give it a try anyway," he said. "And I'll sniff around a bit and see if I can't find the place I saw. It's around here somewhere. I'll take an oath on that."

Jane drew a deep, labored breath and said in a small, flat voice: "You believe it's the Falcons, don't you?"

"They weren't there in my *huesh*, lass, that's for certain. But, yes, I do. As I read it, now they've finished with York they'll move in for the kill on Corlay. Nothing else makes half so much sense. My guess is they'll simply do it and argue the toss later. After all, what's to stop them?"

"But *why*, Magpie?"

"It's like Francis said, Janie. They're scared witless of you Kinsfolk. Remember what that crazy loon of a deaf priest called you? 'Devil's spawn.' I'll never forget the look on his face as he said it. His eyes were going all ways. He was gibbering mad with fright. And when men are that scared all they can do is kill."

"Kill," she echoed dully. "Killing and hate and pain. Oh, Magpie, will it *never* end?"

"Maybe, one day. Perhaps we'll live to *huesh* it yet, Janie. You and me together, hey?"

Jane twisted sharply in her chair and pressed her right hand down hard against the side of her womb. "Oh, how he kicks," she whispered. "Are you in such a hurry to be born, little fool? Don't you know there's nothing for you out here except heartbreak? Lie still now. Hush."

The Magpie smiled. "And just what makes you so sure he's a boy?"

"Do you really need to ask? Didn't your mother *huesh* it so?"

"Aye, she did that," he agreed. "The night you and Thomas were spliced. Lord, but it seems a lifetime ago, doesn't it?"

Jane lifted the pipes and held them up before her in the firelight. "Tom, Tom, you piper's son," she murmured. "Shall I finger you a lullaby on your father's pipes, boy? Will that make you lie still?"

She set the instrument to her lips and arranged her fingers upon the stops. Then, frowning a little abstracted frown, she drew in her breath and, hesitantly and very softly, she began to play.

Chapter Two

The Secular Convention of York which took place in that cold, northern city during the last week of November A.D. 3018 was summoned by Cardinal Constant on his return from Italy and was presided over by his lordship in person. As well as the fifty-two marshals of the Secular Arm drawn from the seven Kingdoms there were also present, by special invitation, at least a score of emissaries from overseas. Representing as it did well over a third part of the forces of the Church Militant throughout European Christendom there could be no question that the Convocation of 3018 was a most formidable gathering. Predictably much of the discussion was devoted to the

purely technical problems besetting a complex secular
organization—mundane matters of communication, of
finance, of inter-departmental co-operation—and it was
not until the evening of the penultimate day that the eight
most senior Marshals assembled around a long table high
up in the York Falconry for the meeting which was
ultimately to prove one of the most significant in the whole
history of the Church.

For this occasion the Cardinal—a tall, thin-featured
ecclesiastic who wore his gray hair cropped so close to his
skull that he appeared almost bald—had discarded his
scarlet robes in favor of the black vestment of the Secular
Office to which his dual rank of Chief Falconer entitled
him. Apart from a golden ring on the middle finger of his
right hand he wore no personal adornment of any kind.
Indeed his appearance on entering the room was so austere as to make the Marshals appear overdressed. He
nodded to them, assumed his position at the head of the
table, and indicated by a sign that they might take their
seats. When they had done so he glanced swiftly around
at the assembled faces and said: "Gentlemen, you are now
assembled in Privy Conclave. We have summoned you
here tonight because we wish to discuss with you certain
matters of High Policy. Anything spoken in this room is
under strict Oath of Confidence. Is that understood?"

The Marshals indicated corporately that it was.

The Cardinal nodded. "As you all know, immediately
prior to our departure for Turin in April we caused to be
published an Edict of Proscription outlawing the heretical
sect known as The Kinsmen. We delegated the immediate
prosecution of this Edict to the Bishop of Leicester. We
now intend to call upon him for his report. Lord Simon,
you have our undivided attention."

The Marshal thus addressed inclined his head in acknowledgment, rose to his feet and cleared his throat. His
voice when it emerged was pitched in so high a register
that it immediately explained his familiar nickname of
"Signor Castrato." "As you know, my Lord, I have long
made the prosecution and eradication of hersey my particular province. For several years before you, in your
wisdom, decided to move against the Kinsmen I had made
it my duty to discover as much as I could about this sect
which I had always regarded with profound suspicion. I
have on file at Newbury sworn attestation of their indulg-

ing in sorcery, alchemy, diabolism, sortilege, thaumaturgy, necromancy and the Thirty Two Unnatural Practices, together with—"

"Yes, yes," interrupted the Cardinal. "You may take it for granted that we are all familiar with the *Codex Iniquitatis*. Just tell us what steps you have taken to prosecute the Edict."

This mild rebuke brought a flush to the Bishop's sallow cheek. "I was coming to it, my Lord."

"Tell us about those Grays of yours, Simon," growled a voice down the far end of the table.

The Cardinal raised an admonitory finger and nodded for the Bishop to continue.

"Having perused your personal letter and the Edict, my Lord, I realized that speed was of the essence. My earlier inquiries had provided me with a list of names, prominent among which were those of two Kinsmen—the ex-Falcon Gyre, and the piper, Thomas of Norwich. Both these men had been intimate associates of the old Tale Spinner, Peter of Hereford who, since the death of the Boy, had been chiefly responsible for the propagation of the cult. After the old man's death certain relics of the Boy passed into the keeping of these two men. One of these relics—a document known among the Sect as *Morfedd's Testament*—I was particularly anxious to obtain since I had every reason to believe that it contained information which would prove of inestimable value to me in the execution of your Lordship's command."

The Bishop paused, removed from his sleeve a lace-bordered handkerchief, and dabbed at his upper lip, though whether for dramatic effect or from physical need it was difficult to be sure. Having restored it to its place he coughed and continued.

"The task of recovering this so-called 'Testament' I entrusted expressly to Brother Andrew, a man of impeccable credentials and a true servant of our Faith as he had proved to my complete satisfaction during his four years' tenure of the office of Chief Examiner at Newbury. I placed him in command of a detachment of those Falcons, known as the Gray Brotherhood, whom I had personally selected and reserved for Special Service. They picked up the tracks of the Kinsman, Thomas of Norwich, in the Western Borders and pursued him across Wales, where they just failed to prevent him from slipping aboard a ship bound for Brittany. Thanks be to God this vessel was driven ashore on the rocky coast of the First Kingdom and all hands were lost. But the Devil looked after his own. This Kinsman survived and found succor with a family of Kinsfolk on the Isle of Quantock. Here Brother Andrew contrived to flush him out once more. The Gray Brotherhood finally ran him to earth at Broadbury on the Isle of Blackdown whither he had fled in the company of a young sorceress. The fugitives were captured and flung into the local prison to await the arrival of Brother Andrew."

Again the Bishop paused and cast a glance down the table to where the Cardinal sat, chin in hand, listening impassively to this recital.

"There the matter would undoubtedly have ended, my Lord, had not the Arch-Apostate, Brother Francis, appeared on the scene and persuaded the officer in charge of Broadbury Fort to grant him access to the prisoners. The report of what actually transpired is sadly confused, but there can be little doubt that all the black arts were employed. In the ensuing confrontation both Brother Andrew and the Kinsman Thomas of Norwich were killed and the Apostate and the sorceress vanished to reappear later in the infamous Sanctuary of Corlay."

"And the Testament?" inquired the Cardinal mildly. "What became of that?"

"I can only assume, my Lord, that they took it with them."

"Very well. Continue."

"The ex-Falcon Gyre died on Black Isle in the Western Borders before we were able to reach him and we have since tracked down and eliminated a further seventeen of the Kinsmen. I am confident that no priest of the Sect will be found today throughout the Seven Kingdoms. To all intents and purposes, my Lord, the Kinsmen have ceased to exist. We have rooted them out completely."

"And the Gray Brotherhood? That has now been disbanded?"

"I am holding the Special Service in reserve, my Lord. An arm so dedicated is of inestimable value to our cause."

This was too much for one of the Marshals who burst out with: "They're nothing but a pack of cut-throats, Simon, and you know it! The whole of Exmoor is still seething! Just tell us what good our cause has been done by your giving those carrion a secular license to hang, burn and rape! I beg your forbearance, my Lord, but some of us do feel very strongly on this matter."

"You exaggerate as usual, Richard," returned the Bishop, resuming his seat. "At no time did the Grays exceed their authority. They were licensed to act only against the heretics and that they have done most effectively."

"Are you telling us that *all* the Kinsfolk were made fair game? As I understood it the Edict outlawed only their priests—the Kinsmen."

"In questions of heresy," said the Bishop suavely, "such nice distinctions are all but meaningless. The Grays carried out their orders in the best interests of our Faith, and they have taught the backsliders a most salutary lesson."

"And brought the whole Secular Arm into disrepute throughout the Kingdoms."

"That may be your opinion, Richard. I doubt whether our Lord Cardinal shares it."

"Well, allow me to inform you, Simon, that in June I was summoned to New Exeter Castle—*summoned,* mark you!—and called to account for the deaths of no fewer than twenty-seven of Earl Robert's liege subjects. Twelve had been hanged; nine burned alive in their homes; and the rest raped and mutilated. As a direct side-effect of that little private *auto-da-fé* which you authorized five of my own men have since been murdered—the last only six weeks ago!"

"It's true, Simon," said another voice. "I've had a very unpleasant session with Lord Northumberland."

"And me with Winchester," put in a third. "I hold no brief for the Kinsfolk, but it's a fact that the Second Kingdom came close to a state of Civil Riot on account of your precious Grays."

"What would you have then?" retorted the Bishop furiously. "Are you all so lily-livered that you must quail before some petty, puffed-up civil Lordling who is out of pocket by a few wretched tax-payers? I tell you, gentlemen, I have dossiers at Newbury which would make my Lords of Kent and Winchester tremble in their shoes could they but read them! The point at issue is not the rotten eggs which may have been broken in the process but the dish which has resulted! The Grays have lanced the poisonous imposthume of Kinship, gentlemen, and you would do well not to forget it!"

The silence which followed this outburst paid impressive tribute to Lord Simon's passion. It was broken by the Cardinal remarking drily: "And what of Corlay, my Lords?"

The Marshals eyed one another covertly but none seemed anxious to venture an opinion.

The Cardinal allowed several seconds to elapse before he said: "Let us put it another way, gentlemen. Lord Simon has informed us that he has eliminated seventeen Kinsmen. In the circumstances we rate that a very creditable performance. But we have the best of reasons for believing that less than a year ago there were something over two hundred members of the Sect proselytizing throughout the Kingdoms of the west. That leaves, by our computation, rather more than a hundred and eighty Kinsmen still unaccounted for. What can have become of them, gentlemen? Where have they all gone?"

"Abroad, presumably, my Lord."

"Precisely, Richard. From whence they will assuredly return. Gentlemen, we have but wounded our serpent, not destroyed it."

There was a soft susurration of in-drawn breath. It sounded not unlike the whisper of a breeze among the topmost twigs of a forest on a still, summer's evening. No one said a word.

The Cardinal made a steeple of his long, bony fingers and tapped them against his pale lips. His cold, dark eyes slid pensively along the double row of faces. "Well, Simon," he said at last, "have you no observation you wish to make?"

The Bishop opened his mouth then closed it again without speaking and shook his head.

"Richard?"

The Senior Marshal for the First Kingdom moistened his lips. "Believe me, I take your point, my Lord," he murmured, "but I must confess I do not see how Corlay could be said to fall within our secular province. The Isle of Brittany is an independent Kingdom. Any official move we made against them might prove to have unforeseeable consequences. Besides, we in the First are trade-linked to the Bretons by the Treaty of Finistère, so Earl Robert would be bound to oppose it. We could be stirring up a hornet's nest."

"Go on."

"And there's the Queen to consider—Elise . . ."

"Yes?" prompted the Cardinal gently. "What about her?"

"A heretic, certainly, my Lord, but everyone knows she's given her shield and sanction to Corlay. Dare we risk provoking open conflict? The Bretons are a fiercely independent people. Might we not drive them wholly into Kinship? I fear the Church might stand to lose more than she could gain."

The Cardinal regarded his lieutenant somberly. Of all his senior Secular Officers, Richard, Lord Marshal of the First Kingdom, was the one he found most attractive as a man. He had qualities of openness, of warmth, of bluff, soldierly plainspokenness that were conspicuously lacking in some of the others. For this reason alone Constant might, in different circumstances, have felt tempted to be lenient with him, but instinct warned him that this was neither the time nor the place for such self-indulgence. Altogether too much was at stake. When he spoke his voice had the icy cutting edge of a whetted scythe.

"You speak of gain and loss as though we dally our time away in some childish game of hazard! Has it not yet penetrated to you, Richard, that in the guise of this pernicious heresy our Faith confronts an adversary infinitely more formidable than any she has faced in all the years since Her first foundation? What Luther, Calvin, De Solero, Mountjoy, Fabian and all their legions failed to achieve, this whelp of a Boy with his puny pipe and his ridiculous White Bird has been threatening to accomplish single-handed!

"For eighteen years we permitted a cancer to burgeon at will within our body—even within our very heart! We fostered it, nurtured it, encouraged it to spread its malignant cells far and wide throughout the healthy flesh of living Christendom. Blinded by our pride, by our overweening confidence in our ability to contain it, we refused to accept the evidence even when it was staring us in the face! We chose to claim him as our own—our little saint —Blessed Martyr Thomas of York—True Son of the Faith—Holy Child of Innocence—Sanctified Worker of Miracles and all the rest of the clap-trap!

"Oh, there's no denying that we reaped a golden harvest with our duplicity. Did we not challenge Lourdes? Turin even? And all the while we closed our eyes against the truth that was there under our very noses. We refused to see that those hordes of feather-pated fools who came flocking to the Minster gates were coming not to York but to the New Jerusalem! For them this Boy was never the Way to the Truth, *he was the Truth itself!*

"None are so blind as those who refuse to see. The cataract was finally cut from my eyes by Brother Francis, my own Private Secretary. I had sent him first as *advocatus diaboli* to contest our little martyr's very first miracle and then off on a fact-finding mission into Cumberland with instructions to ferret out the Boy's history. The track our Brother Francis followed from Cumberland to York became his devil's road to Damascus. He was tempted and he fell. Having embraced Kinship with all the fanatic fervor customary to the apostate he is now lodged with his whore in Corlay from whence he pours forth his poisonous Epistles of Encouragement to the Faithful.

"The longer that tumor is allowed to breed unchecked, the stronger the hold the cancer of Kinship will take. *Ergo —it must be cut out!* Every single morsel of corrupt tissue must be excised. There is no other course open to us. All that remains to be settled is how this most vital piece of surgery is to be performed. It is for this that we are gathered here tonight, gentlemen. This is the task before us."

Lord Marshal Richard slowly raised his downcast eyes from the table before him and was confronted by the covertly smirking features of Bishop Simon. The sight smarted even more than the lash of the Cardinal's tongue. *Servus servorum Dei,* he reflected bitterly. Not for him to question why Almighty God in His infinite wisdom should have chosen such a one for his servant. He did not doubt that this job would be done. The Apostate was probably as good as dead already. Strange how many men were eager to kill in the name of their faith compared with those willing to die for it. I wonder how you'd fare, Signor Castrato, if you were stretched out on one of your own racks? What heresies would you confess to . . . ? Mother of God! The Cardinal was addressing him! "I beg your pardon, my Lord," he muttered. "I was thinking about your Direction."

"And are we to share in the fruits of your cogitations, Richard?"

The Marshal swallowed. "Well, my Lord, I must say that it still seems for the best to me if the job could be done over here. That way there'd be a lot less political friction."

"We are not sure that we follow your precise line of thought."

"Well, say we offer Brother Francis a safe conduct here to York. Give him an opportunity to speak in his own defense. Something that'll tempt him on board ship. Then we can slit his throat at our own convenience. Well, that's the main object of this exercise, isn't it? I mean, he's the one we want out of the way."

"The main 'object of the exercise' as you put it, Richard, is the extirpation of the heresy of Kinship."

"Well, how about a general amnesty, then? That way we could finish off the lot of them."

"*O sancta simplicitas!*" murmured the Cardinal. "And what on earth inclines you to suppose they would ever accept such an invitation?"

"Oh, I don't know. The Kinsfolk have always struck me as a pretty gullible lot. I'd say it's worth a try, my Lord. Besides, what's the alternative? Putting a detachment of Grays ashore in Brittany? If I know anything about the Bretons, Simon's precious bully-boys would be chopped into mincemeat before their boots were dry."

"Well, Simon, what do you say to that?"

"Naturally I do not share his opinion of the Special Service, my Lord. But, as you know, logistics is hardly my province."

"I think Richard's right, my Lord," said the Marshal for the Second Kingdom, delighted to have an opportunity of getting one back at the Bishop. "The Grays may be all very well when it's a question of unarmed civilians. Against seasoned Breton troops it could be a very different matter."

There were murmurs of assent from around the table. The Bishop of Leicester was finding himself singularly short on friends.

The Cardinal was moved briefly to wonder at the strength of the antagonism which the Bishop's minions had aroused. Such reports as had reached him in Italy had contained no mention of civil unrest in the Kingdoms. But one of the penalties of attaining to high office was that your servants tended to tell you only what they thought you wished to hear. He sighed quietly. "We must confess, gentlemen, that we find your counsel disappointingly negative. Can it be that we have failed to impress upon you the true urgency of this matter? Rumors are now rife that Corlay is shortly to witness some novel and miraculous manifestation on a par with the advent of the Boy himself. Surely there is no need for us to stress what that could imply?"

Bishop Simon coughed gently for attention. "My Lord, it is my opinion that our object can be achieved without recourse to any overt military action on our own behalf. For these four months past I have been in close and regular communication with Dom Fabricant of Guincamp, confessor to Duke Alain, the Queen's cousin. The Duke is no friend to the Kinsfolk. I am confident that, with a modicum of encouragement, he would undertake to smoke them out for us."

"Indeed?" murmured the Cardinal. "And what precise form of encouragement have you in mind?"

"Gold," said the Bishop. "The Duke's appetite for it is virtually insatiable."

The Cardinal nodded. "In the light of Richard's observations it would certainly be preferable if the Secular Arm were not openly involved. Presumably this could be arranged?"

"I am certain of it, my Lord."

"And how long would it take?"

Lord Simon essayed a rapid mental calculation. "Six weeks?"

"As long as that?"

"If we are to be sure of success, my Lord. It will mean working through intermediaries—agents of proven loyalty. We dare not risk a leak or we could find our birds flown before we strike."

"That must be avoided at all costs," said the Cardinal. "The last thing we can afford is any perpetuation of the myth. This time the ghost must be laid for good and all. We charge you, Lord Simon, to see that it is done."

The Bishop of Leicester bowed his head. *"Deus vult,"* he murmured. "Your wish is my command, my Lord."

Chapter Three

Late in the afternoon of the third day following his arrival at Corlay, when a cold north wind was mourning for the nameless dead and the western sky resembled a raw, red wound, the Magpie finally found what he was looking for. Acting upon a suggestion from one of the local Kinsfolk he had struck out to the southwest, climbed up into the hills behind the castle and penetrated to the upland wilderness known as the *lande*.

Even to one long familiar with the highland wastes of the Seven Kingdoms this bleak, windswept plateau seemed to possess an awesome melancholy all its own. There was something profoundly daunting about the place, something immeasurably ancient and elemental. It was almost as though the land itself were a living creature brooding darkly back to an era long before the coming of man. Viewed in the waning light the stalks of the dead cottongrass might have been the hairs on the back of a giant's hand; these stony gullies, folds and wrinkles of some ancient and alien skin. There was no sign of human habitation anywhere. For league upon league the plateau rolled away into the dim distance. And yet, even as he gazed out across it the Magpie knew beyond all possibility of doubt that this was where it would happen.

Like a hound questing a scent he began to cast about for some visible clue which would lead him to the site of his *huesh*. He found nothing. Realizing that it would be dark in less than an hour and that it would take him all of that to get back to the castle, he nevertheless picked his way out over the tangled heather, heading for an outcrop of rock from whose summit a solitary, leafless thorn beckoned like a bony finger against the inflamed sky.

A carrion crow leapt up with clattering wings, gave a hoarse croak of alarm and was swept away by the gusting wind. By the time the Magpie had clambered to the top

43

the bird was already invisible in the gathering dusk though its reproachful cries still lingered on the cold air. Shading his eyes against a sudden spearing gleam from the west, the Magpie squinted out across the waste and saw at once that a long shallow valley had now been drawn into his view. Halfway down it, seeming to crouch against the slope as if in mortal dread of discovery, was the *bergerie* his informant had spoken of—a low, stone hut, roughly thatched in bracken. He gazed upon it for a full minute, marking it in his mind, then he scrambled back down the rocks and began to retrace his steps.

The sun had long since set by the time he regained the castle precincts and his face was wooden with cold. From the thick cloud flock which the wind was whipping down from the north snow was already beginning to fall. The flakes swirled in the invisible eddies and currents around the high walls and turrets of the château, and wherever a lamp or window gleamed they appeared to congregate and hover like swarms of golden bees.

He hurried across the inner courtyard and up the stairs to Jane's room where he found her talking to Francis. She glanced up as he entered and her eyes met his in an unspoken question.

The Magpie unfastened his wet cape and flung it on to a peg behind the door. He rubbed his hands together and then scrubbed at his numb cheeks. "That wind hides wolves," he muttered. "Their teeth are sharp."

"Where have you been?" asked Jane.

He thrust out his hands to the flames. "Up on the *lande*. Do you know it?"

"No."

"A God-forsaken place if ever I saw one."

"And what took you up there?" asked Francis.

"I was talking to André the crookback this morning. He said he remembered an old *bergerie* up there. I thought I'd take a look."

Jane stared at him. "You've found it, haven't you?" she said softly.

The Magpie nodded.

"Found what?" asked Francis. "A *bergerie?*"

"His *huesh*," said Jane. "That's what he's been doing these past three days. Hunting for his *huesh*."

Francis checked a smile. "Ah, yes," he murmured. "I

recall him speaking of it the other day. I confess I found the concept somewhat fanciful."

"All I know is that the *huesh* happens," she said. "If it didn't I wouldn't be here."

"Wouldn't be here?" he repeated. "Oh, come now."

Jane drew a deep breath. "Listen, Francis. After I took Thomas to Blackdown the Falcons caught me. The Magpie *hueshed* that. If he hadn't the crows would have killed me. Instead *he* killed *them*. Now do you follow?"

Francis gazed at her as if in the twinkling of an eye she had transformed herself into some quite different person. "Those two Falcons who vanished . . . ?" he murmured, turning to the Magpie. "That was *your* doing?"

"Aye," growled the Magpie, "and I'd do it all over again if I had to."

"But how does that . . . ?"

"Tie up with the *huesh?*" said the Magpie, helping him out. "Why, man, it's as plain as the nose on your face. Like she said, if I hadn't *hueshed* those two buzzards upon her I'd never have been on hand in Culmstock to prick them out."

"But how . . . ? What is it you do?"

The Magpie shrugged. "You don't *do* anything," he said. "You can't force a *huesh*, Francis. It comes of its own fancy. But sometimes you know you have to be there on hand for it. That's so, isn't it, Janie?"

Jane shivered, recalling how she had been dragged down into the Jaws to hunt with frozen fingers for the body of a drowned Kinsman among the storm-tumbled sea-wrack.

"Is it some kind of clairvoyance then?" pursued Francis. "A sort of second sight?"

"Aye. Something of the kind, I daresay," said the Magpie indifferently. "But to us it's the *huesh*."

"Us? Surely you're not telling me that Jane has this gift too?"

"You mean she hasn't told you?"

Francis shook his head. "Not a word," he murmured.

The Magpie glanced up at the girl who was staring into the flames, lost in some sad, remote dream of her own, and his face softened. "There's never been another like her," he said. "That lass would read tomorrow as you'd read a book. Even my old Mam couldn't hold a rushlight to her. Eh, Janie?"

Jane withdrew her gaze from the fire and turned her gray

eyes upon him. "That's all over now, Magpie," she said. "I want no more of it. I told you that."

"Aye, so you did," he agreed, "but I'll wager you've not got the choice, my lass. We're none of us that free. Besides, you can't have forgotten what you told me of the Bird."

"I've not forgotten."

"Then how comes it you've never thought to ask yourself why you were the one chosen?"

"Who told you I hadn't? Not I."

"Well, then?"

Francis had been listening to this exchange with ever deepening perplexity. "What does he mean, Jane?" he said. "What choice is this he speaks of?"

"Why don't you ask him?" she replied wearily. "You surely can't expect me to answer for him."

"You heard my lady, Magpie. Will you not enlighten me?"

"Yes," said Jane. "Tell him, Magpie. Let's hear what he makes of it."

" 'Twas her notion, not mine, Francis. But you are Kin so maybe it'll make some sense to you."

"And he's studied Morfedd's Testament, haven't you, Francis?"

Francis nodded.

"And am I not Old Morfedd's Bride of Time?"

"I believe it to be so, yes."

Jane's eyes were glittering bright with pent-up tears. "And my bridegroom, Francis? What does the Testament tell us of him?"

"The White Bird of Kinship is the Bridegroom. You know that, Jane. We have often spoken of it."

"Am I not then truly wed to Time itself?"

"In symbol only, Jane. None could be wed to Time."

"But how if it were something more than that? If this" —she slapped her stomach—"were the child of the *huesh?* How then?"

"The child of the *huesh?* What does that mean?"

"You heard Magpie ask me why I thought I had been chosen for this?"

Francis stared at her.

"Well, he thinks it's because I'm *huesh.*"

"And what do you think?"

"I think it's because the Bird needed that gift which was lodged in Thomas and the one which is in me. It wanted the two gifts brought together in a single spirit. One poor, new, innocent little spirit. That's what I think, Francis."

"Why have you never spoken to me of this before?"

Jane sighed. "Because it would have meant tearing open the wound all over again."

"But surely you must realize that this sheds a completely new light on all that section of the Testament?"

"I've never even thought about it, Francis. But I expect Brother Charles will be pleased."

There was the sound of footsteps on the turret stair and Alison appeared at the doorway carrying an earthenware jug. Snowflakes still glinted on the shawl which she had wrapped around her head. *"Voilà!* Feathers of the White Bird!" she laughed, shaking them off. "It is falling quite hard now."

"Is it settling?" asked the Magpie.

"No, it is just wet and horrid. See, I have brought us some spiced ale. I'll set it down by the fire to warm."

The Magpie rose to his feet, walked through into the dark bedchamber and peered out of the window. Snow had already begun to drift dimly up against the iron bars of the casement. He unfastened the latch and leaned out but could see little except a blurred gray fog of scudding flakes and the pale gleam of the distant lake.

He returned to the fire just in time to hear Alison saying: ". . . four of them. From Guincamp I think they said."

"What's that?" he demanded. "Who's from Guincamp?"

"Four men, La Pie. Down at the outer gate. They were talking to Alexandre."

"Did you know them?"

"Me? No. I never saw them before in my life."

"What did they want?"

"How should I know? Shelter from the storm I expect."

The Magpie frowned and fingered his grizzled stubble of a beard. Then he walked across to the door, lifted down his cape and draped it over his shoulders. "I'd better go and take a look," he said. "Put that wedge in the door behind me, Alison. And don't open it unless you're sure you know who's on the other side."

"Oh, La Pie, what an old woman you are! You see bandits everywhere."

"Just you do it, lass," he said grimly, and his suddenly

altered tone made them all stare at him. "I hope I'm wrong," he said, and with that he was gone.

"Do as he says, Alison."

"But he is being absurd, Jehane!"

"Then give me the wedge and I'll do it."

"Oh I'll *do* it," said the girl tossing her head. "But I still think he is being stupid."

"What is it he's so anxious about?" asked Francis.

"He believes the Falcons are planning to move against Corlay," said Jane.

"Are you serious?"

"*He* is."

"But why, Jane? Surely he must know that the château has been ordained sanctuary. Who would dare to violate it and risk the Queen's wrath?"

"It's not that," she said.

"Well, what then?"

She looked at him and then made a curious little gesture with her hands, slowly unfolding her slender fingers, one by one, as though they were pale, slim petals. When they were spread wide, exposed, defenseless, she said: "It's his *huesh*, Francis."

Francis blinked. "I don't understand," he said. "Are you telling me he has *foreseen* this attack?"

"Oh, no. It wasn't like that. He *hueshed* us both in the snow. Himself and me. He said something was on fire in the sky. And I think there was some sort of a hut too. That's how it is with the *huesh*, Francis. It's just a bright flash—a picture. A sort of frozen dream." She looked up at him and smiled faintly. "You don't believe it will happen, do you?"

"How can I, Jane? To accept such a thing would mean conceding that we have no free will, no choice; that everything is preordained. But that is the very opposite of what the Boy taught us. How *can* I believe it?"

"But it happens, Francis. It always has."

"Always?"

She stared into the fire and her face became very pale and still. "No, not always," she whispered. "I *hueshed* finding Thomas washed up drowned on the shore. That didn't happen. It should have but it didn't."

"And yet you still believe in it?"

She nodded. "I have to, Francis. The *huesh* is part of

me—part of what I am—of what's happening to me. I can't *not* believe in it."

"So what are you going to do?"

"How do you mean?"

"Well, if what the Magpie said does come to pass—and I really don't see how it's possible with you in the condition you are—it must mean your leaving Corlay."

"Leave Corlay!" exclaimed Alison. "Has everyone gone mad? How can she leave Corlay? Just look at her, you fool! It is crazy! Impossible! Why, the baby may come tomorrow—tonight even!"

Jane laughed. "He will be late, this one. First sons always are. Doctor Robert says it won't be till the end of the month."

"Ach, Doctor Robert!" scoffed Alison. "What does he know about it? He is only good at delivering baby cows! I tell you it will be soon, my pet. I, Alison, know it. Was I not right to the very hour with Madeleine?"

"You were."

"Yes, I was," affirmed Alison. "And I am right with you, too, Jehane. So let us hear no more of this nonsense, Brother Francis. Leave Corlay, indeed! I shall give that La Pie a slice of my tongue when he comes back. Just you see if I don't."

Ten minutes later there was a knocking at the door and the Magpie's voice called: "It's all right. It's me. Magpie."

"Ha!" exclaimed Alison bounding to her feet. "I have a good mind to leave him out there in the cold and teach him a lesson."

She slid the wedge out of the latch and pulled open the door. "Ugh, how wet you are! Don't you dare shake yourself over me, you gray dog! And what's this crazy story I hear about Jehane leaving Corlay? Come on! Out with it!"

With one swift and totally unexpected movement the Magpie had caught her by the back of her neck. Holding her locked rigid like a rabbit he bent her backward, leaned his face over hers and growled: "Listen to me, girl. You breathe so much as a single word about that and you're like to noose Jane's neck and your own too! I mean it, Alison. Keep a lock on your pretty tongue. A steel lock. D'you understand?"

Alison nodded dumbly and he released her, saying: "I'm sorry if I scared you, lass, but that's the message, so don't you forget it."

"What's happening down there?" demanded Jane. "What did you find out?"

The Magpie refastened the door and turned toward her. "There are twelve strangers in Corlay tonight."

"*Twelve?* Are you sure?"

"Quite sure. I slipped down to the lodge and checked with Alexandre. They've been arriving in dribs and drabs all afternoon. Ones and twos for the most part. That lot Alison saw was the biggest. They told him they were pony-packing a load of fleeces down from Guincamp to Loudeac and got caught by the storm."

"Well, why shouldn't they be?" said Francis. "It's likely enough."

"Perhaps. Perhaps not. But you'll allow that twelve way-farers up here at this time of year is a thought over the odds. And doesn't it strike you as curious that not one single face among them was familiar? Twelve complete strangers."

"Oh, La Pie, why are you trying to scare us like this?"

"Because I'm scared too, lass," he said simply. "I daresay you've never seen a chicken house after the foxes have been through it. Well, I have, and it's not a pretty sight."

Jane got up from her chair and moved round behind it. Gripping it by the back rail she leaned her weight forward, breathing hard and deeply.

"What is it?" asked Francis. "Are you feeling all right?"

She nodded. "My back's aching, that's all."

Alison hurried across and started rubbing her hands up and down her friend's spine. As she did so a bell began to toll, signaling that supper was about to be served in the refectory.

Francis rose to his feet. "It is my Grace Night," he said. "I must not keep them waiting."

"Who's playing tonight?" asked Jane.

"Philip, I think. Yes, I'm sure it's Philip."

"Then I shall go with you," she said. "Your grace I could forgo but not Philip's piping." She caught the Magpie's anxious eye and smiled wanly. "It will be all right, Magpie, my dear," she murmured and touched him on the cheek. "You see, I'm not like Francis. I *have* to believe in your *huesh*."

Chapter Four

During its long history the refectory of Corlay had passed through innumerable transformations but all of them had been superficial. Fundamentally the Great Hall remained as it had originally been conceived, almost two thousand years before, in the mind's-eye of that Master among Master Masons, Roger de Vaucours, when Eric of Cahaix had commissioned him to design a dwelling fit for his paramour Marguerite la Blanche. From its minstrels' gallery troubadours had once vied with each other in elegant flattery of the delicate ladies who had wandered the lawns and the apple orchards and with their own white hands had fed white bread to the white swans on the lake. But everything passes. In time even the songs are forgotten. And then only the ghosts are left.

Sitting at the Magpie's side in the Great Hall and listening to Philip of Aubusson piping songs of the Old Times it seemed to Jane that she could feel the spirits of the long-vanished past thronging all about her in the flickering candlelight. In her fancy she seemed to hear their voices, faint as the twittering of distant birds, and, glancing idly upward, she perceived that it was indeed no fancy at all. Two sparrows had found their way into the hall and were fluttering and cheeping among the high rafters. She watched them for a moment, following them dreamily with her eyes as they flittered back and forth, in and out of the swathes of shadow cut from the stone walls by the massive oak trusses, until her attention was suddenly caught by a different movement—a section of the darkness quietly shifting high up among the shadows of the upper gallery. As she stared up at it she saw it move again and then, as though a ghost had breathed cold breath upon her neck, she realized what it was. The little door to the upper gallery had opened and closed and someone had slipped through. Yet not once before in all the months she had

51

been eating in the refectory had she ever seen anyone up there. She frowned, and lowering her head she looked all down the length of the supper table trying to work out who was missing.

"What is it, lass?"

"There's someone up there in the top gallery, Magpie. I'm sure of it."

"Don't look up again," he murmured. "Just tell me where."

"At the far end," she whispered. "Over the kitchens. High up."

There was a momentary pause, then: "Aye, you're right. But there's more than one. Two I make it. Quick now, lass. Tell me how many strangers you see at table."

"I'm not sure. Six, I think."

"And two up there leaves four to make up the tally," he muttered. "Can you spot the others?"

She shook her head. "Oh, Magpie, what does it mean?" she whispered. "What are they going to do?"

"We'll not be stopping to find out," he responded grimly. "So soon as this tune ends and they bring in the new dishes, we'll slip out. Aye, there's another of 'em! Up there, standing back in the doorway right behind the piper. Got him?"

"By the curtain?"

"That's him. The others'll all be around somewhere. Now listen to me. Tell Alison you think your pains are starting. Get her to help you out. I'll follow you up to your room as soon as may be. If they see the three of us quitting together they'll maybe start something."

"What do you mean? Start what?"

"I don't know yet, lass. You just do as I say. Right?"

She stared at him, opened her mouth as if to object, and then turned away, leaned forward across the table and whispered something to Alison. Next moment Alison had vanished. Rather than make the long circuit all round the table to Jane's side she had simply ducked down and crawled underneath. As she was emerging the piper finished his tune. There was a surge of movement in the body of the hall, some clapping and several cries of *"Encore!"* in which the Magpie joined while he watched anxiously out of the corner of his eye as the two girls made their way to the door beneath the minstrels' gallery. He saw Alison twist the iron latch ring, saw Jane put her hand on the door and then, with a pang like a spasm of sickness in his gut, he guessed what had happened.

Jane glanced back at him, her face as pale as milk, and then said something to Alison. At the same instant a Kinswoman server leaned past the Magpie's shoulder, placed a steaming bowl of vegetables on the table before him and turned away. As the piper launched into a new tune the Magpie gathered up the bowl and carried it off down the table. The moment he came within earshot of the two girls he hissed: "Out through the kitchens! Don't run! *Walk!*"

Jane seized Alison by the hand and they scuttled away past the Magpie. As he watched them pass all down the length of the Great Hall and eventually disappear into the kitchens he knew that he had just endured the longest minute of his life.

He set down the bowl he was still holding and then noticed that he was standing directly behind Francis. Bending down he put his lips to the priest's ear and whispered: "There's devilry afoot. The enemy are among us. They've barred the doors. Make for the kitchens. It's your best chance."

Francis's head twisted up over his shoulder. His mouth gaped slackly. "What?" he spluttered. "What?"

"You heard me, man."

As the Magpie straightened up he saw two men he did not recognize rise from the table and stroll casually toward the kitchen doors. He gripped Francis hard by the shoulder. "Too late for that now," he growled. "Up to the gallery."

"You're out of your mind!"

The Magpie shrugged. "Jane's already away. You wish to stay and die that's your affair."

He turned his back and, feeling his skin gathering itself into gooseflesh, sauntered across to the foot of the wooden staircase that led up to the minstrels' gallery. He guessed that his own life now hung from one solitary, fragile thread—the enemy's confidence that none of the Kinsfolk would suspect what was afoot; that they could safely wait until every man was in position and then, at some pre-arranged signal, begin the butchery. And yet, strangely enough, at that moment he felt neither pity for the Kinsfolk nor horror at what he guessed was to befall them. All his emotions had become subjugated to an overriding, ice-cold rage.

He gained the gallery just as the piper brought his encore to a close and bowed in acknowledgment of the applause. Smiling, the Magpie moved forward as if intent upon speaking to him. Suddenly he turned on his heel and skipped up the shallow flight of steps to the partly curtained archway where previously he had glimpsed the lurking figure of a man. At the precise instant his outthrust hand touched the arras a piercing whistle shrilled down from the upper gallery at the far end of the hall.

In one swift reflex movement the Magpie ducked, snatched the knife from his boot, and hurled himself forward. His head struck his concealed adversary square in the midriff and bundled him over backward. The metal crossbow which the man had been holding flew from his grasp and clattered to the stone-flagged floor of the passage. Even before it had come to rest the Magpie's blade, jerked upward with the full, jolting force of his right arm, had sunk up to the hilt in the soft, unprotected flesh beneath the bowman's chin. His arms and legs contracted in a fierce, spasmodic shudder. They were still jerking as the Magpie wrenched the blade free and thrust it twice more for good measure through the tough, cow-hide tabard and into the still pumping heart. Then, his hands slippery with spurting blood he ripped off the leather bandolier of crossbow bolts and slung it across his own shoulder.

The whole frenzied episode had lasted less than a minute but in that time an indescribable pandemonium had erupted in the Great Hall as Constant's hired executioners set about their grim business. From their stations around the walls they loosed their bolts into the defenseless Kinsfolk with a terrible and pitiless precision. Surprise was absolute. Those who fled for the doors found them barred from without and they were picked off even as their fingers scrabbled at the latches. Unable to escape the deadly hail, men, women and children ran this way and that, shrieking and screaming in terror. Some dropped to their knees in anguished prayer, but such prayers as they voiced were never answered. Only those fortunate few who fled for the minstrels' gallery escaped with their lives through the solitary rift in the wall of death which the Magpie's knife had prized open.

In less than ten minutes from the loosing of the first bolt the massacre was complete. The assassins picked their way down the hall, deftly slitting the throats of any who still showed signs of life. When the stone floor ran red as the gutters of an abattoir they dragged the wooden stools, the benches and the tables into a great pyre under the gallery. They tore down the tapestries from the walls and stuffed them into the kindling. Over the wreckage they poured barrels of oil which they rolled in from the kitchens. And when all was completed to their professional satisfaction they set fire to it with flaming brands which they plucked from the hearth.

The first thing which caught the Magpie's eye as he emerged into the courtyard was a dark, double row of footprints in the thin mantle of freshly fallen snow. Clutching the crossbow to his chest he sprinted for the steps of the Queen's Tower. As he gained the outer door he risked a swift backward glance in the direction of the Great Hall. Through the wind-swirled snowflakes the lights gleamed out brightly but there was no sign of pursuit. He slipped inside, panted up the twisting turret stairs and rattled the door. "Are you there, Janie?"

He heard footsteps and the scrape of the wooden bolt being withdrawn. Then the door was opened by Alison. She gave a shrill squeal of alarm as she caught sight of him. "Oh, my God! Your *hands*, La Pie!"

"Where's Jane?" he demanded, flinging down the bow.

Alison pointed to the bedchamber.

"Is that you, Magpie?"

"Come on, lass. We've got to get out of here. They'll be on to us any minute."

"Oh, Magpie, I can't. It's started."

"What's started? What d'you mean?"

"The baby's coming. I felt it when we were running from the hall."

"She has started her labor," said Alison. "It is like I said."

The Magpie stared at her blankly. "How long has she got?"

"How long!" repeated Alison vaguely.

"Before it's born, you fool!"

"I do not know."

"An hour? Two?"

"More, I think. Perhaps a day."

He thrust aside the curtain and entered the bedchamber. "Janie, love. You trust me, don't you?"

"You know I do."

"Then up on your feet, lass. Wrap yourself warm and come with me. I swear you're worm's meat else."

"Oh, Magpie! What are they doing?"

"Think not on that. Move, lass. *Move!*"

"Help me, Alison."

The Magpie stripped off the bedding, bundled it up and trussed it into a tight roll. As he worked he drove the two girls on with his tongue. At his bidding Alison fetched a copper pan which he contrived to lash to the bedroll. Jane found some candles which she thrust into his knapsack along with the pipes he had brought her. In less time than could have seemed possible they were descending the turret stairs.

"We daren't risk the courtyard now," said the Magpie. "Is there a way out on the other side?"

"From the King's Tower," said Alison. "But where do you take us, La Pie?"

"To the only place I know where we'll be safe from those carrion," he replied.

When they reached the foot of the stairs he chanced a quick peep through the barred spy-hole in the outer door. One of the doors to the Great Hall was now standing ajar and he could hear faint sounds of banging coming from within but he saw no one. Slightly easier in his mind he slid the shutter to and told Alison to lead them out.

Five minutes later they emerged from a concealed postern at the foot of the King's Tower. Straightway the wind leapt upon their backs as though it would pick them up and carry them away in its teeth. "They'll not venture far in this," observed the Magpie, "and it will help to cover our tracks. How goes it, Janie?"

"All right," she murmured. "I'll tell you when I need to rest."

"There's my brave lass," he said. "We'll not let the buggers beat us. Set us on the shortest path to the *lande*, Alison."

"The *lande!* You cannot take her up there! You will kill her for sure."

"Get moving, girl. Or do you plan to freeze us all to death before we've even started?"

"Go on, Alison. Please. Do as he says."

With snow flurries whipping around them they trudged off toward the woods which clothed the slopes behind the château. When at last they came to a clearing among the trees the Magpie called a halt. They turned and looked back.

Alison, who up to that moment had never wholly accepted what he had told them, let out a wild sob of distress and flung her arms around Jane. "Oh, my poor Corlay!" she wailed. "Why have they done this? Why?"

One end of the roof of the Great Hall was collapsing inward. As the blazing timbers buckled and crashed a fountain of sparks gushed upward and huge, forked dragon-tongues of orange flame licked at the low clouds. Fretted thin by the wind the sound reached them as a series of faint, far-off explosions; the smoke as a new bitterness upon the bitter air.

The glow in the sky was still visible when they reached the edge of the plateau some two hours later. By then Jane was at the limit of her endurance. Supported though she was on either side she was still frequently compelled to sink to the ground for rest and, despite her resolution, as the pains grew more severe she groaned in anguish. Even so they made progress and at last came to the lip of that shallow valley which the Magpie had first set eyes upon only hours before. There Jane could go no further. However strenuously she willed it her exhausted legs simply refused to carry her. She subsided into the snow and the tears welling weakly from her closed eyes trickled in faint silvery trails down her frozen cheeks.

Unable to rouse her the Magpie stripped off his burdens and flung them aside. Stooping over Jane he gathered her up in his long arms as though she were a child. Hugging her to his chest he plunged off down the slope toward the hut, leaving Alison to snatch up the bedroll and the knapsack and stumble after them.

Later, when he tried to recall that part of the nightmare, even the Magpie could never really explain to his own satisfaction how it was he found himself standing before the door of the *bergerie* when, in his own mind, he was wholly convinced that he had taken no more than a dozen paces into the gully. At the time he did not bother to question it. He set Jane down, forced open the door, then picked her up again and carried her over the threshold like a newly wed bride.

"Lie you there a moment, lass," he panted. "I'm away back for Alison."

The words were hardly spoken before Alison herself appeared at the doorway gasping out some wild nonsense about the White Bird.

"Aye, well, you're here," he said. "What we need now is light and a fire."

He took the knapsack from her, rummaged inside it and drew out a candle and his flame-maker. He spun the wheel till the sparks sprayed and the tinder began to smolder. Ten seconds of coaxing and a tiny flame was flickering up. He touched the candlewick to it and, a moment later, the sprightly shadows were leaping across the walls.

It was then that the Magpie became aware that the hut was warm. At first he had assumed that it simply felt so in contrast to the bitter cold of the plateau, but now he knew that in no way could that be held to account for the fact that his breath was not even visible as mist in the wavering candlelight. Yet, such was his nature that he did not bother to question why it might be so, he simply accepted it as an inexplicable piece of good fortune on a par with Jane's spying of the bowman in the high gallery.

Holding the candle above his head he paced the length of the hut and discovered a hearth ringed with dead embers and above it a stone chimney in which an iron pot was hanging from a double chain. Some bundles of dry faggots were stacked to hand and two wooden shelf-beds had been built into the walls on either side of the fireplace.

He set down the candle in a smoke-blackened niche, unstrapped the bedroll and spread it out on the boards. Then he moved back to Jane, picked her up once more and carried her across to it. "We'll have a fire going directly," he said, laying her down gently. "But first things first, hey?"

She opened her eyes and her lips twitched into the faint tremor of a smile. "This is the place you *hueshed?*" she whispered.

"Aye, love, this is it. 'Tis no palace, but at least it's safe. They'll not think to hunt for us up here."

Alison pulled a handful of dry bracken from the other bed, laid it on the hearth and piled the cold embers around it. She selected a dead stick from a faggot, stamped it into pieces and arranged them in a rough pyramid above the embers. Then she touched a dead bracken frond to the candleflame and roused the kindling into spluttering, crackling life. "We'll need water, La Pie," she said. "Is there any?"

"Aye, there's bound to be some in the gully. How much do you need?"

"A lot."

"I'll take the big pot," he said, unhooking it from its chains and peering into it. He lifted out two metal porringers and a large bowl which were nestling inside. He set them down by the hearth and disappeared into the night.

Alison laid more wood on the fire, saw that all was well, and then turned to Jane. "He is a good one, that La Pie," she said. "He growls a bit fierce sometimes but you he loves, Jehane, like a good gray dog loves his master."

Jane nodded. "How long do you think it will be?"

Alison did not know but she had wit enough not to admit it. "By daybreak, I think," she said. "Lie on your side and I will rub you. It will help."

Jane rolled over and faced the stone wall. Alison began massaging her diligently. "When La Pie comes back I will ask him to try and fix something for you to pull on," she said. "We did that for Madeleine. It helped her a lot at the end."

Jane drew in a sudden, fierce breath, stiffened, and groaned aloud. "Ah-h-h," she gasped. "It hurts! It hurts!"

"No! No!" cried Alison. *"Il faut relâcher, p'tite!* Not stiff! Inside you must first stretch, . . . stretch! There. That is better. So. Breathe deep . . . deep."

Jane panted and sighed as the wave of pain slowly withdrew, gathering its dark strength for a fresh assault. "Poor Francis," she murmured. "How he was looking forward to this. He believed it would all be so beautiful. Like a rose bursting into flower, he said. A flower! I feel like an animal. An ugly, smelly animal. And I'm afraid." She turned over and caught hold of Alison's hand in hers. "Shall I tell you something? I never really wanted this baby. I only wanted Thomas. Does that shock you?"

"No," said Alison. "But when the baby is born you will love it."

"How can you be sure?"

"It happens. And the Bird will have it so."

"The Bird! The Bird did not save Corlay."

"It saved *us*, Jehane. It brought La Pie to us. It has brought us here."

"Ever since Thomas was killed," murmured Jane, "I've

stopped praying to the White Bird. I don't trust it any more."

"Shh!" whispered Alison. "How can you say such a thing?"

"But it's true," said Jane. "And the Bird knows it is. I trust Magpie far more than I trust the White Bird. It could have spared Thomas and my mother and father but it let them die. Now it has done the same to Francis. All those I love it takes from me. If I love this baby it will take that too."

"You don't know what you are saying, Jehane. You must not talk like this. It makes me so frightened to hear you."

Jane let go of the hand she was holding and turned her face back to the wall.

A minute or two later the Magpie reappeared bearing the iron pot. He hooked it on to the chains and a few drops of water trickled down the side and hissed among the embers. "How goes it, Jane?" he said, moving to her side.

"Like a snail," she replied wearily. "I think maybe he's changed his mind about coming out."

"He is doing fine," said Alison, piling more wood on to the fire. "The pains are coming quicker now."

Even as she spoke Jane was wrenched by yet another fierce contraction, and from then on they came rolling in at regular intervals like storm waves of increasing violence each one of which broke over her and left her breathless and gasping.

Alison bailed some of the water out of the pot into the saucepan and set it down in the middle of the flames. As soon as it began to whisper she said: "We must tear up one of the sheets, La Pie, and put some pieces into the boiling water."

"What for?"

"Because that is what one must do. Always. Doctor Robert says so. It is to make sure they are clean. Now you must lift her up and I will pull the sheet out from under her."

They managed it easily enough between them and then Alison tore the cloth into rough strips. The other half she folded and laid to one side.

"How often have you done this?" asked the Magpie.

"Four times," said Alison. "The first two times I only

stood and watched, but with Berthe I did a lot and with Madeleine I did almost everything." She leaned over Jane and said: "In a minute I will feel in you to see how things are, my pet. I promise you I will be gentle. But first I must wash my hands and arms."

She rolled up her sleeves above her elbows then poured hot water into the largest bowl. Having dipped a piece of the sheet she began scrubbing briskly at her hands and fingers. When they were bright pink she shook them dry, turned back to the bed and, very gently, eased her right hand up inside Jane's body.

Jane gazed up into her friend's abstracted face and read the relief she saw there. "All's well, then?"

"Yes," said Alison smiling. "He is head first and well down. Just as he should be."

Jane reached up, pulled Alison's head down and kissed her. "Bless you, my golden bird," she whispered. "Forget all I said just now. I didn't mean it."

Alison returned her kiss and laughed. "I had forgotten already. Now may I have my hand back please?"

In the early hours of the morning Jane's labor began in earnest. Under Alison's instructions the Magpie had scrubbed the dried blood from his own hands till, he averred, they were cleaner than they had ever been in his life. Only then was he allowed to bend over Jane and let her grasp hold of him whenever she felt the need of something to pull at. He gazed down at her ashen face, saw the sweat standing out in blisters and the veins wriggling like blue worms across her temples as she gasped and strained to rid herself of her intolerable burden, and he sensed dimly that his whole life's purpose had been to be where he was standing now, that every twist and turn of the *huesh* had been designed for nothing else except to bring him to this point in time and space to watch a young girl squealing in torment like a stuck pig while he stood by unable to do anything more to help her than mutter empty useless words of encouragement.

A long hour passed. The candle guttered out and they lit another. Out on the *lande* the wind had dropped. In the soft panting interludes between each contraction they listened to the faint shaking of the iron lid on the simmering pot; the shift and shuffle of the logs as they settled on the hearth. So quiet had it become within the hut that it almost seemed that they could hear the beat of each other's heart.

Jane asked for a drink of cold water and the Magpie took one of the metal porringers, went outside, and found that the sky had begun to clear. He crouched beside the dark, gurgling rivulet, dipped the bowl and scooped up a frosty shimmer of stars. Staring down at it he became lost in an unfamiliar dream in which, for a timeless moment, he seemed to be floating suspended halfway between two heavens and knew not which was which. It was then that the whispering began.

At first he thought it must be the murmur of waves breaking far off along the southern coast which was being carried to his ears by some freak effect of the cold night air, but he dismissed the notion almost as soon as it had occurred to him. He rose to his feet and carried the bowl back to the hut. On the threshold he paused briefly and listened again, and this time he wondered if he were not hearing some sound which existed only in his imagination.

He closed the door behind him, kicked the snow from his boots and walked over to the bed. "I've brought you a bowlful of stars, lass," he said. "The sky's full of them out there."

He slid an arm under Jane's shoulders, helped her up and held the bowl to her lips. She swallowed a mouthful then panted as though she had run a long, hard race. Her eyes seemed to have changed into two dull gray pebbles sunk deep into two dark holes in her head. Strands of her bright, brown hair, blackened by her sweat, were plastered lankly across her pale cheeks. It seemed to the Magpie as though he were watching her youth drain away before his eyes. For the first time since he had set foot in Brittany he felt himself assailed by a sudden fearful doubt. Laying Jane back gently on the bed he caught hold of Alison's arm, drew her away to the far end of the hut, and whispered: "Are you sure everything's all right?"

"I think so, yes," she replied. "Why do you ask?"

"She looks so terrible."

"What did you expect? It is hard work having a baby, La Pie."

"Aye," he muttered, "I can see that. How much longer will it be?"

"I do not know. Not long now, I think. Come. She needs us with her."

They returned to the bedside and the Magpie took up his former station. "Do you want another drink?" he asked.

Jane shook her head. "I just want it to be over," she muttered. "Here we go again." She gulped a huge breath, her face screwed itself up like a tightly crumpled ball of paper, and the veins seemed to leap out on the backs of her hands as she gripped and strained downward with all her might.

"Good! Good!" cried Alison. "I see his head now! Just so much." She joined her finger and thumb into a small circle and held them up. "Rest now, Jehane. I must wash you round about. Then we finish it together, yes?"

She turned away to the fire, picked up a bowl and was carrying it over to the bed when Jane suddenly jerked up her head and said: "Listen!"

The Magpie stared down at her. "What is it, lass?"

"Ssh," she whispered. "There! Don't you hear it?"

Under his hands the Magpie felt hers trembling like lutestrings. "A sort of whispering, is it?" he asked.

She shook her head. "Music," she breathed. "Listen! Listen!"

Alison, practical as ever, set down the bowl, wrung out a steaming cloth and began to make all ready for the delivery. When she had done she took the Magpie's knife and dropped it point foremost into the pan of boiling water. Then she moved back to the bed, spread the folded half-sheet beneath Jane's thighs and laid her ear flat against the rigid, drum-tight belly. It seemed that what she heard was music enough for her. "When the next pain comes," she said, "you must push like never before. But when I say stop, you stop the pushing and pant like a dog. You understand me, Jehane?"

Jane sighed and closed her eyes and felt, deep inside her, as if an ebbing tide had begun slowly to turn. She felt it flooding quietly back into all the invisible fissures and crevices of her being, brimming, and dark, and huge. And as she felt it come so she felt her old familiar fears slipping away from her. He had come back for her. She was no longer alone.

A tremendous surge of joy intense far beyond anything she had ever known was lifting her up in its arms and driving forward, carrying her onward in triumph. In a moment she had swept clean through her agony and far, far beyond it. The scream she left behind was not part of

her any more. She learned the secret blood-red beauty of
the rose that lies in the heart of the howling storm; and in
that one fierce moment she became truly elemental—nothing and everything—with the sounds of piping and happy
laughter everywhere about her.

She came floating back to her senses to feel something
warm and wet wriggling upon her naked belly. She reached
down, felt it, and knew it to be her own living son. With
the Magpie's help she raised her head and looked at him.
"Tom, you Piper's son," she whispered huskily. "You look
just like a little red frog."

"Oh, how can you say such a thing?" exclaimed Alison
indignantly. "He is beautiful! Far more beautiful than
Madeleine's David, aren't you, my pet?"

The baby let out a lusty wail of distress as she deftly
sponged him clean, dried him, and then wrapped him in
her own shawl and presented him to Jane's breast. His
lips puckered eagerly about the nipple, he gripped his
mother's finger fiercely in his tiny hand, and he did not
seem in the least concerned that she was weeping.

Chapter Five

A thin feathering of ice, scarcely more than a transparent
filigree, floated upon the dark surface of the water in the
stone tank high up in the Queen's Tower. On the lip of the
limestone conduit which drained the southern quarter of
the slated roof above, a drip slowly gathered. For a long,
quivering moment it hung as if undecided, then dropped.
A hole the size of a baby's fist appeared in the frozen
tissue and a barely perceptible crescent of a ripple fanned
out across the surface. Half a minute later a second drop
followed. Then, as the sun rose higher in the eastern sky
and touched the topmost slates of the lower roof, the snow
crust began to melt more rapidly. Twinkling rainbow tears
pricked out along the fringe of the lower slates, blinked,
and vanished into the stone gutter. In the dark tank below

the ripples spread more and more rapidly, and the delicate ice flowers trembled, rocked, and shed their petals.

On the paved gangway which circumscribed the water tank a man was lying. A series of dark smears trailing away from his awkwardly twisted body to the threshold of the stone stairway provided some evidence of how he had got there. Adjoining his body a denser stain had congealed. In shape this stain bore a rough resemblance to a lady's pointed shoe. The "heel" of the shoe was resting against a loosely tied bundle of scorched papers. This too was blotched and smeared, and in one place the imprint of fingers could be clearly seen. The "toe" of the shoe had its origin in a vicious wound. A barbed crossbow bolt, fired from above, had pierced the man's left buttock and had lodged itself deep in the hamstring at the back of his thigh. Subsequent movement of the leg had ripped open the muscle and brought about a severe hemorrhage.

But this was by no means the sole extent of the man's injuries. The right side of his face from the cheek to the temple was hideously scarred. The hair on that side of his head and his beard had been charred away almost to the level of the gray, puckered flesh, and the skin on the back of his blackened right hand had gathered itself up into loose papery folds. He was, in truth, a most sorry scarecrow travesty of that Brother Francis who had intoned the evening grace in the Great Hall a mere twelve hours earlier. Yet it was the same man and, despite his injuries, he was still alive.

He owed his survival partly to the Magpie and partly to his own passionate devotion to his new-found faith. The Magpie's whispered warning, even though at the time Francis had discounted it, had enabled him to grasp what was happening when the assassins set about their deadly work. In the mad minutes of pandemonium that had ensued he had fled to the minstrels' gallery, though not quite soon enough to escape a marksman's aim. Dragging his useless leg he had made his laborious way up three flights of stairs to the room which served him as a study. There he had contrived to truss up his own manuscript and to collect the two precious relics of the Boy which he had brought to Corlay. Hobbling back down the stairs he had slipped in a pool of his own blood, fallen heavily and struck his head on one of the steps. When he regained his senses it was to find the whole wing ablaze and his retreat

cut off. Crawling on hands and knees he had somehow
managed to drag himself through the flames and on down
by way of the serving passages until he reached the hall
at the foot of the Queen's Tower.

By this time, unknown to him, Jane, Alison and the
Magpie were already far away. Nor was he aware that,
after a cursory and fruitless hunt for survivors, the enemy
had also fled. Lightheaded with pain, half-blind, and weak
from loss of blood, Francis had begun dragging himself
up the twisting stairs to Jane's room thinking to warn her
of what had happened and urge her to escape. Having
eventually reached her room and found it deserted, he had
summoned up the last remnants of his strength, crawled
on up to the top of the Tower and there collapsed.

Hours later he came back to consciousness convinced
that he was crawling up a long narrow tunnel toward the
sound of a plucked harp. He opened one eye, partially
opened the other and groaned as the scabbed tissue of his
grilled eyelid cracked open to expose the raw, red flesh
beneath.

Rendered visible by the faint smoke haze which origi-
nated among the smoldering charnel of the refectory, a
slim blue lance of a sunbeam was poking through the
eastern slit-window. The sound of the harp Francis slowly
traced to the plangent drip of water falling into the stone
tank against which his head was resting. Very, very slowly
he raised himself on his left elbow, then with his right
hand groped upward for the rim of the tank and began
to pull himself up, propping his left shoulder against the
cold, damp limestone wall. At last he was kneeling with
his chin resting on the parapet. Stretching painfully down
he dipped his right hand into the water, cupped a few icy
drops and lifted them laboriously to his mouth. He repeated this action half a dozen times and then, exhausted
by the effort, sank slowly back to the floor.

After resting for a long minute he began tentatively to
explore the wound in his buttock and thigh. The bolt was
still there, its stiff, blood-matted feathers protruding
through the thick wool of his long coat. He knew he
would have to pull it free but the mere thought of the
pain this would cause him made his head reel. Very gin-
gerly he eased up the skirt of his coat and slid his hand
in underneath. With his fingertips he traced the wooden
shaft of the bolt, found the hard ridge of bruised flesh

which sheathed it and the place where the fanged, razor-edged steel had emerged before slicing its way down into the muscle below. He could not see the actual wound but by the thick pancake of dried blood he guessed that the head of the bolt had severed some major blood vessel. Quite calmly he visualized what he was going to have to do. First he must grasp the bolt by the shaft and pull it backward until the barbs were clear to the thigh; then must raise his knee, seize the exposed head of the bolt and pull the feathered shaft forward and downward through the wound in the buttock.

He mimed through the first part of the process three times and each time his nerve failed him just as his fingers were about to grasp the stiffened feathers. Finally he closed his eyes, prayed aloud for courage, gripped the shaft firmly and jerked it backward.

The pain was almost unbelievable. It felt exactly as if he had drilled a white-hot poker into his own flesh. Driven close to the point of madness he seized the now exposed head of the bolt and heaved. In two abrupt jerks it had torn free and the warm blood was pouring down his thigh. His final act was to staunch the flow by pressing his fingers tight against the wound. Then, lying flat upon the cold stones he let the waves of pain wash over him and sink him back into merciful insensibility.

His swoon did not last long. The fluttering periphery of the pain gradually shrank toward its center and became established as an intense throbbing. As it slowly withdrew he allowed himself to contemplate the possibility of further action. He realized that it was imperative for him to get back down the turret stairs to Jane's room and there attempt to fix some sort of dressing on his wound. But what if the devils were still lurking among the ruins? He could hear no sound apart from the cool tinkle of the water falling into the tank and the throbbing pulse inside his own head. He held his breath and then slowly rolled himself over on to his stomach. The movement proved less painful than he had anticipated. Encouraged by this he slowly drew his right knee up to his chest, lifted himself by his hands, and began to worm his way back toward the stairs trailing his left leg stiffly behind him.

He reached the doorway, gradually inched the door back, and held his ear to the crack. The silence was so profound that it gave him new heart. He pulled the door wide open, turned himself around and, thrusting his wounded leg stiffly ahead of him, began the dangerous and painful backward descent.

It took him twenty minutes and numerous pauses before he eventually dragged himself over the threshold of Jane's room and lay, trembling weakly, on the sheepskin rug before the dead hearth. From there he crawled through into the bedchamber and began to search for a cloth which would serve him as a dressing. In a carved wooden chest he found, neatly folded, two small embroidered sheets which had been stitched by Alison for the baby's crib. He used his teeth to tear one in half, fumbled it into a clumsy pad, and contrived to bind it into place across the still-oozing wound in his thigh. With the other sheet he attempted, less successfully, to cope with the wounds in his buttock. By the time he was done he was shivering uncontrollably and was close to delirium, but some deep-seated instinct for self-preservation still drove him to crawl round to the far side of the bed, to drag the feather mattress down on to the floor and to roll himself up in it.

Francis's own account of what transpired during the next twelve hours was not written down until many years after the events themselves had taken place, and it appears to differ in some degree from the descriptions which others have given of those events. What cannot be denied is that the subjective experience itself, even though its precise nature will probably never be established, has since proved to have been one of the most significant and critical junctures in the whole history of Kinship. Some commentators have even gone so far as to equate it in importance with the Advent of the Boy Himself. What follows is Francis's own description as it occurs in his *Fourth Letter to Brother Matthew* (August A.D. 3042).

". . . Further to these things you saw fit to question me as to the true nature of my Revelation in Corlay which, as you rightly observed, has proved the rock upon which all my life's work has since been founded. Because I know you to be a man of honor and integrity and a diligent seeker after truth, I will do my best to enlighten you, for even though I speak to you of events which occurred fully twenty years ago, yet I can say without dissembling that there has been no single day in my life subsequent to that moment when I have not recalled some part of it in all its mystery and glory.

"First I must ask you to try to picture my condition —severely wounded, weak from loss of blood, badly burned about the face and hands and feverish from the shock of pain and the intense cold. Although it was scarce the ninth hour of the morning and the bright sun was shining in through the casement, yet, as I lay there upon the floor of the Maid's room, racked by spasms of shivering so violent that my teeth rattled in my head, I knew full well that Death's dark doorway was standing open ready to receive me.

"Nor do I use that phrase fancifully. I saw the darkness closing in upon me like the walls of a prison cell from which I should shortly be led out to my final judgment. And I knew that there was nothing I could do to prevent it. Nothing. I was overwhelmed by a sense of loss, of failure, of infinite regret so profound that no words of mine could ever convey it to you. I felt the tears of an unutterable despair well up from my bursting heart and gather in my eyes. All was dust and ashes, waste, futility. Never had I known so bitter, so desperate, and yet so helpless a grief. Truly if hell lies anywhere it lies in the human capacity for regret.

"Fear of death itself played no part in it (that bridge I had crossed a year before when Gyre first showed me the Way just before his own end upon Black Isle). No, this was something of a different order altogether. It stemmed from my aching awareness that I had failed to execute the trust that had been laid upon me first by Gyre, then, through Gyre, by the Boy Himself, and finally by Thomas of Norwich. Their faith had been a living, growing thing: mine resembled a flower perfectly preserved in amber, exquisite to behold, but dead. My passionate quest for the true history of the Boy had been pursued at the expense of all He Himself had ever lived and died for. By remaining at Corlay when I should have been out there in the world struggling with Constant's dark legions on their own battleground I had helped to kill the Boy as surely as if I had loosed the fatal shaft myself. I had failed even to protect the Maid, and I had willfully shut my ears to the divine messenger sent by the Bird to warn me.

"As I lay there shuddering with the bitter tears scalding my seared eyes, I heard Gyre's voice say: *'Art thou not that Black Bird for whom we have been waiting?'*

"At that my heart broke clean in two and the darkness closed upon me.

"Death has many forms; the cessation of physical life is but one of them. I tell you, Matthew, that I died then as surely as if the assassin's bolt had pierced my skull and not my thigh. Only my living sorrow was left to link me to that poor broken thing upon the floor. I rose quietly up and, standing above myself, looked down and felt no more than a sad regret for the body which lay at my feet, a sort of surfeit pity.

"Then, raising my head, I faced the dark prison doors and replied: 'I am he.'

"Slowly and soundlessly the doors began to part until at last they were standing wide open. There before me, unimaginably vast, shimmering in celestial splendor, I beheld the firmament of Heaven. But this was such a Heaven as no living man had ever seen. It far surpassed all human consciousness of beauty. Huge beyond dreams; infinitely remote, infinitely mysterious; arching above me for ever, depth beyond depth. As I beheld it I was racked by a sense of unutterable yearning, a hunger of the spirit so intense that my stunned soul opened before it like a lily to the moon. Eternity was spread before my eyes, and as I reached out to embrace it, I heard the far-off music of piping. I knew it at once for the Boy, for not even Gyre or Thomas of Norwich himself could have wrought such havoc of enchantment upon my fainting soul. The stars wept. Heaven held its breath for wonder. And the sound I had thought I should never hear again was there once more, filling all the echoing caverns of distant space; a sighing, silken downrush of huge invisible pinions, sweeping on and on toward me along the endless corridors of starlight, through the empty avenues of the air.

"The piping ceased: the sound of wings was stilled: a huge, brooding silence hung darkly over me like some enormous wave frozen in the very instant of its breaking. And then it was that through the appalling stillness I heard a child's voice whisper softly and clearly: *'Stay, Francis, I need you.'*

"How can I describe to you the conflict of emotion that filled me at that moment? I stood poised upon the threshold of Paradise about to enter; the world with all its agony and strife, all its endless failures and betrayals lay there at my feet like a shabby heap of soiled, discarded garments. And the choice was mine alone. Yet I knew that if I stepped forward I would be committing an act of betrayal infinitely more abject than any I had ever perpetrated in the whole of my life. The words of a girl I had once questioned about the Boy seemed to ring out clear as a silver bell on a frosty morning—*He came to show us what we have it in ourselves to be . . .* The Boy had surrendered His own precious life for that divine dream: was I now to refuse the surrender of my own death? Dumb as a stone I bowed my head.

"No sooner had I done so than all around me, like flowers bursting open to the sun, I beheld a host of joyful spirits rising upward. I knew them at once for those dear Kinsfolk who had died while I had lived and whose innocent bodies lay even now buried beneath the still smoldering ruins of the Great Hall. No vision more poignant has ever graced my sight as, rooted in mortality, half-blind with grief, I stood and watched them melt away among the stars. And then the stars too faded, grew ever more faint and dim, and the dark shadows came crowding in about me. The last thing I recall was hearing faint and far in the remote distance the fading melody of that exquisite *Lament* which the Boy bequeathed to us just before he died.

"When I opened my eyes again it was to find myself once more imprisoned in this broken, familiar body. Many hours had passed. The casement formerly so bright was now a dim gray rectangle in the darkness of the outer wall. My clothes felt cold and wet to my skin but my fever had burned itself out. Although my wound was still very painful I felt an extraordinary peace of mind. I was wholly and absolutely convinced of the objective truth of my experience—it was, indeed, far more real to me than the reality of

my physical predicament. I saw with a wholly pre-
ternatural clarity what it was that the Boy required
of me and how I must devote the rest of my days to
achieving it. The legions of darkness must be confronted and defeated. Only then would the whole
world be willing to accept the Truth of Kinship. This
was the task for which I had been chosen. And there,
to the best of my ability, lies the answer to your question . . ."

At dawn the next day, a full thirty-six hours after the sack
of Corlay, troops from the Household Guard of Queen
Elise arrived at the sanctuary. Among the small handful
of survivors they discovered Brother Francis and they
carried him back with them to the court at Cahaix where
his wounds were attended to by the Queen's own physician.

The Queen herself spent many hours at his bedside and,
in response to his urgent entreaty, sent search parties out
scouring the countryside about Corlay for Jane and the
Magpie. Three days later a patrol on the *lande* stumbled
upon the deserted *bergerie*. By then the fresh falls of snow
had obliterated any tracks and no one could be certain if
the fugitives had ever reached the place. The general opinion was that they too were victims of the holocaust. It
seemed only too probable.

Despite his grievous injuries Francis was like a man
who is in the grip of some fierce supernatural force. In
next to no time he had succeeded in convincing the Queen
that what had taken place at Corlay was not, as Duke Alain
contended, the work of a band of roving robbers seeking
gain, but was the culmination of a carefully planned attempt to exterminate the creed of Kinship. At his urging
she summoned Alain's confessor, Dom Fabricant, before
her and invited Francis to question him in her presence.

The examination lasted for eighteen hours and by the
end of it Francis was in possession of a detailed confession which confirmed everything he had suspected. And
yet at no point had he employed physical coercion to
extract it. Two faiths had met in psychological contest and
the stronger had prevailed. The new vision of Kinship had
won its first remarkable victory.

The Queen acted swiftly. Summoning the Estates—the
ancient Island Parliament—to Privy Session, she told it

what had happened and received from each Member his sworn Oath of Loyalty to the Crown. Then, having first prudently alerted her Civil Lord Lieutenant as to what was afoot, she armed herself with Dom Fabricant's confession and confronted her cousin the Duke Alain. Invoking her hereditary powers she summarily stripped him of all his estates and public offices and placed him in close custody. That accomplished she dispatched her troops to demand—on pain of instant death for the crime of Civil Treason—the surrender of the keys of every stronghold of the Secular Arm throughout the Kingdom. The surprised Falcons were presented with a simple, stark alternative: surrender to the Civil Force or be banished from the Kingdom for ever—minus your right hand. As far as is known, none elected banishment.

By the end of March everything which had been foreseen by Richard, Senior Marshal of the First Kingdom, had come to pass. Brittany had become the first European Kingdom to adopt Kinship as its official faith; the Island was united as never before in its history; and a new Corlay was already beginning to arise from the ashes of the old.

PART II

FIRST KINGDOM

Chapter One

At eight o'clock in the morning on the first Friday in June, A.D. 3024, a horse-drawn covered wagon of the type once known affectionately as a "prairie schooner" rumbled up the wide wooden gangway of a ferry in the northwestern corner of the First Kingdom. The breeze being friendly and the tide slack it disembarked just over an hour later at the tiny port of Bicknoller on the Island of Quantock where without further ado it set off along the dusty white road which led up to the ancient hill-crest earthwork known as Thorncombe Barrow.

The man who led the horse was the Magpie. A shade grayer in the beard and somewhat more crinkled around his sharp blue eyes he was still indisputably that same man who had spirited Jane and Alison out of Corlay. The boy who trotted at his side was Jane's son, Tom, now a sturdy five-year-old whose untidy mop of light brown curls, wide and generously shaped mouth and square, firm chin owed much to his mother. Only his eyes seemed to claim a genetic allegiance foreign to both his parents, for while Jane's eyes were gray and his father's had been brown, Tom's were as green as emeralds and touched with strange elusive flecks of reddish gold.

How he could have come by such a color was indeed a mystery, but it was not one which gave their owner noticeable concern though it might well have featured as one of those unanswerable questions—"Why don't horses talk? Why is the grass green? Why can't we see the wind?"— which he delighted in posing to his elders. Unlike many children who seem to ask just for the sake of hearing themselves talk, Tom really wanted to know the answers to his questions and few things exasperated him more than to be told: "Because it is so," which, unfortunately, owing to the nature of his inquiries, happened quite often.

The two young women who were seated side by side

on the driver's bench of the lurching wagon were Jane
and Alison, and sprawled in Alison's lap sucking a thumb
and sleepily surveying the rocking, sunlit landscape was
her daughter Marie, nineteen months old, blue-eyed, gold-
en-haired, and known to everyone in the little group as
"Witchet." Her nickname had been wished upon her
shortly after her birth by her father and it had stuck to her
like a burr ever since. He—Alison's legally wedded husband—was none other than the Magpie. They were mar-
ried at Woldingham in the Third Kingdom three months
before the baby was born, a fact attested to by an entry
in the Parish Register, dated August 12th 3022.

Motherhood and marriage suited Alison. She adored
her husband and her daughter and she gave thanks nightly
to the White Bird for her happiness and prayed that she
would soon be blessed with a son. Although this prayer
had not yet been granted she knew in her heart that it
was but a question of time and she was deeply content.

So what of Jane? Who could give an answer to that
question? Certainly not Jane herself. Outwardly she was
still very much the same girl who had surrendered her heart
to the Kinsman, Thomas of Norwich, all of six long years
ago. In the towns and villages of the Kingdoms men still
turned their heads and followed her with their eyes as she
walked past. They were drawn by some ineluctable quality
within her which they sensed but could not fathom; a
quietness; an inner stillness: a mystery.

In spite of what she had confessed to Alison on the
night when Tom was born she loved her son dearly and
had done so ever since the moment she first beheld him.
But the fear which had inspired that dark confession was
still lodged within her like a tiny splinter of ice that would
not melt. And there was something else too, something
she had never mentioned to another living soul, something
she had thrust so far down inside herself that it emerged
only in her dreams and was banished from her memories
of them the moment she awoke.

It had happened when Tom was two years old. He was
cutting a tooth and it made him fretful and kept him
awake. One night while she was having her supper she
heard him whimpering in the next room and went in to
comfort him. She had knelt beside his cot, gazed down at
him and laid her cool hand on his flushed forehead. His
eyes opened and looked up into hers.

Before she was fully aware of what she was doing, and thinking perhaps to soothe him, she had allowed herself to slip down into his infant mind. It was something she had never done with him before, and never again since, for what she had seen was impossible—a brilliant, flickering tumult of memory images, of scenes and people and places which could be no part of his small life's experience. And behind it all was a quivering, star-pricked, velvet-textured darkness, deeper than the deepest night.

The contact lasted no longer than a few bewildering seconds but it had left her inwardly trembling and desperately afraid. She had kissed him, settled him down and had then gone back to the supper table where Alison told her she looked as if she had seen a ghost. If she had, then she managed to persuade herself that she had imagined it, but she never tried the experiment again.

As the Magpie had forecast she recovered the power of *huesh* soon after her son's birth. She did not welcome it but there was nothing she could do about it and from odd remarks he had begun to let fall she suspected that Tom had inherited the gift from her. What he most certainly *had* inherited was his father's gift for music. Almost before he had learned to talk he was picking out tunes on the wooden whistle which the Magpie had made for him. He acquired a habit of wandering off on his own, disappearing sometimes for hours on end, oblivious to the passage of time. They would eventually track him down by following the silver thread of his music through the labyrinth of the woods to find him squatting beneath a tree or perched up on a rock, piping away, lost to the world.

Until September 3022 they had traveled around the southern Kingdoms leading a gypsy life, then the news that the Magpie's old mother was ailing drew them back to Blackdown. There in the cottage in the valley they had settled and Alison's daughter was born. In May the following year Old Mother Patch took to her bed. A few days later she called them all in to her, gave them her blessing, and calmly announced that her time was up. She looked around at them and her ancient eyes, still as sharp and bright as needles, came to rest upon young Tom who was perched in the crook of his mother's arm regarding the old woman curiously. "You'll play me a tune, won't you, lad?"

she said. "Give your old Granny a hand over the threshold? Sit you there."

She pointed to the foot of the bed and there Jane set Tom down. He tucked his legs in beneath him, drew his wooden whistle from inside his woolen jerkin, gazed into the old woman's face, then set the pipe to his lips and began to play.

The melody he chose was so light and gay that the dark little room seemed all at once to be filled with sunshine and butterflies and spring blossom. Hearing it the sadness lifted from their hearts and slipped out through the open window like a wisp of dark fog.

The old woman smiled, nodded, let her head sink slowly back against the pillows, and closed her eyes.

It was in March the following year that Jane sought out the Magpie and told him that the time had come for her to return to Quantock.

"I wondered when that was coming," he replied. "How long have you known?"

"Since Christmas. It's safe now, isn't it?"

"Safe as it'll ever be," he said. "And are we to come with you?"

"Of course you are."

He smiled. "It would have been hard for us to split now, Janie. Have you *hueshed* it out?"

"Rett and Simon will help us. Can you get a message to them?"

"I'll do better than that," he said. "I'll go over there myself and tell them what's afoot. That'll give them a chance to lay some timbers for the roof. The way I read it, lass, we'll do best to trade our way up from Buckfast and aim to home in on Tallon around June. That'll give us the summer to work the fairs and put a few royals by. Or have you some other plan?"

"No," she said. "All I saw was us living in Tallon and the kiln firing again."

And so it came about that in May 3024 the wagon had been loaded up with the winter's produce together with as many tools and household goods as they could manage to pack inside. The goats and chickens were disposed of to neighbors; the cottage securely locked and barred; and they set off down the high road to Sidbury where they boarded a coasting trader which landed them at Buckfast a day later. At the beginning of June they descended upon the little port of Bicknoller on Quantock Isle and began the final stage of their long journey.

It was close on midday when they reached the road which runs white as a bleached bone all down the length of the island's spine. The breeze which had wafted them over the narrow channel was whispering among the heavy-headed roadside grasses and sending silvery shivers dusking across the flanks of the ancient earthwork. The air was warm and sweetly scented with wild flowers, the sky as blue as a starling's egg, and over the high moors to the west puffs of fleecy white cloud had begun to form. They floated serenely away out over the northern channel, trailing little patches of purple shadow across the surface of the glittering water.

The Magpie unshackled the horse from the shafts of the wagon and turned it loose to graze. While Alison set about preparing a meal, Jane took Tom's hand in hers and climbed with him to the top of the mound from where she pointed out various landmarks, among them the Island of Blackdown twenty miles to the south. "The last time I stood up here I was just as old as you are now," she said, "and I rolled all the way down to the bottom."

Tom looked up at her in obvious disbelief. "You didn't."

"Oh yes I did."

"How?"

"Like this," she said, and dropping on to all fours she suited the deed to the word.

Squealing with excitement he launched himself after her. They arrived at the bottom breathless with laughter and dusted from head to foot with yellow pollen. "Now do you believe me?" she panted.

"Were you with *your* mum?" he asked.

"No. With my dad—your grandad."

"Did he do it too?"

"Yes, he did."

"Was he as good a roller as you?"

"Better," she said. "He was rounder." And all at once, remembering him with a sudden, terrible vividness, her heart melted with her loss and she turned away lest Tom should see the tears which had sprung unbidden to her eyes.

At four in the afternoon they jolted over the brow of Cothelstone Hill and had their first glimpse of the roofs of

Tallon rippling in the heat haze far below them. Above the harbor the bare masts of a trading coaster appeared to waver like yellow cornstalks. Out on the Reach, like left-over autumn leaves, two brown-sailed mackerel boats floated becalmed. Beyond them the island of Blackdown was a blue leviathan slumbering peacefully in the dozy warmth of the declining sun.

For Jane it was like re-entering an all-too-vivid dream. Times beyond number she had imagined herself to be standing on this very spot gazing out across Taunton Reach and the Somersea, and always she had turned her eyes aside lest they might catch a glimpse of the ruined shell of the cottage which for so long had been her home and where, six years before, the Gray Falcons had tortured her father and had burned her mother alive. What lay before her now was not the future but the past. She knew there could be no more turning aside. The *huesh* demanded it. And as if she needed to confront her adversary alone and face to face she halted the wagon, climbed down and walked on ahead.

Tom would have run after her but the Magpie held him back. "Let her be awhile, Tom," he said. "Come, you shall ride atop of old Jason and enter Tallon in style."

He swung the boy up on the horse's back and set the drag brake on the wagon. By the time they were under way again Jane had passed out of their view round a bend in the road.

The first sight she had of Kiln Cottage was of the gleam of mellow sunshine from the roof-spine of oak joists which Rett and Simon had already erected in place of the charred timbers. It was as though a smothering weight had been lifted from her breasts. She unlatched the garden gate and hurried down the flagged path calling their names. Then she remembered the boats she had seen out on the Reach and guessed where they were.

Beside the front porch lay a neat stack of newly quarried slates and just inside was a half-empty cask of lime. With her heart thumping painfully she thrust open the door and stepped over the threshold, expecting to see evidence of the carnage everywhere about her. But the once smoke-blackened stone walls had been freshly lime-washed, new wooden ceiling joists were already in place and new floor boards stood propped against the wall waiting to be laid. The only smell was of sun-warmed oak shavings and the clean, acrid scent of fresh mortar. Someone had even thought to scour the rust off the kitchen range.

She wandered from room to room seeking she knew not what, then walked outside into the overgrown wilderness of a kitchen garden and made her way up into the orchard. There, under the old cherry tree, just as the Magpie had told her, lay the grave which he had dug six years ago. The stone had settled slightly crooked and the grass of summer had grown high but she knelt down and with her fingers traced out the rough shape of the Bird and the lichened lettering below: *Pots and Susan Thomson. May 3018*. Even as she read the legend it dissolved away before her eyes in the grief she could no longer restrain.

She was aroused by the sound of piping. Raising her bowed head she saw Tom seated astride the orchard wall. The tune he was playing was new to her and she guessed that he intended it for her ears alone, that somehow he had divined her need and had chosen this way to comfort her. A moment later, as though spurred into emulation, a blackbird perched in an apple tree higher up the slope suddenly unlocked its throat and began pouring its own song into the sunny air. Another answered it, and in a minute the whole orchard seemed to have burst into a blossom of birdsong across which her son's piping wove like a glittering silver thread in a golden tapestry.

Listening, enraptured, Jane knew that she had never really heard Tom play before; that for the first time she was hearing his music as Old Mother Patch must have heard it just before she died, and that in some utterly mysterious fashion he was conjuring some element of her own self with which to enchant her. Her memory groped hazily back into the past for something which Thomas had once told her about the Boy and his divine gift, but what she sought eluded her like a word hovering on the tip of her tongue. Just as she seemed about to grasp it the tune broke off in the middle of a phrase and Tom jumped down from the wall, scampered toward her, flung his arms around her and became her own true son again.

She drew him to her breast, hugged him and kissed him and asked him where the others were. Then, hand in hand, they made their way down toward the kiln yard where Alison and the Magpie were already at work unloading the wagon.

The pottery and the kiln, standing some fifty paces distant from the cottage, had escaped the fate which had befallen it. They had also escaped the predatory attentions of the village children who believed that the place was haunted by the ghosts of the dead potter and his wife and gave it a wide berth. Jane found everything almost exactly as her father had left it on that black day when the Falcons had struck. Even the kiln was still loaded with glazed pots ready for firing and the billets of wood were stacked ready to hand. A thick mantle of sooty dust lay over everything and generations of mice had nested in the straw-filled packing crates, but she knew that in a day or two she could have it all straight again. She would have liked to have made a start upon it right away, but until the new roof was on the cottage they would have to use the pottery as their living quarters.

That evening the twins Rett and Simon arrived with a gift of a dozen fresh mackerel and a jug of ale. They stayed until the small hours, re-living the past and discussing the future. When they left Jane walked with them to the gate. The night sky was a billion frozen twinkling raindrops; the invisible sea a restless whisper. "There are no words to tell you how much I owe you both," she said. "My heart is too full."

"Having you back wi' us again is all that counts, Janie," said Rett. "Tallon's missed her little witch. Remember how you *hueshed* us the haul which broke old Dad's net, hey? What a mad day that was!"

"We'll have the cot all tiled up for you by this time next week," said Simon, "never you fret."

She kissed them both and watched them stride away down the hill. When they were lost to her sight in the shadows she raised her head and looked up into the heavens. "Oh Blessed White Bird," she murmured. "Now do I thank you with all my heart."

Chapter Two

One sunny afternoon in the middle of June 3029, almost
five years to the day after Jane and her son returned to
Tallon, Robert, Earl of Exeter, Lord of the First Kingdom
and the Eastern Isles, brother-in-law to the Duke of Winchester and linked to the Fifth Kingdom through the
betrothal of his eldest daughter to Northumberland's son,
Henry of Doncaster, leaned back in his chair, prized loose
a reluctant morsel of roast pork from its lodging place between his back teeth and said: "Just between the two of
us, Richard, I'm damned certain you wouldn't give a fish's
fart if the gelding broke his neck this minute."

The Lord Marshal of the First Kingdom grinned and
helped himself to an orange from the dish before him.
"Bishop Simon's not the easiest man to love, Robert. I'll
grant you that. But he's clever, and Constant values him."

"More fool Constant then. Simon lost him Brittany."

"That was never proved, you know."

"Oh, come now, Richard! What do you take me for?
You know as well as I do who was behind that fiasco. Hell,
man, I read Dom Fabricant's confession myself."

"Extracted under torture."

"It rang true as a bell, Richard, and well you know it.
I'm only surprised it didn't cost Castrato his head. It would
have done if I'd been in Constant's shoes."

The Lord Marshal tore off a strip of orange peel with
his strong yellow teeth and spat it on to his plate. "You've
heard the news from Switzerland?"

"Aye. Is it true?"

"It's true. Three weeks ago the Secular Arm was officially
disbanded in the last of the Cantons."

"Well, well, well," mused the Earl. "Things are certainly
moving apace. What does the Vatican think about that?"

"They're still counting the cost of Aosta. More than
fifteen thousand dead, I've heard."

Robert sucked in his breath then let it out in a slow, deliberate hiss. "Crazy," he muttered. "Completely crazy. I sometimes wonder how Constant can sleep at nights."

"I don't think he does," said Richard. "I don't think he ever has."

Earl Robert beckoned for more wine. "I don't believe I've ever asked you this before, Richard," he said. "Why did he do it?"

"Promulgate the Edict, you mean?"

"Aye."

The Lord Marshal glanced over his shoulder and, with a twitch of his eyebrow, indicated the table servant.

"Leave the wine on the table, John," said the Earl. "Away off with you."

The servant placed the silver jug between the two lords, bowed and vanished.

"The truth is," said Richard, "I've never really known for certain. It was all tied up with that secretary fellow of his."

"The Apostate?"

"Aye, that's the chap. Brother Francis. I met him once in the old days up at York. Quite liked him as a matter of fact—but don't say I ever said so."

"Well? What happened?"

"Constant—he was still Bishop in those days—sent Francis off as devil's advocate about some supposed miracle of the lad's. To the Cotswolds, I think it was. Or was it Cumberland? No matter. Anyway, Francis got himself pecked by the White Bird and being that kind of a holy fool spoke up to Constant on behalf of the Kinsfolk. I think that's what really opened Contant's eyes. As he read it, if a priest as loyal as Brother Francis could catch the 'flu then nobody was safe."

"But I always thought it was Constant who had claimed the Boy for the Church in the first place."

"So it was. And that's just what made it all the more bitter. Bill Barran had warned him away back what might happen but he hadn't listened."

"How warned him?"

"About the legend of the White Bird. But that's something I can't speak about. Not even to you."

Robert eyed him enigmatically but refrained from comment.

"In my opinion where Constant slipped up was in hand-

ing the Prosecution over to Lord Simon before he left for
Turin. I suppose he thought it would just be a short sharp
operation and the scar would be healed up by the time he
got back. Well, you know all about that. If Simon had had
his way the Grays would have drawn and quartered every
man, woman and child of the Kinsfolk between here and
Forfar."

"That man's a maniac."

"A loyal servant of the Faith, Robert."

"Your own does you credit. But you know as well as I
do what he cost us across Exmoor and through the Isles.
Those Folk weren't traitors, they were loyal, law-abiding,
honest citizens. Are you telling me I'm wrong?"

"I think you know my opinion on that."

"Yes, yes. That's all over and buried now, thank God.
I really let you have it though, didn't I? Does it still
rankle?"

The Marshal laughed. "A verbal box on the ear never
did me any harm. Besides, I felt at least as sick as you did.
It need never have happened."

"That's just what I've always said, Richard. A word in
the right place at the right time. . . . And now look where
we are. Christendom's becoming a cock-pit. All your lord
and master seems to have achieved is to turn sucking doves
into eagles. Between ourselves he's never read this situation
right. He just doesn't seem capable of seeing things in the
round. Take this latest notion of his for instance. If he
honestly expects us to abrogate the Treaty of Finistère he
must be clean out of his mind."

The Marshal raised his goblet to his lips and took a long,
thoughtful sip of the French wine. Then he set the cup
down again and carefully dissected a segment of his
orange. "I was rather hoping you weren't going to say
that, Robert."

"Well, for God's sake, man! What did you expect? Half
the Kingdom's revenue comes from our trade with Brittany! And not just ours either. Winchester and Kent are
equal partners now."

"I know it. And that's precisely what's put the cat
among the pigeons."

"Now, listen to me, Richard." The Earl held up his left
hand with the two first fingers splayed. He gripped one.
"Church," he said. He transferred his grip to the second.

"State," he said. "Two separate fingers on the one hand. But *separate*. Do I make myself clear?"

"Oh, yes. Very clear."

"Because I wouldn't like the Cardinal to get a false impression."

The Marshal sighed audibly—really it was more of a groan than a sigh. "Couldn't you just try to meet him *part* of the way?"

"What are you *talking* about, Richard? The treaty's there in the archive! It's solemn and binding on all parties! Go ahead and read it for yourself if you don't believe me! Damn it, it was even witnessed and blessed by old Bishop Andrew! It's got the Primatial Seal! And don't you forget that you take your full tithe from every single landing at every port in the Kingdom. It would cost the Church at least a thousand crowns a month! That's the real point to bear in mind."

"Forgive me, Robert, but with all due respect I don't really think it is."

"Oh, isn't it? Well, as far as I'm concerned it is. Those Customs and Excise duties buy my civil servants, Richard. Is Constant proposing to pay their wages himself?"

"He is prepared to forgo the tithe."

Robert gave a harsh bark of mirthless laughter. "Oh, sweet heaven! What splendid magnanimity! And where are the other nine tenths going to come from? The air? The bottom of the sea? Or the coffers of the Secular Arm perhaps? Just tell me, Richard. Let me into your secret."

"We realize it will involve the Kingdom in a considerable temporary sacrifice but—"

"No," said the Earl, cutting him short. "You realize nothing of the kind, Richard, because it won't happen. That treaty stands fast and the whole of the First Kingdom stands four-square behind it."

"That's your last word, is it?"

"My first *and* my last. I've never given the idea a single moment's serious consideration. It's just plain stupid. Idiotic. The raving lunacy of some fanatic up in York. Lord Simon, no doubt. Besides, what possible advantage could accrue to anyone? Come, Richard, you're a man of sense, you know what I'm talking about. Haven't you got a property of your own in Brittany? Just tell me one single benefit which the abrogation of the treaty would bring either to the Church or to the State."

"It could bring Brittany to her knees."

"Oh, balderdash! It would simply knit the Bretons tighter together than ever before."

"I'm only repeating what I've been told."

"Told by who? By Constant?"

Richard nodded.

"He's obsessed," said the Earl. "There's no other word for it. Obsessed. He's got birds on the brain."

Richard said nothing.

The Earl poured more wine into their goblets. "You didn't seriously think I'd agree, did you?"

"No, frankly, I didn't."

"And you told him so?"

"Yes."

"Well? How did he take it?"

The Marshal drew a deep breath and slowly exhaled it. "You mean you can't guess?"

Robert raised his goblet. "Well, I can see he wouldn't have been exactly overjoyed."

The Marshal raised his head and turned full face toward his friend. "Robert, he's threatening excommunication."

The Earl choked so explosively on his drink that drops of blood-red wine showered across the table. "*What?*" he croaked from behind a napkin which looked as though it had stopped a hemorrhage. "*What did you say?*"

The Marshal spread his hands. "The message was that if you refused to abrogate the Treaty of Finistère, the Church will have no option but to implement a bull of excommunication against you."

The Earl's complexion was florid at the best of times, now it began to resemble a piece of raw beef. His eyes bulged and his nostrils flared to expose a tangle of reddish bristle. He almost appeared to steam.

Wondering if he were about to witness the onset of an apoplectic seizure, Richard reached out and quietly refilled the Earl's goblet. "Believe me, Robert," he murmured, "this was none of my wishing."

"So," panted the Earl. "So that is to be the way of it. We are to save the soul by hacking the limbs off the healthy body. For that's what it'll be. This isn't just us, Richard, it's Kent and Winchester too. You realize that, don't you? I tell you we've got a raving fanatic on our hands! Well, go on, man? Say something!"

For a wild moment the Marshal was tempted to agree and damn the consequences, but a lifetime's schooling in obedience stayed his tongue. "Let us not be over-hasty, Robert," he said. "You can see as well as I can what's happening in Europe. We've got to stop the rot before it destroys us. Switzerland's fallen; Norway and Sweden are set fair to follow. And Brittany is the core of the infection. If we do not strike now, Christendom bids fair to suffer a defeat from which she will never recover. We'll be back in the Dark Ages and the devil will have come into his own."

The Earl mopped his beard and moustache and dropped the napkin on to the table. He appeared to have regained a measure of control over himself. "Has it never occurred to you, Richard, that if Constant had simply let the Kinsfolk be, none of this would ever have happened?"

"Such speculation is profitless," the Marshal replied. "The fact is that it *has* happened and now we've got to cope with it."

"You haven't answered my question."

"How can I answer it? You know the nature of my Oath."

"I know you've chosen to put your eyes in blinkers, but I suppose that your own affair. But why that should give you and your crazy driver the right to cart us all over the precipice is another matter altogether. Don't you see that if we accede to this threat of Constant's we'll be playing right into the Apostate's hands? What you'll have is civil turmoil in three of your seven Kingdoms. It's inevitable. Our economies are geared to our trade with Brittany. The Treaty of Finistère has brought us nothing but good. We are more prosperous now than we have been for centuries. We abide by the laws. We pay our tithes. We go to mass. And all this you are prepared to pitch overboard. For what? For some obsession, some wild fever in Constant's brain that the Kinsfolk are in league with the devil. All I ask from you, Richard, is one solitary shred of evidence that this is so. Just one."

"One? Are there not fifteen thousand of them lying on the mountainsides at Aosta!"

"Oh no," said the Earl. "That, my friend, is evidence of nothing more than monumental military stupidity. But perhaps you are claiming idiocy as evidence of God's approval? Is that it?"

The Marshal forbore to comment. "I have to report back to York in a fortnight, Robert. What am I to say?"

The Earl pushed back his chair, walked across to the window and gazed out. Above the distant spires of Exminster, the silken banners fluttered bravely against the sunny sky. In the soft green fields which lay between him and the city, horses and cattle were peacefully grazing. Peace; order; stability; a chance for everyone to enjoy the fruits of their labors. This was what you struggled for, what you believed that life was all about. When your time came you died and you were judged by Almighty God. And if you had done all the things you ought to have done, had carried out the responsibilities which He had placed upon you to the very best of your ability, then you went to Heaven. And no doubt, if you were very lucky, you would find that Heaven was very much like this. His was a simple enough creed but it was one which had served him well for the forty years since, as a callow youth of seventeen, he had succeeded to the title and become ruler of the First Kingdom. But now what? Was he just to throw it all away? Was it *really* possible that this crazy Cardinal could get to God's own ear and have him damned to hell without his being able to say a single word in his own defense? Well, the only thing to do was to play for time and hope to find some way out of the mess. He sighed heavily. "Tell your master that I shall first have to consult with Kent and Winchester. By the very nature of the Treaty this is not a matter I can decide upon my own."

"And when will that happen?"

"As soon as may be."

"But *when*, Robert? You have to give me *something* to carry back to York."

"September?"

"The beginning of September?"

"The end. The very last day of the month. Tell him that. And, Richard. . . ."

"Yes?"

"For dear God's sake try to make him understand what this will mean for all of us."

"You know that I will."

The Earl turned away from the window and moved back to the table. "It doesn't make sense," he said gloomily. "It just doesn't make any sort of sense at all."

"What doesn't?"

"What you're doing. What you're hoping to do." The Earl's eyes suddenly narrowed, became thoughtful. "Unless . . . " he murmured.

"Unless what, Robert?"

The Earl brushed his hand through the air and shook his head. "A passing fancy. Nothing." His manner changed to a brisk and businesslike geniality. "Well, to work, Richard. Your news has given me letters to write."

"Are we not to ride then?"

"Ah, I had forgotten. Well, some other day, eh? As you said yourself time is of the very essence."

"True," said the Marshal rising to his feet.

The two men, friends of so many years, so many shared adventures, looked at one another and each knew in his innermost heart that something had changed, that things could never again be quite the same between them. But it was already too late for either of them to do anything about it.

The Marshal set out on horseback for the Falconry by way of bridle paths through Hartcombe Forest. It meant taking in two long sides of an irregular triangle but he was in no particular hurry and the weather was perfect. His interview with the Earl had passed off far better than he had dared to hope and yet he felt no corresponding sense of achievement, almost, in truth, the opposite. He knew that he had failed to make Robert appreciate how vitally important it was that Brittany should be won back for the Faith. Their discussion had concerned itself too much with the means, too little with the ends which justified them. Yet the Earl was a God-fearing man—by all prevailing standards an enlightened ruler of his people—and he had sufficient imagination to appreciate that none of the Kingdoms of Christendom could exist in isolation, that all were integral parts of the closely woven garment that was the Church Militant. Why then had he been so reluctant to espouse the cause of economic sanction when it must have been obvious to him that this was the surest and safest way of achieving the desired objective? The answer, of course, was that Robert seemed to be constitutionally incapable of seeing Kinship for the threat that it was. As far as he was concerned the problem was simply an obsession of Constant's, some sort of grotesque fixation which was driving him on to destroy the very thing he wished to preserve.

The Marshal reined up his slowly pacing horse and sat gazing ahead into vacancy while for a bewildering moment he seemed to glimpse the world through Robert's eyes. He saw a country in which the Church was an outmoded anachronism, useful only because it supplied a framework of social stability within which the loyal subjects of the First Kingdom could thrive and prosper. With a chill clarity the Marshal recalled that appalling interview when he had been summoned to account for the atrocities of the Grays and, for the first time in his life, had found himself being forced by the nature of his Office to defend the indefensible before a man who had always regarded him as a friend. *"A pack of licensed murderers—enemies to God and man alike! If those scum represent your Christianity, Richard, then give me honest Kinship any day! They've done more harm to your cause in two weeks than the Kinsfolk could have accomplished in two centuries!"* And so on and so forth. Well, that storm had blown itself out and over the past ten years he himself had done as much as anyone to bleach out the stains. Provided that the First Kingdom Kinsfolk had kept themselves to themselves and the stubborn ones had paid their recusancy fines, they had been left alone—never exactly tolerated but not overtly persecuted either. And most of them had been perfectly content to trot along to mass of a Sunday just as they had done in the old days when the Boy's star had been riding high in the northern sky. Had he really betrayed his Faith by not turning his Falcons loose upon them? He could not believe it. But there would be several at York who would say that he had, and there was little doubt in his mind that Constant would number himself among them.

He set his horse ambling onward again and thought about this Cardinal whom he had known personally and had genuinely admired for over thirty years. No man alive had done more to restore the failing strength of the Secular Arm throughout the Western Kingdoms. If Constant drove men hard then he drove himself harder. He did not tolerate fools, but he was just almost to a fault. He had had men executed for abusing their authority and had done it with no more compunction than one would expend in the swatting of a fly. He used other men as a stonemason used chisels and when they lost their cutting edge he discarded them. Nor was it true that Constant would never listen to advice; he did, and sometimes he even acted upon it; but neither readily nor very often. Perhaps he was too used to being right himself. Some men admired him; all feared him; none loved him. It was this last incontestable fact which would, Richard guessed, ensure that his Master would never attain to the highest Office of them all. Yet he did not even know if that was Constant's ambition. It seemed likely, but with such a man could one ever be certain that simple ambition was the spur? Richard was inclined to doubt it. It was altogether too human, too prosaic a motive for one of Constant's austere stamp. And he recalled how once, long ago, Bill Barran in his cups had confided to him that he believed Constant's true source of motivation was a desire to re-create God in his own image.

It was then that the Marshal, for no obvious reason, found his thoughts had flickered back along some subconscious conduit to center once more upon the Earl. He frowned as he found himself recalling the way in which Robert had suddenly seemed to check himself in mid-flight, just before he had brought their interview to an end. What was it he had been saying? That what Constant was proposing to do didn't make sense? And at that point he had paused and murmured "Unless . . ." Unless what? What thought had crossed his mind? Unless the plan should prove successful? That hardly stood up in the light of what he had said about the probable effect of trade sanctions. So what could it have been that he had spotted—or thought that he had spotted—which he would not confide? Some ulterior motive of Constant's? Yes, that was possible, though Robert was usually neither shy nor backward whenever he felt that criticism of the Cardinal was called for. So it must have been something in which both he, Richard, and his master were equally involved. Which left only the Secular Arm itself.

With a sharp involuntary shiver the Marshal realized what the connection was, why his idling thoughts had suddenly homed back to Earl Robert. Power was the link! By discounting the threat of Kinship as a figment of the Cardinal's obsession Robert had contrived to rationalize the demand for the abrogation of the Treaty of Finistère. In the inevitable privation and civil unrest which would ensue he had perceived a manufactured opportunity for the Secular Arm to seize absolute control over the civil government throughout the Southern Kingdoms! The notion was, of course, utterly ludicrous, but it would not have seemed so to Robert who had never forgotten (or allowed *him* to forget!) how the Grays had torn through the First, murdering and raping his liege subjects and owning responsibility to none but Lord Simon.

The idea had no sooner occurred to him than he was convinced that it was correct. So certain was he that he would have been prepared to wager a sizable sum in gold that even now the Earl was dictating letters to the Lords of Kent and Winchester apprising them of what he suspected was afoot. For a minute he seriously contemplated spurring back to the castle and attempting to disabuse Robert of such a patently ridiculous notion, but finally he decided against it. For one thing he might conceivably be mistaken, and, for another, if he were right then his action would almost certainly serve no other purpose than to confirm Robert in his suspicions.

The irony of the situation was not lost upon him, but far more hurtful was the realization that, through no fault of his own, he had forfeited the Earl's trust. What the Grays had started Constant had now concluded: the painstaking effort spread out over twenty-five productive years had been effectively reduced to ruins in the course of an hour. But would it have survived the coming crisis anyway? Nothing, he knew, would deflect Constant from carrying out his threat should Robert prove obdurate, and as an infallible recipe for the total annihilation of trust, friendship and co-operation between Church and State, what could be more effective than that?

He turned his horse's head toward the northwest and cantered for home. The air was just as warm and sunny as it had been all day, yet to the Lord Marshal it seemed to have become distinctly chill. He was oppressed by a premonition of dark storm clouds gathering themselves below the horizon. Nor was his sense of unease lightened in the least when he happened across a deserted clearing on the outskirts of the forest and saw, sketched out in rough and forceful lines of chalk upon a rock face, the sign which was growing daily more familiar throughout the western world—the symbol of the hovering White Bird of Kinship.

Two and a half weeks later, on the first Monday in July 3029, the three Senior Marshals of the three Southern Kingdoms were received by Cardinal Constant at a morning audience in the New Falconry. Not one of the three officers was pleased to find that Bishop Simon of Leicester was also in attendance. They were even less enthusiastic when, after they had kissed the Cardinal's ring, they were informed that he had received an urgent summons to the Vatican and that during his absence in Turin the Office of Chief Falconer, the supreme secular authority for the Seven Kingdoms, would be vested in the Bishop. It was for that reason, Constant explained, that Lord Simon was being made privy to their counsel since it would be necessary for him to be fully cognizant of the matters they were met to discuss.

As they took their seats at the table the Cardinal directed their attention to a large map which was mounted upon the wall opposite the windows. It represented the whole of Western Christendom since the Drowning. Each Kingdom bore a small pinned emblem—either a scarlet cross or a black circle. Richard was amazed to see that not only Switzerland was spotted with black but also the Island Kingdoms of Normandy and Bethune fronting the Channel, as well as the Northern Pyrenees and the whole of Scandinavia.

"But is this true, my Lord?"

"*De facto*, Richard. That display is based on the reports which have just reached us from Turin. Our present intelligence is that Normandy will declare for the Apostate before the end of this month; the others probably before the year is out. Indeed, for all we know, Sweden may already have done so. The news from Switzerland has traveled fast."

"It's incredible!"

"It is certainly the most pessimistic analysis possible," said the Cardinal. "We wish everyone to be fully conscious of the critical nature of the situation. The time for complacency is long since past. We are now reaping the bitter harvest sown by our failure in Corlay. Well, gentlemen, to business. What news do you bring us?"

Richard glanced quickly around the table, saw that none

of the others seemed anxious to set the top spinning, and said: "As soon as I received your instructions, my Lord, I made haste to acquaint Earl Robert with your proposal. As you may imagine he was not what I could call enthusiastic."

The two other Marshals signified by murmurs that they had met with a similar response from their respective Civil Lords.

"Well, go on."

"We discussed the matter at some length. When it became obvious to me that he was set firm in his opposition I informed him of the ultimate sanction you were preparing to invoke. Naturally he was profoundly shocked."

"What did he say?"

"I cannot recall his exact words, my Lord—they were, in truth, somewhat intemperate—but he did express the opinion that to him it seemed like a case of lopping off the limbs to save the soul. When I pressed him for an answer he insisted that he would first have to consult with Kent and Winchester upon the matter. He has promised to let me have their joint decision by the end of September."

"*September!*" cried the Cardinal. "By September Normandy itself may well have fallen! What does the fool think he's playing at? Either that treaty is abrogated by the end of this month or Earl Robert will find himself upon the high road to hell! The same goes for Winchester and Kent! Is that understood?"

The Marshal drew a deep breath. "My Lord, I do not see how this is possible. The Treaty of Finistère has been signed and sealed by all three parties. Even with the best will in the world Earl Robert could scarcely be expected to—"

"Perhaps we did not make ourselves sufficiently clear, Richard. Either the Earl abrogates that treaty forthwith or we shall do it for him."

"We?" echoed Richard. "But, my Lord, the Treaty of Finistère is a *civil* covenant—a contract of the State."

"Precisely. So it may well prove necessary for the Secular Arm to assume full civil control."

As though suddenly bereft of the powers of speech the Marshal stared dumbly back at him and it was left to Bishop Simon to comment drily: "The plans for such a contingency have already been drawn up, Richard. I have them here with me."

"But this is sheer lunacy!" Richard exploded. "We will simply be plunging the Kingdoms into civil war! Forgive me, my Lord, but I cannot see anything but disaster arising from such a desperate course! At one stroke we shall be depriving them of their laws, their livelihood and their liege lords! And for what? For something only one man in a hundred among them will even *begin* to comprehend! My Lord, with all my heart let me beseech you to reconsider this decision."

"You are overwrought, Marshal," responded the Cardinal coldly. "Do you imagine that we have not spent many weeks in fasting and prayer while we pondered upon the alternatives open to us? Your own report has merely served to confirm us in our chosen course. Earl Robert's loyalty to our sacred Cause has long been suspect. Be warned now lest you yourself become corrupted by his example. *Vigilate et orate.*"

Richard made token obeisance, lipped a silent penitence, and felt as if a leaden weight had dropped into his breast. At that moment he knew a loneliness more acute than anything he had ever felt in his life. He realized well enough that neither of the other Marshals would dare to speak out even though at first meat that very morning they had all three been in complete accord as to the political folly of the proposed course of action. He reflected bitterly how he had dismissed this very possibility as the purest lunacy when he had fathered it upon Earl Robert's fevered imagination, and now he himself was to become one of the instruments by which it was to be implemented. As he listened to Bishop Simon outlining the plan which had been drawn up by the Inner Secretariat it seemed to him as though it were all happening in a dream from which he would shortly wake. It was as though his mind had been taken over by two distinct voices one of which repeated over and over again his Solemn Oath of Obedience, while the other quietly insisted that Robert had been right all along and that Constant and Simon and all the rest of them had simply gone stark raving mad. He suspected that one of the voices must belong to the devil but he was no longer capable of judging which it was.

When the audience ended and the Marshals were taking their leave Simon drew Richard to one side and murmured: "Could we have a word in private, Marshal, before you depart for New Exeter?"

"It seems I'm yours to command, Bishop."

"True," responded the Bishop with a thin smile. "Come then. Let us take a glass of wine together."

He led the way down to the floor below and along an echoing stone corridor to the room which served him as an office. A young Falcon with blond curly hair and girlish features was seated at a desk making entries in a ledger. He jumped to his feet and saluted as the two men entered.

"Fetch us some wine, Peter," said the Bishop. "The Bordeaux. Pray take a seat, Marshal."

"Pretty boy," observed Richard when the lad had left the room. "Where'd you find him?"

"Peter? Oh, I brought him with me from Leicester," said the Bishop, restoring his files to a shelf. "He has some quite remarkable talents for one of his tender years."

"I can believe it. Well, what is it you want to talk to me about?"

"Practical matters of policy chiefly, Richard. I have been mulling over what you said in the audience. Your observations had a certain utilitarian force which was not entirely lost upon me."

"Oh yes? And which observations were those?"

"When you gave it as your opinion that we would plunge the Kingdoms into civil war."

"You think we won't?"

"On the contrary. Unless we are very careful indeed I think it more than likely that we shall."

"Well, in God's name, man, why didn't you say so? I could have done with a bit of support in there."

"I should have thought that was obvious even to you, Richard. To have spoken out then would have implied that I was in accord with your general thesis, which, if I'm not mistaken, was of total opposition to the whole policy."

"You're in favor of a takeover?"

"Yes, of course. Providing it can be achieved with the minimum of upheaval the advantages will be overwhelming. At one stroke the whole of the southern coast will be welded into an impregnable bastion. The three Kingdoms will become a stronghold of the Faith. Today they are nothing but a breeding ground for heresy."

The young Falcon reappeared bearing a tray on which was set a flask and two crystal goblets. He poured out the wine, presented the tray to the Marshal and the Bishop, then returned to his desk.

Richard raised his glass to the light then set it to his lips. "This is one of the minor pleasures you'll have to forgo when the treaty is torn up," he observed.

"A small price wouldn't you say?" returned the Bishop.

"To us, maybe," said the Marshal, "but not to those whose livelihood it represents. I wonder if the Cardinal realizes just how much he's asking of the Kingdoms. Things look very different from up here, you know."

"They will accommodate themselves to privation quickly enough. And we will take good care to see that they appreciate who is responsible. I will be astonished if within a year there are any Kinsfolk left between Launceston and Canterbury."

The Marshal nodded. "You could well be right at that. A scapegoat's always a welcome diversion in times of hardship. But you'll achieve that end without having to usurp the civil authority. As soon as the Lords appreciate that Constant's in deadly earnest they'll come to heel meekly enough. You'll get your precious abrogation all right, Simon, never you fear."

The Bishop set down his glass and dabbed the gleam of moisture from his lips. "My dear Richard," he sighed, "why must you be so willfully obtuse? Surely you understood what the Cardinal was saying? We do not wish *them* to abrogate the treaty. That is something we have every intention of doing for ourselves. In effect their opposition is providing us with the ideal pretext for our action. I should have thought that was obvious."

"But when I tell Earl Robert of Constant's ultimatum, he'll agree to do it. He won't like it, but he'll agree. I'm sure of it."

The Bishop nodded. "Precisely, Richard. And therefore you will *not* tell him. Instead you will make all the arrangements which we have outlined in the contingency plan. When we give you the signal you will, ah, execute them with all that practical expertise for which you are so justly renowned."

Richard blinked. "I see," he said. "Am I to take it that that's an order?"

"Yes, Marshal. That is an order."

Richard turned his head and gazed out of the window toward the Minster. Across the blue heavens a solitary cloud shaped like a curled white feather sailed silently upon its way. Far below him an oblong patch of slightly paler grass on the Precinct lawn was all that was left to mark the grave where the body of the Boy Thomas had once lain. "How long have we got?" he asked.

"Six weeks."

"It's not enough."

"On the contrary, if anything it is too much. Our aim is complete surprise. The longer we delay the less chance we have of achieving it. Surely you must appreciate that."

The Marshal nodded. "And the signal?"

"I shall deliver it in person, Richard."

"What does that mean?"

"It is my intention shortly to announce a public tour of inspection of the Secular Arm throughout the Southern Kingdoms. That will give you an excellent opportunity to deploy your forces to our best advantage, without arousing undue suspicion. You will also make arrangements for me to pay a courtesy call upon the Earl, for which you will insist upon the maximum security. It is all down in the sealed schedule we have prepared for you. Open it on your return, study it well and carry out its instructions to the letter. That is all you have to do. Now, another glass of wine before you go?"

Richard shook his head.

"As you please."

The Bishop rose to his feet and extended his hand. The Marshal touched it in the briefest possible token of civility and walked to the door. As his fingers fastened upon the latch the Bishop said, "Discretion, Richard. Let that be the watchword. It would be most unfortunate if the Earl were to get wind of what we are about."

The Marshal muttered something inaudible and strode from the room.

Accompanied by his two aides Richard quit York that same afternoon. Two days' hard riding saw them across the Pennines, and early on Thursday morning they boarded the *Speedwell* at Preston. The black sailed, three-masted longship was one of the fastest vessels in the Secular Fleet and despite the fact that the wind was blowing from an unfavorable quarter she had docked in New Bristol by noon on Friday. Here the Marshal and his companions transferred to a sloop which flitted them across the Somersea to Porlock. They stepped ashore on the First Kingdom shortly before six o'clock. Two hours later Richard was back in his private quarters within the New Exeter Falconry.

A number of letters had arrived for him during his absence but he ignored them until he had bathed and changed into a fresh uniform. Then, seated in his favorite chair before the window embrasure which afforded him one of the most beautiful views in the whole city, out across the moors to the far distant Eastern Isles, he helped himself liberally to the bread, cheese and strong ale which his servant had laid out for him and began to glance through the waiting post.

Most of it consisted of official reports of one kind or another but one different letter caught his eye. It was addressed in a round, familiar hand to *"Richard, Lord Marshal, The Falconry"* and bore the words *"PRIVATE"* and *"WITH ALL HASTE"* in bold capitals. He examined the seal, then, smiling faintly, he broke the wax with his thumb nail, unfolded the stiff paper and read—

> *My Dear Lord Richard. I know that you are very busie and have many important matters to attend to but I beg you grant to me a few moments with you alone for I am sorly trubbled in my mind and needs must speak with you. If you could send me word when this might be I will hasten privily to any meeting place you chose. But I besech you for your owne dear sake do not fail in this your own beloved God-child*
>
> *Alice*

There was no date, and the misspellings and general tenor of the message betrayed every sign of haste and of the "sorly trubbled mind" of which the writer spoke. The Marshal rang for his servant and asked him if he could remember when the letter had been delivered. He was told that it had been brought on Tuesday afternoon by a messenger from the castle.

The Marshal nodded, thanked the man and dismissed him. Then he glanced through the letter again and wondered what it was that was so distressing Lady Alice, the third in line of succession of Earl Robert's four children. Compared with his own immediate problems he doubted whether hers could amount to anything very serious, but he was extremely fond of his young God-child and guessed that she would be impatient for his reply. He scribbled a note to her apologizing for the delay and informing her that he would be exercising in the park next day and would make a point of going down the Royal Ride at about noon.

He sealed his message and gave orders for it to be delivered forthwith, then, having told his servant to see that he was not disturbed he bolted his door, took up the schedule that Lord Simon had given him, broke open the seal and with a sinking heart began to study the orders within.

During the night the weather changed. Soft veils of thin, misty rain were drifting in across the westward moors when the Marshal mounted his favorite horse and cantered out toward the castle by way of the south gate of the city. A sun as vacant as a blind man's eye slipped palely in and out through the low clouds. Within minutes the moisture had gathered in minuscule pearls along the Marshal's eyelashes and eyebrows and had dulled the sheen of the steel studs upon his black leather corselet and his gauntlets.

He reached the broad grass track of the Ride just as the Minster chimes were sounding the hour of noon. There was no sign of young Alice so he set his horse into a canter toward the forest, guessing that she would be waiting for him there. And so it proved. As he passed out of sight of the castle and the trees were beginning to close in upon him he heard a shrill, boyish whistle. Glancing back over his shoulder he saw a slender figure, dressed in a hunting tunic of dark green leather, urge her pony out from a covert and come galloping after him.

He reined in his horse and raised his right hand in amiable salute. "Well met, my lady," he called. "You got my message then?"

She smiled tremulously. "Ride with me to the West Lodge, Richard. We can talk there."

"Can we not talk here?"

She shook her head and sent a flicker of raindrops sprinkling from her hood. "Come. I'll race you!" she cried, and the words were scarcely uttered before she had kicked her heels into her pony's flanks and was away off deep into the woods.

The Marshal grinned, waited until she had gained a

fair start, then urged his own horse into a gallop and thundered after her.

He caught up with her and passed her a full minute before they reached their destination and he was already on foot awaiting her when she came scampering into the clearing which housed the hunting lodge. She jumped nimbly down, flung her pony's bridle over the stone hitching post, then taking the Marshal by the arm, conducted him up the steps to the door.

"Well, at least it's drier here," he observed as they stepped inside. "And no more than the odd mouse to run tattle. So what's this great secret that needs so close a cell?"

"I am afraid," she whispered. "Sore afraid. For I love you much, Richard, and I do not wish that you should suffer harm."

The Marshal gazed down at her in blank astonishment, wondering if he could possibly have heard her right. "*I* come to harm, Alice?" he repeated. "But how should this be?"

"I cannot tell you that."

He frowned. "Is this some jest?"

"No, no," she insisted, seizing his gloved hand in both of hers and gripping it so tight that he heard her small fingers crack. "I speak true, Richard. Oh, you *must* believe me!"

He gazed into her pale, strained face and saw that her eyes were glittering like stars. "Come, sweet lass," he said gently. "Sit you down here beside me and let us have this matter out. What is it you fear? Is it something you have heard?"

She opened her mouth as if about to reply then shook her head wildly and burst into tears. At that he hefted her bodily up on to his lap as if she had been a puppy and held her cradled in his arms. "Aye, you spoke true, little maid," he murmured. "You are indeed sore troubled and I think I dare hazard a guess as to why. Your heart is being rent in two, eh? Is that not it?"

He sensed rather than saw her shivered nod of assent and felt a fresh upsurge of that deathly sickness of the spirit which was becoming so familiar to him. His arms tightened around her quivering shoulders and he gazed out over her head to where a fringe of raindrops gathered in slow tears before weeping from the overhang of the roof.

It seemed to him that they could well be God's own tears of despair at the invincible folly of his children. "Tell me just one thing if you can," he murmured into her ear. "When is it to be?"

"I know not," she whispered.

"And is it only me?"

Alice shook her head.

Suddenly, grotesquely, he found that he was laughing—genuine, bubbling laughter that sprang from some unknown source so deep within himself that he could not have stayed it even if he had wished. It had dawned upon him that all Bishop Simon's cunning schemes were worth even less than the paper they were written on. They had already been forestalled. And there was nothing he could do to halt the rumbling passage of events even though he stood oath-bound to try and would, in all likelihood, noose his own neck for his pains. In some strange way he felt almost cleansed, absolved, and lighter of heart than he had felt for weeks. He drew the glove from his right hand and lifted Alice's head with a finger crooked beneath her chin. "Fret not, sweet maid," he murmured. "Whatever God wills then that is what will be," and he kissed her on her rain chilled forehead.

"What will you do, Richard?"

"Do?" He smiled wryly. "I think I had best make it my business to pay my respects to your father, before he sends someone to call upon me."

"You will not tell him that I—"

"Nay, lass. What do you take me for? I'll not breathe a word of it. But how came you by your intelligence?"

"I overheard them talking."

"Who?"

"Father and some other men who came."

"And who were they?"

"I know not. One, I think, was Uncle Matthew's secretary. I did not see his face."

"This was on Tuesday last?"

"On Sunday."

"But your note was sent on Tuesday."

"Yes," she said. "I knew not what to do. I was so afraid for you and Father both. All Sunday night I could not sleep for thinking of it. And Monday was the same. On Tuesday I rode out alone and prayed . . ."

"Go on."

Alice colored faintly and shook her head.

"You went to Church?"

Again the blonde head shook.

"Where then?"

"Into the forest. A place I know of. A secret place. I cannot tell you more, Richard."

The Marshal stared at her, looked as if he were about to say something and then appeared to change his mind.

"And then I knew what I must do," she said simply.

"Someone told you?"

"Does it matter?"

"Someone did though."

"Yes," she said with a sigh. "Someone told me that I must talk to you; that I must tell you what I knew and then all would be well. They said that you were a good man and it was for that I had been sent to them. So I went back and wrote that note to you. Did I do wrong?"

"Only a bigot would say so," he replied. "If I read this particular text aright, between the two of us we may contrive to save a thousand lives."

They rode back by separate ways for prudence' sake. When the Marshal reached the Falconry he did not go directly to his quarters but turned aside and entered the deserted chapel. He knelt before the altar, crossed his forearms over his chest and closed his eyes.

An hour later he was observed to re-mount his horse and ride off in the direction of the castle. Belted at his side was his gold-hilted Sword of Office. Otherwise he was dressed exactly as he had been when he had ridden to meet Lady Alice.

If the Earl was surprised to see him he concealed it admirably. He shook him warmly by the hand, offered him wine and inquired how he had fared in York.

Richard spread his hands. "Do you need to ask?"

"Constant still holds constant then?" said the Earl and chuckled at his own joke.

"Adamant's closer to it, Robert."

"Aye, well, we've come to expect no less. You told him what I thought?"

"I did."

"It made no difference?"

"None."

"Well? What happens now?"

The Marshal gazed at him then, very slowly and deliberately, he unbuckled the broad belt from which his Sword of Office hung, pulled it free of its hooks and handed all —belt, scabbard and sword—to the Earl.

Robert stared at it in open-mouthed astonishment. "What means this, Richard? Have you taken leave of your wits, man?"

For answer Richard thrust his right hand inside his corselet flap and drew out the Sealed Orders which Lord Simon had given him. He passed them over without a word.

"What's this?" demanded the Earl.

"I want you to read those, Robert."

Still looking at the Marshal as though he were some wonder at least the equal of a talking horse, the Earl laid the sword down on the table beside him and took the documents. He glanced at the top one then back to Richard. "But these are marked highly confidential. Are you sure—?"

"Read them."

The Earl swallowed hard and began to read.

Five minutes later he dropped the sheaf of papers on to the table beside the sword. "Mother of God, Richard," he muttered. "They'll burn you alive for this."

"Not if you have me executed first they won't."

The Earl glanced up at him sharply. "Why do you say that?"

"You have the sword there ready to hand. Do you wish me to kneel?"

The Earl snorted. "If your neck's as thick as your head I'd never hack it through. Sit down, man, while we both take a firm hold of our senses. How much do you know?"

"Only what I can guess."

"Then, in God's name, Richard, what brought you here to me?"

"I found that I could only take so much, Robert. Perhaps I've damned myself to hell for it. I hope not. But the sword's still there to hand if you want me to find out."

"And just what do you suppose that would solve? Your problem perhaps, but not mine. Did you not guess something of this kind was afoot?"

"No. Not till I reached York. I won't say it hadn't crossed my mind but, frankly, it seemed too crazy to credit. I even told Constant as much. Come to think of it it's a wonder he didn't see fit to end it then and there." He paused. "It's even occurred to me that he's guessed this might happen."

"Constant has?"

"Aye. I suppose it does sound crazy. But when I was on my way over here just now I found myself recalling the legend of the White Bird. You asked me about it, remember? Well, one of the verses in that prophecy the Kinsfolk call 'The Testament' tells how a black bird with wings of scarlet flame will one day set fire to its own nest. Half an hour ago it struck me how that black bird might be none other than Constant himself: that the course he is set upon is bound to lead to the destruction of Christendom."

"You're crazy."

"Well, perhaps I am. But not in their way. I want no more part of their kind of madness."

The Earl picked up the sword and weighed it thoughtfully in his hand. "You're no earthly use to me without this, Richard," he said. "Put it back on."

"As you wish."

The Earl poured out two fresh cups of wine. He handed one to the Marshal and said: "We drink together, Richard. There can be no turning back now. You and I must pledge blood loyalty one to the other. In life; in death; in the sight of God. Are you with me?"

They clasped arms and each drank off his wine in a single draft.

The Earl set down his empty cup and remarked: "I suppose you realize that you have just stepped back from your own grave."

"I guessed as much," said the Marshal. "When was it to have been?"

"Next Saturday. A tragic accident on the hunting field. We saw no other way, old friend."

In spite of himself the Marshal shuddered retrospectively. "Do you mind if I have another drink?"

"You deserve it. Fill 'em up."

Richard did so. "Will you let me propose a health?"

"Your own, eh? Go ahead."

"To Alice."

"Alice? Why Alice?"

"Am I not her God-father?"

They drank the toast, grinned at one another, and then the Earl said: "Now, my General, with all speed you and

I must fashion a plan of campaign. Tell me exactly how many Falcons you command and whether they can be trusted to follow you."

One shimmeringly hot noon early in August when the air seemed to dance a jig above the flagstones on Porlock jetty, a black-sailed troop galley crept under oars into the harbor, its pennant hanging limp as a scrap of seaweed above the mainmast. Orders were bawled; hawsers winched fast; a gangway rolled out; and the sweating Falcons who had been mustered into a guard of honor upon the quay sprang to attention as Lord Simon, Bishop of Leicester, Acting Chief Falconer of the Seven Kingdoms, stepped ashore and raised his right hand in lack-luster acknowledgment.

The Lord Marshal for the First Kingdom strode forward and brought his gloved right fist across to the left side of his chest. "Welcome ashore, my Lord," he said. "Did you have a good voyage?"

"Appalling," said the Bishop. "The wretched rudder broke and we were becalmed for two hours off Cheltenham. It was like an oven."

The Marshal clicked his tongue sympathetically. "How many men have you brought with you?"

"A platoon."

"So many? Are they all Grays?"

"Of course."

"You should have let me know, Simon. We've made provision for only a dozen. I haven't got the transport for a platoon."

The Bishop shrugged. "They'll soon forage up mounts for themselves. They're used to that."

"And have the locals up in arms before we've even started? Why cause needless friction at this stage?"

"Well, it's either that or they take over your men's."

"They've got legs, haven't they?" retorted the Marshal. "Let 'em march. It's not more than ten kilometers to the barracks."

"March? In this heat? Quite out of the question! We need them fighting fit not half dead before they get there!"

"Your orders made no mention of any platoon of Grays in your entourage, my Lord. In fact they specifically state that we are to provide your escort. That's exactly what we've done. On my own initiative I made allowance for a dozen extra as a personal bodyguard. It seemed more than adequate in the circumstances. Furthermore, I should point out that we are well behind schedule as it is. We're due to pay our formal respects to the Earl in two hours. So unless you intend to scrap that part of the plan here and now, I suggest you make haste to select the twelve you wish to accompany you and give orders for the rest either to remain aboard or to make their own way to the City on foot."

The Bishop had not been spoken to in this fashion for longer than he cared to remember, but he knew the man he was dealing with and, wisely, elected to swallow his anger. He swung round on his heel, summoned the young Ganymede he had chosen for his aide and told him to pick out twelve experienced men for personal escort duty and to order the rest to prepare to march to New Exeter.

Half an hour later a flickering mirror high on the crest of Dunkery Beacon relayed the news to the castle watch-tower that the Head of the Secular Arm and the Lord Marshal of the First Kingdom were on their way.

Riding at the Bishop's side Richard took the opportunity to inquire when the Cardinal was expected back from Italy.

"Sometime next month, God willing," replied the Bishop. "His health is no longer of the best. The success of our enterprise will prove a tonic to him."

"Was this operation his idea or yours, Simon?"

"His, of course. He called me in to supervise the work of the Secretariat and one thing led to another. Had he not been summoned to Turin he would probably have insisted on being here in person today. Have you encountered any problems at your end?"

"None as yet."

"You anticipate some?"

"In my experience, Simon, nothing ever proceeds exactly according to plan. Man proposes: God disposes. So far everything has gone smoothly and the reports from the Districts augur well. My aim throughout has been to avoid unnecessary bloodshed at all costs. That way we will be most likely to win the civil co-operation we'll need. Speaking for myself I could wish you'd left your Grays behind."

"On the contrary, Richard. I assure you they will prove a salutary reminder that the Church is not to be trifled with!"

"Perhaps. But we in the First are blessed with long memories."

"So much the better. It will make the essential task of purification that much easier."

The Marshal glanced sideways thoughtfully. "I've been wondering if that was coming," he said. "You're intending to turn them loose, are you?"

"They have their instructions, Marshal, just as you have yours. But there's no harm in my telling you that we intend to set up a Special Court of Examination in New Exeter within the next week or so. From all I hear it will not be short of material either."

"Oh? And what do you hear?"

"Heresy is running rife throughout this Kingdom, Richard. There is corruption even at the very highest levels. You will be amazed when you learn whom we intend to call before us."

"Indeed? And may I be allowed to—"

"All in good time. But you will do well to prepare yourself for some shocks."

"I'm grateful for the warning, my Lord. It's always a comfort to be prepared for the worst. Now, if you'll excuse me, I'd better have a word with Captain Blackwood. After all, we wouldn't want any last minute hitch, would we?"

A gaily striped and flag-bedecked awning shaded the saluting base which had been set up in front of the gateway leading to the inner courtyard of the castle. It was there that the Earl Robert, Lady Margaret and three of their four children were seated in readiness when word was brought to them that the visitors had been sighted approaching.

"About time too," growled the Earl. "All right. Sound the first call."

High on the battlements a trumpeter raised a silver bugle to his lips and blew the "Stand To Arms."

The Household Guard, shouted up to attention, brought their crossbows smartly to the "Shoulder Arms." Only the most observant eye would have noticed that each weapon was drawn, cocked, and ready to fire.

The clatter of iron-shod hooves and the jingle of harness was heard at the outer gate. A moment later the Lord Marshal and the Chief Falconer appeared framed in the stone archway. As they dismounted and made their way on foot toward the saluting base, the Earl rose to his feet and came down the steps to greet them. It was the cue for six trumpeters to rattle the castle windows with a blistering fanfare.

The escorting Falcons marched in two abreast and took up their pre-arranged positions: the Grays in the center of the arena, and the Marshal's men ranked behind them.

The Earl shook the Bishop by the hand, nodded to the Marshal and said: "Carry on, Richard. You know the drill."

The Marshal saluted, stepped two paces backward, unsheathed his sword and swept it upward in a glittering arc against the blue sky. "For God and the First Kingdom!" he yelled. "Present . . . *Arms!*"

The falling sword flashed in the sun like broken glass.

There was a sudden flurry of activity. Before even one of them knew what was happening the Grays found themselves surrounded, disarmed and gripped fast by the Household Guards.

Grinning broadly, the Marshal sheathed his sword and turned to the Earl. "They are yours to command, my Lord."

"Excellent, Richard. Excellent. Bishop Simon, I have to inform you that you are now a prisoner of the First Kingdom. You will shortly be called upon to face trial on a charge of attempted insurrection. I need scarcely remind you that that is a capital offense."

The Bishop's face defied description. He stared first at the Earl and then at the Lord Marshal. Not a single word did he utter. No words, not even those to be found in the vocabularies of the damned could have expressed his feelings at that moment.

Chapter Three

The news of what was happening in the capital took some days to reach the Isle of Quantock. Since it followed hard upon a disquieting rumor that a regiment of the dreaded Grays was abroad in the land it was not difficult for the islanders to discount it as wishful thinking even though the man who brought the report to Tallon swore blind that he had been standing in the crowd outside the City Hall when Earl Robert was proclaimed Defender of the Faith and Head of the Secular Arm throughout the First Kingdom. The combers of Tallon debated among themselves what this might mean and most of them concluded that it would bring nothing to their advantage.

Scarcely had they digested the information before the coaster *Goshawk* called in from Salisbury with the even more extraordinary tidings that the Second Kingdom had risen in open rebellion and pitched battles were being fought between the forces of the Civil Government and those of the Secular Arm. With their very own eyes, so the crew maintained, they had seen the Downton Falconry ablaze and three Falcons dangling by the neck from the public gibbet, each with a placard pinned to his breast bearing the message *"An enemy of the Kingdom."* The Duke of Winchester had proclaimed Martial Law and a dusk-to-dawn curfew throughout the land. Trade was at a standstill. Honest citizens went in fear for their very lives.

When the *Goshawk* tied up, Tom, by now a lad of ten and a half years, was down at the quayside helping Rett and Simon to check over their nets, and he was well to the forefront of the little crowd which congregated to marvel at the news the crew brought ashore. He had no very clear idea of what Martial Law was, but he was alert to the buzzing excitement generated by all the talk of momentous events.

Bursting with the news he scampered away up the steep

street to the pottery, arriving so out of breath that it was fully half a minute before Jane could manage to get any sense out of him. When she did she was quick to relate his story to the rumors from New Exeter and to wonder what it could all portend.

For hundreds of years the Secular Arm had both upheld and symbolized the supremacy of the Church throughout the Kingdoms of the west. It had become synonymous with political stability, with the fixed order of human affairs, with degree, with authority, and with fear. Above all with fear. Its historical roots lay back in the decades of turbulent anarchy which had followed the Drowning, when by faith, self-discipline, and dedication to a noble ideal the Church Militant had gradually achieved its aim of imposing order upon chaos.

But the victory had been costly. Dissent had been suppressed with a ruthlessness unknown since the dictatorships of the twentieth century. Printing, publishing and all forms of technical innovation had been decreed Church prerogative, infringement of which was to be punished by death. Scholarship, other than that permitted within the strict confines of Orthodoxy, had virtually ceased to exist. And all this had been made possible through the power of that Secular Arm whose grim motto *"Hic et Ubique"* was to be found riveted in characters of burnished steel above the doors of every Falconry in Christendom. Now that inflexible authority which for so long had stood supreme was being challenged and was apparently crumbling like wormeaten timber. But what would arise to replace it? And how many would have to die before that happened?

Over supper that evening Jane discussed the latest tidings with Alison and the Magpie. Michael, Alison's three-year-old son, had been put to bed, but Tom and Witchet sat with pricked ears listening to all that was being said.

In the Magpie's opinion what was happening in the Second Kingdom would make little difference in the long run. "The great lords will carve it up among themselves. The most that ordinary folk can hope for is to find a few scraps left on the side of the plate after Winchester has picked over the bones."

"But the Kinsfolk," said Alison. "Surely they'll be free from persecution now."

"I shouldn't count on it. My guess is the Folk may find themselves nicely to hand if things don't work out so well and someone has to answer for it. If I was Kin and in the Second right now I'd lie very low and keep mum till I was quite sure which way the wind had set."

"I don't think Francis will let them do that," murmured Jane. "It's not his way."

"You could be right at that," agreed the Magpie. "I wonder, did anyone ever think to tell Francis that he'd got more than a touch of the Constants himself?"

"What do you mean, Magpie?" Tom asked.

"Well, I reckon something happened to Francis when Corlay was fired. Maybe the flames tempered him somehow, made him harder, gave him a cutting edge. Eh, Janie?"

"I don't know," said Jane. "I don't care to think about it."

"Why not, Mum?"

"Because it's all over and done with, pet. What good would it do to anyone to rake that up all over again? Francis went his way and we've gone ours."

"Does he know you're still alive?"

"I don't suppose so."

"You've never written to him?"

"No."

"Then how do you know he's changed?"

"Oh, we hear things about him from time to time."

"What sort of things?"

Jane smiled faintly. "They say he's a great man now—almost as great as the great Pope himself. Not a bit like the Francis we used to know."

"Are you afraid of him?"

"Afraid of Francis? Good heavens, no! What a strange thing to say." She gazed at her son thoughtfully and then shook her head. "I don't know though. Perhaps I am a bit. I've never really thought about it. I suppose I'm a bit worried about what he's become. I wouldn't know what to say to him if I met him."

Alison laughed. "I would. I'd say: 'Who's darning your socks for you, Francis?' You remember those holes, Jehane?"

"I remember how you used to spoil him. You were always knitting things for him or sewing on his buttons. Sometimes I wondered if you were in love with him."

"Me! With Francis! *Sacré Oiseau!* What an idea!"

"Look, Mum's blushing!" cried the delighted Witchet. "Are you jealous, Dad?"

"Fat lot of use that would be," said the Magpie with a grin. "It was all over between them the moment she clapped eyes on me."

"What *did* happen to Francis?" asked Tom. "Do you know, Magpie?"

"They say it was a near miracle he got off with his life. His face still bears the scars of that night. Not only his face either, I daresay."

"I'd really like to meet him," said Tom.

"Well, perhaps you will one day."

"Oh, I will," replied the boy. "I have to."

In the sudden hush that descended upon the room Jane turned to her son. " 'Have to'?" she replied. "What do you mean, 'Have to'?"

Tom wriggled uncomfortably. "I don't know," he muttered. "I just said it. But I'd like to meet him, Mum. Really I would."

"So would I," averred Witchet stoutly.

"She's just saying that," observed Tom crushingly. "She's a copy cat."

"No. I'm not! And you're Tom pig!"

"Pig yourself!"

"Outside the both of you," growled the Magpie. "I'm counting to three. One . . ."

When the kitchen door had banged shut behind them Jane said: "You heard him, Magpie. What do you think?"

The Magpie stroked his chin. "Does it matter?"

"It does to me," said Jane.

"You mistake me, lass. All I mean is that if Tom speaks true there's not a thing in the world any one of us can do about it."

Jane picked up a crust of bread from the table and began abstractedly to shred it into crumbs. "I think it's that that I dread more than anything," she said.

"What is?" asked Alison.

"That one day he'll come to me and say: 'Goodbye, Mum. I've got to go now.' "

"But why should he do that?"

"Because he has to, maybe. Just recently he's taken to asking me all sorts of questions about his father. Strange questions. And about the Boy."

"He's asked me too," said Alison. "He wanted me to tell him all about the Kinsmen. And about Corlay."

Jane nodded. "Sometimes I get the oddest notion that he's just been lent to me—that he isn't really mine at all . . ."

"That's just moon talk, Jehane."

"Is it?" Jane glanced up and caught the Magpie's eye. "I once read Tom. When he was a babe. I didn't really mean to. It just happened."

"Go on," he said curiously.

"It didn't make sense, Magpie. I saw things which shouldn't have been there—that weren't part of *him* at all. It was like finding Carver in Thomas—a stranger hidden in someone I loved. For years I've tried to pretend to myself that it never really happened with Tom—that I'd just dreamed it or something. But it *did* happen. And now I'm beginning to wonder just what it was I saw then—who he *really* is."

The Magpie ran his fingers through his thinning hair. "Are we to know the answer?"

"That's just it," she replied. "I don't know it myself. And nothing will ever make me go back there to try and find out."

"So what *did* you see?"

"Places. People."

"That's all you can tell us?"

"Magpie, *I didn't know who they were!*"

"None of them?"

She shook her head. "At the time I wondered if one of them might have been the Old Tale-Spinner—or maybe even Morfedd the Wizard. But whoever they were those weren't my child's memories. They *couldn't* have been."

"Tom never said anything?"

"Not to me. But then I've never dared to ask him."

"Would he know, do you think?"

"Thomas never really knew about Carver. He just got him mixed up in his dreams."

"And what does young Tom dream about?"

"Of being a piper like his dad."

"I didn't mean that."

"But it's true. Tom really does dream music. He's often told me so. Sometimes he gets furious with himself because he can't make it come out the way he's heard it in his sleep."

"He does marvelously well for all that."

"Not by his own reckoning, he doesn't. For Tom it always seems to be on the other side of the hill—out of reach. He begged and begged me to let him have his father's pipes, and when at last I gave in he'd no sooner put them to his lips and blown a few notes than he burst into tears and flung them across the room."

"Yes, I remember," said Alison. "I'd never seen him in such a temper. He sulked for days. Even Witchet wouldn't go near him."

"You never told me this," said the Magpie.

"Well, you were off trading when it happened," said Alison. "And he got over it."

"What about the pipes?"

"Oh, I hid them away again," said Jane. "They weren't hurt."

"So what was it all about?"

"He never really told me. I thought at first it was because they're twinned for a Kinsman's tongue, but now I'm almost sure that wasn't it. I think Tom must have somehow been expecting them to be something they weren't—something very special he'd pictured in his own mind. But all he ever said to me was that they weren't tuned right."

"What did he mean?"

"I don't know. And he wouldn't explain. Perhaps he didn't even know himself."

"He would've known, all right," said the Magpie. He tapped his forehead. "He's got it all up here and to spare has young Tom. Ask Rett if you don't believe me."

"Oh, I believe you. But why Rett?"

"He reckons young Tom's brighter than a fistful of new royals. Thinks the world of your lad does Rett. And of you too, come to that."

"That's right, Jehane," said Alison. "Haven't I told you so a hundred times?"

Jane laughed. "Is he paying you to do his courting for him?"

"Not enough, it seems," said the Magpie. "What have you got against him, Janie?"

"I've got nothing against him. I'm very fond of Rett. I just don't want to marry him, that's all."

"You can't mourn Thomas forever, lass. It's more than ten years now. Besides a lad needs a father."

"Did you need yours?"

"Aye, I did. But he wasn't up to it. And Rett's no Jack Patch. He can give you something you both need and he asks nothing more than the chance to prove it."

"He is in love with you, Jehane," said Alison. "You know that's true."

"I know he *says* he is," retorted Jane. "He wants me to go and live with him. But why should I? Give up my own home and the pottery! Rett's welcome to share my bed but it will stay *my* bed."

The Magpie laughed. "Have you told him so?"

"He knows."

"And what did he say to that?"

"That I didn't realize what *I* was asking of *him!*"

"That's his pride, Jehane. He is afraid men will say he is a pet rabbit."

"Then he's a bigger fool than I took him for," said Jane hotly. "And you can tell him as much next time you see him." So saying she thrust back her chair and strode out of the kitchen leaving Alison and the Magpie grinning at one another.

Throughout the remainder of that year the shock waves from the Southern Kingdoms reached Tallon as a series of diminished ripples. Of these the strongest by far were those generated from New Exeter. In the first week of September the Magpie loaded his van with four crates of Jane's pots and set out for the capital. When he returned four days later he brought with him an ill-printed two-penny broadsheet. It was the first of its kind that any of them had ever seen which did not carry the official *Imprimatur* stamped upon it. In its place was the Earl Robert's coat of arms and below it in bold black type the stirring injunction: *Tell The Truth And Fear No Man.*

The main story, which occupied two of the four columns of print, purported to be an eye-witness account of the trial by common jury of the arch-traitor Simon, Bishop of Leicester, on the charge that he did in his own mischievous person plot and plan the treacherous subversion and overthrow of the Civil Government of Our Most Noble Lord and Ruler, Earl Robert the Blessed, Defender of the Faith, Prince of the First Kingdom.

The Chief Witness for the Prosecution was that erstwhile Lord Marshal of the Secular Arm, Richard of Hawk-

ridge, who now as General in Chief commanded the Earl's
forces throughout the Kingdom. He described to the court
how he had received sealed and secret instructions from
the Bishop who, as Acting Head of the Secular Arm
during Cardinal Constant's absence abroad, was his immediate Superior in Office. These instructions (produced as
Documents in Evidence before the court) contained a
detailed plan by which the forces of the Secular Arm were
to usurp the authority of the Civil Guard throughout the
Kingdom and, most iniquitously, to incarcerate the Noble
Earl Robert together with all the members of his family.

Horror stricken by the evidence of such diabolical
treachery the honorable Lord Marshal had galloped
straightway to the castle where he had laid all before the
Earl. Having sworn a solemn and binding oath of undying
liege loyalty he had then contrived to engineer the brilliant
counter-stroke whereby the authority of the Secular Arm
was privily transferred to the Civil Power where, with
Divine Approval, it was rested.

The Accused, who had sustained certain complex frac-
tures of the lower limbs during his pre-trial Examination,
was graciously permitted to give evidence in his own defense from a seated position. His replies were uttered in
a low voice and were rendered somewhat indistinct by the
fact that most of his teeth were missing. He admitted the
truth of all the charges brought against him, acknowledged
his own signature upon the Documents Offered in Evidence
and also upon the detailed Confession which was read out
to the court and then formally presented as part of a Depo-
sition in Plea for Clemency.

The Judge summed up damningly and the jury conferred
briefly *in situ* before pronouncing a unanimous verdict of
Guilty Upon All Charges.

Before passing sentence the Judge paid heartfelt tribute
to Lord Richard without whose Noble Loyalty and Prompt
Action the fate which had so recently befallen the Third
Kingdom would in all likelihood have been theirs also. He
then summarily sentenced the Bishop to be hanged by the
neck until he was dead. Twenty four hours later his head
was to be severed from his body and his body was to be
butchered into four separate quarters. The pieces were to
be displayed above the five gates of the city to serve as a
warning to all like-minded traitors.

There followed a solemn prayer in which the prisoner

had been observed to join most tearfully and affectingly and the court had then dispersed amid scenes of general jubilation and thanksgiving.

The rest of the broadsheet was given over to news from the provinces and consisted in large part of Protestations of Loyalty from various ex-Captains of the Secular Arm who were now sworn Servants of the State. There was also an Official Notice of a Census and Hearth Tax Assessment scheduled for Lady Day in March of the following year, and brief references to an embassy from the Second Kingdom and a trade mission from Normandy.

To these meager items the Magpie was able to add some hearsay news of his own concerning the fate of those Gray Falcons who had accompanied the Bishop on his ill-starred mission. Rumor had it that they had attempted to fight their way back to Porlock but had been pursued by Lord Richard's men who had caught up with them and cut them to pieces near Berry Castle, almost within sight of their goal.

The reference to the fate of the Third Kingdom which the Judge had seen fit to include in his address to the court was explained a week or two later when a coasting trader called in at Tallon with the grim news that the Duke of Kent had been overthrown and his Kingdom had fallen under the absolute control of the Secular Arm. In the purge that had followed over a thousand Civil Officers were reputed to have lost their lives and the bonfires of the Inquisition were still burning. Scores of the Kinsfolk had fled across the sea to Brittany taking with them nothing but the clothes upon their backs, while hundreds less fortunate were left languishing in the prisons of the Secular Arm awaiting the trial to which there could be only one outcome.

It was at this point that Constant returned to York. The illness which Bishop Simon had hinted at was now written plainly upon his face. He was being consumed from within by an invisible malignancy which left him unable to stomach anything more substantial than slops. Even his own body seemed to have turned traitor. He held audience while racked by an agony which often rendered him well nigh speechless, and all those who knelt to kiss his hand could not but remark the unwholesome, sickly scent of physical corruption which seemed to exude itself like a pungent oil from the wasted, papery flesh. Only his eyes remained as they had always been, steel gray, and as cold and glittering as February ice.

When the news of Lord Richard's defection had reached him his only comment had been to call for the bell, the book, and the candle and personally to pronounce the dreaded sentence of Maximum Excommunication, followed by the decree that henceforth the Marshal's name was never to be mentioned in his presence. But there were those who whispered that they had heard, from behind the locked doors of his lofty eyrie in the Falconry, the sound of the Cardinal's footsteps pacing up and down in the long watches of the winter night and the forbidden name of the traitor being groaned aloud in a terrible agony of the spirit. For long periods during the day Constant would sit motionless before the window gazing down upon that area of the Minster precinct where the body of the Boy had once lain, and at those times none cared to approach him for fear of what they might find etched upon his gaunt and ravaged face.

The day of the Cardinal's death was as cold and as hard as any in living memory. All that week ice floes had formed on the Sea of Goole to be driven ashore by the bitter northeast wind. The spiky plates lay in an untidy jumble along the frost-rimed beaches. Nudged and chivied by the tides they grated and crackled like the racked bones of the damned.

And so, in the end, Constant died as he had lived, without mercy to himself and with his desolate eyes fixed upon the crucifix which was held before them. No one present at his death bed knew exactly when the tortured spirit left him, and no one knew for sure where it had gone.

In the months immediately following the Cardinal's death a wholly unfamiliar hesitancy—at times it could almost have been called a genuine doubt—appeared to have afflicted the leaders of the Church throughout the western Kingdoms. Whispers began to be heard, even within the confines of the Sacred College itself, that the policies which Constant had both advocated and prosecuted with such passion were producing effects almost diametrically opposite to those which their author had intended. Voices were heard pointing out that in those Kingdoms which had espoused Kinship as their national faith, the True Church and her spiritual officers had not been subjected to persecution. It was the autonomy of the Secular Arm which had been contested. The published "evidence" of sectarian oppression by the Kinsfolk had always been secretly acknowledged to be suspect, and, in the vast majority of cases, was openly admitted to have been fabricated for purposes of propaganda.

In the autumn of that same year a pamphlet began to circulate among scholars attending the orthodox universities of old Europe. With the innocuous title *A Perspective of the Christian Dilemma* and written above the anonymous signature *"V.O.V."* (*"Veritas omnia vincit"* or *"Truth conquers all"*) it argued the case for the historical evolution of religion by pointing out how, in its earliest years, Christianity had contrived to absorb the ancient pagan cults into the corpus of the Church where, eventually, they had withered away and been forgotten. Not until the Medieval Church had become so fossilized in form, so doctrinally rigid that it was incapable of further assimilation, had it chosen the path of direct opposition to those reforming movements which had grown up within it. The outcome had proved disastrous. The Protestant Reformation and the ensuing counter-Reformation had resulted not in a true revitalization of Christian faith but in destructive schism and, ultimately, in abject surrender to the legions of Godless scientific materialism.

Annihilation of the whole human race had been avoided at the eleventh hour only through the Infinite Mercy of God and the release of those titanic cleansing forces of Nature which, by effectively reducing mankind once again to a primitive tribal level, had re-created the conditions out of which a truly Christian civilization could once again arise. And once again the lessons of history had been fatally ignored. No sooner had the Church established itself as the dominant force in society than dogma had thickened into a rigid carapace which had effectively stifled any further spiritual development. Now it found itself in the very position once occupied by those ancient pagan cults. It too was on the point of being absorbed into something greater than itself. Was it not time to ask, in all humility, whether the Holy Catholic Church had not finally achieved its divinely ordained purpose by providing the foundation and the stable social framework upon which an even nobler edifice could arise?

The reaction of the Vatican to *The Christian Dilemma*

was a foregone conclusion. It was condemned out of hand as a work of Satan. To be found in possession of a copy constituted a grievous mortal sin. The gentle and diffident Benedictine monk who had written it communed at length with his own conscience and, some years later, entered upon that marvelous correspondence with Brother Francis which was eventually to become known the world over as *The Letters to Brother Matthew.*

But *The Christian Dilemma* is significant as presaging a trend which was to become ever more pronounced in the decade following Cardinal Constant's death. It was in truth the very drift which the Cardinal himself had seen foreshadowed in Brother Francis's defection, the same which had driven him on in his relentless persecution of the Kinsfolk and, at the end, had so haunted his final days and nights. It could perhaps be expressed as his realization that the fundamental appeal of Kinship was not to the worst elements in mankind but to the best. It called to those very qualities to which the Church had paid dutiful lip-service over the centuries while its main energies had all been concentrated upon the consolidation of its own absolute temporal authority. For was not the very concept of "Papal infallibility" synonymous with hubris? In how many lonely cells and cloisters throughout Christendom was that particular battle for the souls of the Faithful fought and lost? No one will ever know for certain but it must have run into many thousands. And of those thousands many eventually came to travel the road to Corlay.

Whether the advent of the era which has since come to be known as the Second Renaissance was ever truly appreciated as such by those who experienced it is still matter for scholarly conjecture. Probably it was not. To very few is the gift given to see themselves as history will see them. The vast majority find it quite hard enough to see beyond the ends of their own noses. Yet a vague, uneasy sense that great tidal changes were astir in the world was surely present in some degree in almost every citizen of the western Kingdoms and even in those who inhabited the dim regions far beyond. It was a time of portents and rumors, of hopes and fears and doubts. But these were all experienced against the familiar background of a day to day expediency, dominated as it always had been by the necessity to earn one's bread. Abstract speculation was a luxury reserved for the leisured classes, and in a society which was still fundamentally feudal, this meant in effect the Church or the landed aristocracy, both of whom were constitutionally opposed to the contemplation of change. There was, in addition, one major inhibiting factor which cannot be overlooked—the knowledge buried deep in the consciousness of every human adult of what had happened in the distant past.

For a thousand years the Church had preached that the Drowning was God's punishment for straying from the path of orthodoxy—a doctrine which could be accepted either as fact or metaphor depending upon the degree of your intellectual sophistication. What could not be denied was that it had happened, for the physical evidence was still lying there beneath the waters. Curiously enough, the actual physical causes of the catastrophe had never been contested—the massive build-up of carbon dioxide in the earth's atmosphere leading to drastic modification of the planetary albedo with consequent melting of the polar ice-caps—but the whole global concept was in itself so far removed from day to day human experience as to be virtually meaningless to all but a very few. What men did accept was that the disaster had been a direct consequence of their forefathers' failure to control the forces they had unleashed upon the world, and so, blended in with anticipation of impending social change was a very real sense of apprehension as to just what that change might ultimately entail.

Even someone as stoical by nature as the Magpie was not entirely free of it. "Things will happen because they must and there's not much we can do about it," he informed Tom. "But that doesn't mean we don't have to make a choice now and again on our own account. That's what the *huesh* teaches us, Tom. We're a part of something bigger than ourselves, but we still *are* ourselves."

"Have you ever broken a *huesh*, Magpie?"

"Not when I was sure of it. Once or twice when it sort of fell betwixt and between I've let it go."

"What did you think would happen if you *did* break it? Properly, I mean."

"Don't ask me, lad. Nothing as like as not. I don't really think I'm that important."

"But you saved Mum's life, didn't you?"

"Who can be sure?"

"She is."

"Ah, well. That's different. What I mean is none of us can be certain, *really* certain, that she wouldn't have come through on her own. Francis did."

"Do you mean the *huesh* is a sort of luck thing?"

"Aye, you could say that. Luck's chiefly a matter of being in the right place at the right time. I once missed a north-bound barque out of Croydon because an axle broke on the van. Had to wait two days before I got to board the next one. That barque I missed went down in a squall twenty leagues out into Bedford Reach and every man-jack she carried was drowned."

"And you hadn't *hueshed* it?"

"Not so much as a glimmer. It was just pure luck—whatever that is."

Tom frowned and scratched his freckled nose with one of the peeled willow sticks which the Magpie was using for the chairback he was constructing. "It must have been the White Bird," he said finally.

The Magpie grinned. "Why, there's a thought! He drilled right through the axle like a woodpecker! 'Struth, that's never struck me before!"

Tom laughed in spite of himself. "Oh, you know what I mean, Magpie."

"I do?"

"Of course you do. You just won't admit it, that's all. You only say things like that to tease Aunty Alison."

"Ah, you've noticed that, have you?"

"It's because you love her, isn't it? People always seem to tease the ones they love the most."

"Like you and Witchet?"

"I was thinking more of Mum and Rett."

The Magpie gave him a quick, bright, sideways glance. "Were you now?"

"Why yes," said Tom. "I'm sure Mum loves him. She just won't let herself believe it yet, that's all. But she will."

"And what makes you so sure?"

Tom turned his head and gazed out of the barn door toward the distant, mist-wrapped grayness that was Black-down. "If I tell you, will you promise to keep it a secret?"

"You know me, Tom."

"Well, it's because I have to go away soon, Magpie. Someone's coming for me."

The Magpie stared at him.

"I think Mum knows about it. I'm not sure but I think she does."

"But go *where,* lad?"

"Away from Tallon. That's all I know, Magpie."

"Then who's this someone who's coming?"

"A Kinsman."

"You've *hueshed* that?"

The boy nodded.

"It'll break her heart, Tom. You're all she's got."

"No," said Tom, "that's not true. She has you and Alison and Witchet and Mike, and soon she'll have Rett too. I won't go till that's happened."

"It's not the same, Tom. You're her only son."

"She'll have other babies. And I'll come back again one day."

It seemed to the Magpie at that moment that he was seeing this child plain for the first time in his life and the sensation it evoked in him was very close to awe. It was almost as if their ages had been reversed and he had become the child. He heard Jane's voice saying: *"Sometimes I get the oddest notion that he's just been lent to me —that he isn't really mine at all"* and he wondered if it could really be true. "How long have you known this?" he asked.

"About a year," said Tom. "I *hueshed* the Kinsman coming that day I took Witch nutting up on Lydeard Hill."

"And when's it to be?"

"This summer sometime, I think. You won't say anything to Mum, will you?"

"You've got my word on that, Tom. But like you said I wonder if she hasn't *hueshed* it for herself. It seems likely enough. But she'll never tell a *huesh* these days. Have you noticed that?"

"She's *never* told me one ever," said Tom.

The Magpie did not exactly break his promise to Tom but there can be little doubt that his decision to seek out Rett and urge him to come to terms with Jane was inspired by what the boy had told him. After he had done it he was moved to wonder whether this had not been Tom's intention all along. Nevertheless he put forward his case so persuasively that Rett forsook his scruples, and, having ascertained when Jane was likely to be working alone in the pottery, he called in on her.

She was three parts of the way through throwing a batch of jugs and she glanced up as he appeared at the doorway and gave him a fleeting smile. "Just let me finish this one," she said. "It won't take a minute."

He leaned his shoulder against the door-post and gazed in at her. She was wearing a shapeless old canvas smock that had once belonged to her father. It was at least twice as big as she needed. Her bare arms and her face were smudged with red clay slip, and her soft, bright hair had been dragged back and snared by a length of coarse twine. While she worked, the tip of her tongue stole out between her teeth as if to observe what her hands were up to. Rett was utterly entranced.

Jane finished shaping the body of the jug, trimmed off its base, freed it from the wheel-head and lifted it on to the wooden rack at her side. Then she sat back and dropped her hands into her lap. "Well," she said. "And a very good afternoon to you, kind sir."

"Are you too busy right now, or can I talk to you, Janie?"

She glanced down at the balls of clay still waiting to be thrown and then up at him again. A faint smile flirted at the corners of her mouth. "What's it about?"

"Us."

"Ah," she said and the smile broadened into a grin. "Are you sure you want to?"

"That's why I'm here, lass. Si and young Tom have the boat all to theirselves this afternoon. Witchet's along wi' 'em."

"But not you."

He shook his head. "I'm up here a-purpose to talk wi' you."

"Well, go on then. Talk."

Rett's glance flittered around the workshop as if seeking for some secure point upon which to alight. Finally it settled for the shelf of newly thrown jugs beside Jane's right elbow. "Did you hear that Si and Maggie have clicked again?"

"That's nice," she said. "Maggie wants it to be a girl, doesn't she?"

Rett nodded. "It'll make things a bit awkward in the cottage though—seeing as how they'll be needing the extra room and all."

"Yes, I suppose it will. But not yet awhile, surely?"

Like one launching himself full tilt down a mountainside Rett plunged: "So I got to thinking about what you'd said, Janie, and . . ."

Jane nodded, holding back her amusement with the utmost difficulty. "And?" she prompted.

"And—and I thought to myself, Rett you're a silly sod, don't you give a bugger's cuss what anyone else says, it's her you want not them, so you get up there and tell her so right quick afore someone else does." His gaze unriveted itself from the line of jugs and anxiously sought her face. "So here I am," he concluded lamely. "Is it on, Janie?"

Jane was tempted momentarily to feign ignorance of what he meant but found she lacked the heart. "You mean you're asking me to marry you?"

"Aye. That's it."

"And you'll come and live up here?"

"I will."

"And I'll keep the pottery?"

He nodded.

"An equal kinship? Share and share alike? What's mine is yours: what's yours is mine?"

"Aye, Janie, my love, that's the way it'll always be between us, I promise you."

She laughed happily, held out her clayey hands to him, and they sealed the most welcome compact with a kiss.

The wedding took place at the end of May in Aisholt. The Magpie, who had not set foot inside a church since his own wedding, gave the bride away, and it seemed as if almost every man, woman and child in Tallon was there on hand to see him do it.

The weather being fine the reception was held according to long-standing comber tradition down on the quayside at Tallon. The fishing boats had all been decked out with bunting and green branches; a traditional arch erected from spars and draped nets strewn with flowers; vast quantities of food, ale, and wine had been set out on trestle tables; and on a platform constructed out of planks and barrels the village musicians took their places with young Tom in their center. As the bride and bridegroom appeared walking hand in hand down the steep cobbled street to the waterfront, Tom raised his pipe to his lips, nodded to the others, and set the party alight.

The combers of Tallon were still recalling that celebration years later. It became a sort of trusted yardstick by which the success of others was gauged—the *ne plus ultra* of wedding festivals, supreme, unmatchable. And yet no two people could be found to agree precisely wherein its ultimate perfection lay. A quality of magic overhung the memory like a dust of golden pollen. Was it the wine? or the food? or the dancing? or the laughter? or the feeling in the air that the dark and lingering ten year old shadows had finally been dispersed? Or was it the music?

Ah, that music . . . ! Rheumy old eyes would mist with reminiscence. "Aye, blast me, how they did play! Durned if ever I've heard finer! The Aisholt Minstrels couldn't have held a snuffer to 'em. And that little lad of Jane's—what's his name?—you know the one I mean, him as went away—Tom, aye, that's the chap. Young Tom. Oh, a wizard he was with a pipe! A real little wizard! Take hold of your very own heart could Tom and drag it right up into your throat. I tell you those fingers of his could coax salt tears to your eyes or set your feet spinning so's it seemed they didn't belong to you no more. Magic, I tell you. Magic. Dance? Lord bless us I'll say so! Without you'd been there you'll never know what dancing's all about. I tell you straight I never footed like that neither 'fore nor since. 'Struth I'll wager a hatful of gold royals we'd all be there a-footin' it still if we'd had the say in't . . ."

The sun set and the moon rose and hung like a globed lantern, full-faced, low down over the Somersea. The barrels were hopefully tilted to relinquish their final reluctant dribbles; beneath the tables the dogs nosed around for fallen scraps; and the old people gathered together in little clusters and swapped monstrous lies with one another. A full hour earlier Rett and Jane had said their farewells and climbed the hill taking the children with them and leaving the Magpie and Simon to see the party out.

It was close on midnight when the Magpie decided to call it a day and set off in search of his own bed. The moon was bright enough to cast sharp shadows on the lime-washed walls, the air so still that the threads of silver smoke rising from the chimneys seemed to tether the drifting stars, and almost without realizing that he was doing so he found he was remembering the night when Tom was born and he had scooped the night sky into a bowl and carried it in to Jane. It might have happened yesterday or a whole lifetime ago. People came together, clung awhile, drifted apart. Some died young, some old. The lad would be off soon, not a doubt of that, and he'd carry some part of all of them with him wherever he went. Like enough he'd take poor Witchet's heart. No single damned thing stayed still long enough in this world for you to make up your mind about it one way or the other. He snorted aloud and muttered: "God damn it, Patch, you're drunk," but he knew it was not really so—his mind was as clear as it had ever been—it was just that he was so sharply aware that a whole chapter of his life was about to close and that there was no way those pages could ever be turned again except in memory.

He reached the top of the street and paused to regain his breath. Ahead of him the white road ribboned away up the flank of Cothelstone Hill. Silvered by the moon-light the trees were huddled like sheltering sheep. And away in the distance he saw a shadow move on the brow of the hill, too far off to be told for man or beast. He shivered as though someone had trodden on his grave, felt a sudden fierce male hunger for Alison warm beside him in his bed and he turned gratefully toward the cottage gate.

Chapter Four

On a bright blue morning in the second week of August a trading barque from the Southern Irish Isles put into the port of New Barnstaple on the northern coast of the First Kingdom. Among the passengers who stepped ashore was a man traveling under the name of Marwys. Thin-faced, bearded, with pale blue eyes, he might have been almost any age between twenty and forty, but he was in fact thirty-two. By trade he was a wood carver: by calling a Kinsman. He stood on the quayside and looked about him. He saw the familiar busy sights of a trading port; the color-washed houses clambering upon each other's shoulders; the tawny hills billowing up behind. Smiling to himself he hitched his leather backpack high on his shoulders, hooked his thumbs securely under the straps and set off into the town.

It was market day and the main square was thronged with farmers and traders who had traveled in from the outlying districts. Marwys bought a cheese pasty and a bowl of creamy milk from one of the stalls. Intrigued by his unfamiliar accent the young woman who served him asked him where he hailed from. He told her he came from Switzerland.

"And where's that, m'dear?"

"A long way away," he replied. "Over the sea."

She shook her head wonderingly. "You've come from there now?"

"No," he said with a smile. "Now I have come from Ireland."

"Ah."

"And before that from America."

Her eyes widened perceptibly. The furthest she had ever traveled was to New Exeter. "America," she breathed. "What's it like over there?"

"Very big," he said. "Their lakes are bigger than our seas. The men are all three meters tall and the cows are as big as elephants."

"What's elephants?"

Marwys laughed. "I am looking for a place called Tallon," he said. "Can you help me to find it?"

"What sort of a place is that?"

"A village, I think."

"Is't hereabouts?"

"I know not. It is by the sea somewhere."

"You'd best ask of old Ben, yonder," she said. "If anyone knows, he will. Me, I never heard tell on't."

Marwys thanked her, paid for his breakfast, and approached the old man.

Old Ben had heard of Twichet and Telford and Torrington and Tawton and a dozen others besides but not a Tallon among them. " 'Taint this side New Exeter," he assured Marwys. "That's for sure. Reckon you'd best go 'n' try on t'other, m'dear."

Before setting out Marwys explored the market. Having found a stall which sold trinkets and ornaments he unshouldered his pack, rummaged inside it and pulled out a lumpy bundle. He untied the strip of linen by which it was fastened and unwrapped the parcel to disclose a dozen or so exquisitely carved little wooden figures, not one of which was bigger than a finger's length. Some were human; most were animals—a fox, a deer, a rabbit, a cow, a squirrel, an otter with a salmon in its mouth. He beckoned to the stall owner who leaned over, glanced at the figures, and then, his interest aroused, came out from behind the counter and peered at them curiously. "Clever," he said. "Where d'you get 'em?"

"I make them," said Marwys.

"Is that right? You're selling then?"

Marwys nodded.

"How much?"

"I sell only two," said Marwys. "You choose."

"How much?"

"What will you offer?"

The man lifted up one of the figures and examined it more closely. "I'll give you a quarter a-piece."

Marwys shook his head.

The stall owner selected three: a fox, a deer, and an old woman. "A full royal for those then."

"For two, yes."

The man shook his head and was about to hand back the carvings when something, some quality in the workmanship stayed him. He turned the figure of the old woman over between his fingers. "How long did you take shaping her?"

"Babushka? About a week." Marwys held out his hand for the little figure, preparing to do up the bundle and restore it to his pack.

"All right," said the man. "I'll take her. And the others too. A royal and a half."

"Two, only two," said Marwys holding up two fingers. "The old woman and one more."

"You're a coddle, you are," said the stall holder. "A proper coddle. Make it the fox then."

Marwys set the chosen figures down on the stall and the man took a purse from his breeches pocket and counted out four silver quarters.

Marwys tested each coin carefully between his teeth then nodded and stowed away his bundle. Before he was even clear of the town the stall owner had disposed of the statuette of the old woman for twice what he had paid for it and was cursing himself for not having asked more.

The Kinsman spent that night lying upon a bed of bracken high up on Exmoor under a roof of stars. Before settling down to sleep he took from his pack a set of pipes similar to those which the Magpie had once brought to Jane. Holding them by a hand at either end he raised them high above his head so that they lay dark across the twinkling Pleiades and he murmured softly in his native tongue: "Bird of Dawning, I am here. I listen." Then he set the pipes to his lips and played a snatch of melody, breaking off with the tune drifting in the air like a purpose unfulfilled.

He became very still, his head tilted slightly on one side and his eyes closed. Then he repeated the same haunting little phrase, again breaking off at the identical point until it seemed as if the very air itself ached to complete it for him.

Three times he repeated it and at the third, so faint and far away that it could almost have been the ghost of an imagined echo, he heard three pure notes fall like silver drops into the harmonic pattern and complete it.

Marwys smiled, drew in a deep, deep breath, and opening his eyes to the stars began to play.

He awoke shivering shortly before sunrise. His leather jacket was soaked with dew and all around him mist lay like drifts of dense white smoke in the dips and hollows of the hillside. He thrust aside the piled bracken which had served him for a blanket, climbed stiffly to his feet and began leaping up and down and beating his chilled arms across his chest. Alarmed by such untoward activity, two draggle-tailed moorland sheep started up bleating out of the mist and scampered off, bucketing away through the fog-smoke like two extraordinary legless bundles of woolly flotsam. So curious and comical was the sight that Marwys burst out laughing, and at that precise moment the first rays of the rising sun gilded the high cairn on Hoar-oak Hill. He took a wheaten bread-cake and a sour green apple from his pack, settled his cap on the back of his head and set off down the hillside toward the high road to the east.

Shortly before noon he entered the capital of the First Kingdom through the West Gate, passing beneath the black iron hooks from which the Bishop of Leicester's severed left leg and thigh had defied the beaks of scavenging crows for many a dismal month. Today a bright silken banner fluttered above each gatehouse celebrating the first anniversary of the Kingdom's successful bid for independence, and on the steps outside the City Hall a drum and trumpet band was playing martial music.

Marwys sought out the office of the Land Tax Commissioner, reasoning that if anyone would know the whereabouts of Tallon he would. The old clerk to whom he addressed his inquiry had records of three hamlets answering roughly to that name, but only one of them was on the coast. "T-A-L-L-O-N," he spelled out, peering up at Marwys over his spectacles. "Population at last census, two hundred and fifteen souls. Hearths sixty-two. Lies in the parish of Aisholt on Quantock Isle. Forms a tenth part of the Squiredom of Merridge and bears a fealty of twelve bows. Hah, used to be ten, I see! Port tax in abeyance. Doesn't say why. No boats maybe. Hardly seems likely though, does it? Well, that's about it, young man. There's your Tallon, I'd say."

"Thank you," said Marwys. "And where is Quantock Isle?"

The old man closed up the tome he had been consulting and restored it to its shelf. "East of the Brendon Spine," he said. "Lies out in the Somersea. You can take a ferry across from Monksilver. Tallon's right down at the southern end as far as you can go. Step off it and you'll be swimming in the sea. Here, I'll show you."

He beckoned Marwys down to the end of his office where a map of the First Kingdom was hanging, and pointed out Quantock Isle. "The ferry plies between Monksilver and Bicknoller," he said. "That's your best way. Tallon's there—no, *there*. That's it! Used to have quite a reputation for smuggling and general lawlessness in the old days. All that coast did. Independent lot the combers."

Marwys smiled and nodded, then asked casually: "Would there be Kinsfolk thereabouts?"

The old man turned, ducked his head and squinnied up quizzically at the Kinsman over the lenses of his glasses. "Oh, I daresay," he murmured. "One or two, no doubt. Those the Grays missed."

"Who are the Grays?"

"Were, sir. Were," corrected the old man. "Ten years back they came and hunted down the Kinsfolk like rabbits around those parts. The Gray Falcons they called themselves. Vultures might've been nearer the mark. Ah well, that's all over now and done with, God be thanked. We live in happier times now, heh? Happier times."

Noon the next day saw Marwys on Quantock, drawn thither by a dream which he had dreamt all of nine months before among the fiery autumn hills in far off Vermont. He had set out at once for New Concord seeking a ship on which he could work a passage to the place he knew only from the memory of the voice whispering to him of *"Sea-girt Tallon, dwelling of the Bride of Time."*

Then had followed months of frustration, fretting for the winter ice to relax its grip along the eastern seaboard, and at last a wretched passage, battling against contrary winds in an ill-founded tub which had barely managed to struggle into Killarney and had spewed him out like a sick Jonah, delirious with shipboard fever, on to the Irish shore. There for interminable weeks he had languished until the last of the poison had crept reluctantly from the marrow of his bones and he had begun to recover his strength.

And then the call had come again, sighing to him from the reeds which fringed the long, dark Irish lakes; whispering down the glittering corridors of the cloud-pillared sky; borne to him in the lonely cries of the sea-birds; always beckoning him on to where the white road of his dream lost itself in the blue distance—*sea-girt Tallon . . . Tallon . . . Tallon.*

The moment he stepped ashore at Bicknoller Marwys sensed that his journey was nearly done. There was no need for him to ask which way he should take because he knew that he had traveled this road before. It was as though a strong wind blew at his back thrusting him on.

He climbed the hill to the ancient earthwork, stood where Jane and Tom had stood six years before, and turned his face to the south. As he did so he heard, faint but crystal clear, thrilling upon the sunny air, the opening phrases of the melody which was as familiar to him as the pulse of his own heart. Three times they came to him and after the third he took out his own pipes, set them to his lips and knotted up the broken thread.

"What's that you're playing?" asked Witchet. She was seated in a nest of grass at Tom's side on the eastward flank of

Lydeard Hill nursing a battered wooden doll which the Magpie had made for her five years before.

"It hasn't got a name," he said. "It's just a tune."

"Is that why you keep stopping?"

"Shh," he commanded. "There! Didn't you hear?"

"Hear what?"

"Listen!"

Witchet's brow puckered into an elaborate parody of intense concentration. "The sheep, you mean?"

"Sheep!" he groaned. "You're a sheep."

"Well, I can't hear anything else except grasshoppers."

Tom rose to his feet and shading his eyes from the dazzling sun stared into the distance.

"What can you see?"

"Nothing."

"Are you sure it's today?"

"Yes."

"How can you be sure?"

"I just am, that's all."

She climbed to her feet and stood beside him, a stocky, sunburned little figure in a faded canvas frock, the downy hairs on her bare arms bleached to pale silver by the long suns of the summer. "Tom?"

"What?"

"Take me with you."

The boy made no sign that he had even heard her.

"Please, Tom?"

"Don't be silly," he said. "You know I can't. I've explained all that."

The corners of her mouth drooped pathetically; her blue eyes grew large with tears. "Please, Tom."

He turned and gazed down at her, then put his arm around her quivering shoulders. "It's no use crying, Witch. And I'll be back soon. I've promised you, haven't I?"

"It's not the same," she mumbled, butting her small blonde head into his chest like a lamb seeking its teat. "What'll I do when you're not here?"

"You'll have Mike. And next year there'll be Mum's new baby."

"It's not the same. They're too little."

"Well, Tammy then. She's your best friend, isn't she?"

"She's not you."

"Come on," he said. "Cheer up. I'll play you something. What would you like?"

He sat her down in the grass beside him and smudged away her tears with his fingers. Taking up his pipe he turned full face to her. "Look at me, Witch!"

Reluctantly she raised her sad eyes until they met his own, then with fingers still dewy from her grief he began to play.

Jane was puddling raw clay in a wooden trough outside the pottery when she heard voices coming down the path toward the cottage. She looked up, saw a tall, bearded stranger flanked on either side by the two children, and she felt her heart miss a painful beat. He carried a pack on his shoulder; his jacket and leather hose were gray with the dust of the summer roads; his eyes were the color of an April sky reflected in running water; and she knew him even though she had never seen him in her life before.

"Mum, this is Marwys. He's a Kinsman."

Aye, what else could you be, she thought as the stranger doffed his cap and bowed to her. "Greetings, Kinsman," she said. "And welcome to Tallon."

At the sound of her voice Marwys raised his head and stared at her. Then he took a couple of paces toward her, knelt on the stones at her feet and bowed his head once more. "Thou are she," he murmured. "Truly thou art she."

The children gazed from one adult to the other in bewilderment, completely at a loss.

"And you the Wanderer," replied Jane. "Truly you have taken your time."

"A long hard journey, Madonna."

"Aye," she said. "From the world's edge was it not?"

"The world's edge," he repeated. "For how long have you known?"

"Ever since Thomas first told me the Testament, I suppose. And you?"

"The Call came to me nine months ago."

Jane reached down and helped him to his feet. "I thought perhaps Francis had sent you."

"Brother Francis? But he believes the Bird has claimed you. Did you not know?"

"I guessed that was it," she said. "I wasn't sure."

"They have built a shrine to you in Corlay. I have prayed before it."

Jane laughed. "And were your prayers answered?"

"Yes. When first I heard your son play an hour ago."

The smile died on Jane's lips. She drew a deep sighing breath and said: "And who is going to teach him? You, Marwys the Wanderer?"

"You do me great honor," said Marwys. "I only wish the choice were mine."

"Who then?"

"I will take Tom with me to Corlay. There he will join the school and a tutor will be appointed by the Council."

Jane nodded. "When will you leave?"

"The school opens in the second week of September. Would you say it is a week's travel from here to Corlay?"

"Less," said Jane. "Until then you shall be our guest."

No three weeks in Jane's life ever passed more quickly than those before Tom left. Having come to terms with the inevitable almost without realizing she had done so, she surprised herself as much as anybody with her lightness of heart. She occupied herself in making Tom a complete new outfit of jacket and hose of soft leather, to which the Magpie contributed a superb belt adorned with a buckle of wrought brass together with a pouch purse for either hip. Alison contrived a cap modeled upon Marwys's to which Tom had taken a great fancy, and Rett got the Aisholt cobbler to fashion his step-son a pair of doeskin calf-boots which became the envy of all the lads in Tallon.

On the last evening they held a family party in Kiln Cottage. For the farewell feast Tom chose his favorite roast lamb, mint sauce, and tender young finger-beans, with apple dumplings and cream to follow. When everyone had eaten their fill the table was cleared and carried out into the next room, a jug of mulled wine was produced and Tom and Marwys played their pipes for the dancing.

Later Marwys went out and returned with the bundle of carvings which he had displayed to the stall owner in New Barnstaple market. From it he selected a deer which he presented to Alison; a rabbit he gave to young Michael; the otter with the salmon in his mouth went to Witchet in exchange for a kiss; and then, turning to Jane he unwrapped a separate treasure which brought gasps of astonishment from all who beheld it. It was a figure of the Bird of Kinship hovering on outstretched wings, its head turned to one side and drooping slightly as if in sorrowful contemplation of what it beheld beneath it. "It is for you,

Madonna," he said, handing it to Jane with a smile. "So that you will remember the Wanderer in your prayers."

"It is beautiful," she murmured. "Never have I seen anything more lovely. When did you make it, Marwys?"

"When I was lying sick in Ireland," he replied, "it came to me so in a vision. Later I found the wood waiting for me by the lake shore. I had only to release the spirit which was locked within it." He turned away and retrieved his pipes. "Now, Tom, let us show them what we have been practicing. Are you ready?"

Tom nodded.

"This is the Boy's *Lament for Morfedd*," explained Marwys. "By rights it should be rendered on two sets of twinned pipes, but such is Tom's skill that I do not think you will heed the difference." So saying he set his instrument to his lips.

Of all those who heard that performance Witchet's reaction was by far the strangest. Curled up in a dark corner of the room, clutching the wooden otter which Marwys had given her, she drifted off into a waking dream where she seemed to be wandering lost in a strange, gray, unfamiliar world in which she was seeking for someone or something which she could not quite remember. Doors opened and she glided through them to discover other doors, but none held the thing she sought, and when the music ended and she returned to her own true self she still did not know what it was she had been looking for. Later, when Tom sought her out and asked her if she had liked their playing she said with a puzzled frown: "What playing?" which could hardly have been the answer he had expected. Then she had taken his hand in hers and whispered to him with an intensity which was totally foreign to her: "Tom, if ever I'm lost, promise me you'll come and find me."

"What on earth do you mean?"

"I'm not sure," she confessed. "Just that, I think."

"You're drunk, Witch. I saw you having a go at the wine."

"But you will, Tom? Promise me."

"All right, you boozer," he replied with a grin. "I promise. Now show me your otter."

At first light next morning Tom and Marwys prepared to board Rett's boat and cross to Chardport which was to be their first port of call on their way to Brittany. Jane, Alison and Witchet came down to the quayside to wish them God-speed and safe journey.

Wisps and tendrils of autumnal mist were curling off the quietly lapping water in the harbor basin as Jane took her son into her arms and held him close. "I have some things here for you, my love," she said, dipping a hand into the deep inner pocket of her cloak. "There is a letter to Brother Francis. And here is a gold royal for your journey. And there are these." She drew out the pipes which had belonged to Tom's father. "You do not have to take them unless you want to."

Tom flung his arms around her and hugged her with all his might, not trusting himself to speak for the pain of the love he felt for her at that moment. Then clutching the gifts, he quickly ducked away, kissed Alison and Witchet and jumped down on to the rocking deck where he stowed the articles away inside his pack.

Rett hoisted the brown mainsail. Simon cast off the mooring ropes and sprang aboard. As the stirring breeze nudged the boat away from the harbor wall toward the open sea, Witchet trotted the length of the quay as if tugged along by an invisible line which Tom held in his hands.

Well over an hour later she climbed up into the cherry tree in the orchard behind the cottage. By screwing up her eyes she was just able to make out the tiny brown sail, smaller now than a butterfly's wing, far out on the Somersea. And then it was rinsed away by the tears which her aching heart could no longer contain.

PART III
HERITAGE

Chapter One

At the extreme tip of the Breton headland known as *L'Index* which juts out into the Sea of Nantes and points southward toward the far-distant *Hauteurs de Gatine* a young man was sitting with his knees drawn up and his back resting against the scaly bark of a storm-twisted pine tree. Lying open beside him on the carpet of dead pine needles was a small notebook made up of several sheets of parchment which had been stitched rather amateurishly into a limp leather cover. The exposed page had been scrawled into a series of makeshift double staves, the first pair of which was flecked with the ciphers of a musical notation. In his left hand the young man was clasping those same twin-barreled pipes which had once belonged to his father, the Kinsman Thomas of Norwich. His right hand held a well-chewed stub of pencil. Every now and again he would raise his tousled head and gaze out across the water in the direction of the nearest of the islets which together comprised the *Archipel Lanvaux.*

In a rocky cove some ten meters below him and about thirty paces to his left a second youth was wading bare-legged in the shallow water. Around his neck was slung an open-weave basket into which he was dropping handfuls of the feathery red seaweed known locally as "Judas' beard." His name was David Ronceval and he was Tom's closest friend. The two of them had been constant companions ever since they had first arrived at Corlay on the same day seven and a half years before. Since then each had visited the other's home during the annual summer vacations. Their close companionship had earned them the nickname of "the Heavenly Twins" and it had been a foregone conclusion that once their period as Probationers in the communal dormitory was over they would elect to share a study cell.

Between the two of them there flowed a deep undercurrent of real affection, though temperamentally their characters were very different. At seventeen Tom was a bewildering mixture—prone to black moods, fierce fits of frustration, and wild outbursts of ecstatic joy which at times bordered upon hysteria. He was also gifted with flashes of profound insight, moments when he achieved an imaginative identification with others which seemed almost supernatural, and his careless generosity had long been a by-word among his fellow students.

David was as equable as Tom was effervescent. He had once referred to the two of them as "the oak and the ivy" though he had refrained from saying which was which. His mind was both placid and logical, and this, together with a dry sense of humor, sometimes made him seem more detached than he really was. He cared deeply about his calling—far more deeply indeed than Tom, who, in their numerous discussions about the true nature of Kinship, was only too willing to take upon himself the role of devil's advocate and had even been known to contend that Brother Francis's secret ambition was to be elected Pope.

Quite early on, the friends' paths of study had diverged, for David had no natural gift for music and Tom cared about very little else. At the end of their second year David had elected to specialize in medicine and Tom had contrived to skip a whole year of academic study in order to concentrate upon mastering the pipes. No sooner was his tongue healed from the painful operation known as "twinning" than he had set about demonstrating his prodigious aptitude for that instrument which had become almost as famous a symbol of Kinship as the White Bird itself.

Within two years he was already the acknowledged equal of even the most accomplished of his tutors who, in private, agreed that it could only be a matter of time before he quite outstripped them. There was even some talk of applying for a special dispensation to allow him to graduate without having to undergo the examinations in History, Latin and Mathematics which formed part of the course, but this had been firmly vetoed by the Council on the grounds that it might be establishing a dangerous precedent.

At the end of their final year each student at Corlay was called upon to present the Council with a piece of original work from his own hands. These, known as the *dona-tionem,* constituted a symbolic expression of that basic tenet of Kinship which had gained popular currency in the phrase: "What is mine is yours." Ever since Christmas Tom had been hard at work perfecting an elaborate quartet,. and David had been slaving over a medicine which was destined for the sanatorium and was derived from vast quantities of red seaweed by a tedious process of distillation.

It was not mere chance which had brought them both to *L'Index.* In the last two weeks they had already paid no fewer than three visits to this very spot. Tom had been drawn there by the imperious summons of the *huesh,* and David, long familiar with his friend's uncanny gift, had elected to accompany him. Had additional incentive been needed it would have been supplied in abundance by the sheer natural beauty of this place where the sea-breeze whispered in the tops of the pines and the Atlantic rollers exploded thunderously in silver spray across the long sand bars at the mouth of the nearby river.

Hearing a sudden shout, David looked up and following the direction of his friend's pointing arm masked his eyes against the wave-glare and peered out to sea. He saw a little white-sailed skiff skimming like a swansdown feather across the glittering jostle of April waters which separated the islets of Lanvaux from the mainland. He could just make out a tiny figure leaning perilously outward to balance the frail, flitting cockleshell of a craft. "I see it!" he called. "Is that the one?"

But Tom was already scrambling down the steep bank into the cove where a fishing boat had been dragged up above the high tide line. "Help me get her afloat!" he cried. "Quick, Dave!"

The unmistakable urgency in his friend's voice overrode any qualms David might have felt. He waded ashore, dragged off his basket of weed and dropped it on the stones. Together they began lugging the cumbersome craft down to the water's edge.

"What are you going to do?" panted David.

"We," grunted Tom. "You'll have to come too. It'll need both of us."

David scrambled aboard, found his feet ankle deep in rain water, and began fumbling a pair of oars into the foremost tholes. Tom thrust the boat out farther, hauled himself in over the stern and seized the second pair of oars.

In a minute they had drawn clear of the shelter of the headland. The boat began to pitch and toss in the choppy waters of the channel. Tom darted a glance over his shoulder and saw no sign of the skiff.

"Well?" demanded David peering into his anxious face.

"She's over."

"Can you see it?"

"Not yet. But just keep pulling. She'll cling on."

"You're sure it's a she?"

"It has to be."

Ten minutes' hard rowing took them out into mid-channel. Tom called a halt while they both scanned the surface of the sea. "The current's taking us west," panted David. "Hadn't we better pull further over?"

"It'll be taking her too," replied Tom. "Hold still. I'm going to stand up."

With one hand clutching his friend's shoulder he rose to his feet and almost immediately said: "I can see it! Over there to the left. About five hundred meters." Letting go of David he cupped his hands round his mouth and yelled out in French: "Hold on! We're coming!" Then, without waiting for a response he resumed his seat and bent once more over the heavy oars.

Hardly anything of the capsized skiff was visible above the surface but its position was betrayed by a patch of unnaturally calm water. They saw a dark head lolling alongside the submerged mast. As they drifted alongside David shipped his oars, leaned over the side and grabbed. "Let go!" he shouted. "Let go! I've got you!"

But the girl's hands were locked about the spar in so tense a rigor of panic that it took the combined efforts of both of them to prize her free and they all but capsized themselves in the process.

They hauled her inboard and tumbled her like a water-logged sack into the bilges where she lay inert, her blue lips gulping weakly against the tarred boards while they gazed down at her and fought to recover their breath.

David crouched down beside her, took hold of her wrist and felt for the pulse. "She's as cold as a fish," he said. "Lend me your jacket."

Tom stripped off his leather jerkin and passed it over. As David was wrapping it around her, Tom leaned over the side again and with the aid of an oar succeeded in retrieving the painter of the skiff which he secured to a cleat.

David glanced up and told him he was out of his mind if he thought they could tow it back to shore.

But Tom had spent his childhood in and around boats of all kinds and he had no intention of letting this one go if he could help it. He first contrived to release the sail then, having hauled it aboard, he proceeded to maneuver around till he had hold of the top of the mast. He dragged it clear of the water and then began slowly handing himself along it until eventually it rose high above their own boat and the little shallop was floating right way up, awash to the gunwales.

"And what now?" asked David, impressed in spite of himself.

"I'll bail her out," said Tom. "There's a bucket under your seat."

In a surprisingly short time the shallow skiff was floating high enough in water for them to tow it in. Tom flung the wooden bucket down beside the still motionless figure of the girl and grinned at his friend. "No comber worth the name ever lets a good boat go unless he has to. Back to your oars, you idle slug!"

They were more than halfway home before the girl began to stir. She rolled over and brought up a noisy bellyful of bile and sea-water.

"Well done, lass," said Tom cheerfully. "Better out than in."

The girl coughed and subsided with a groan. From time to time she could be heard retching feebly but it was not until they regained the shelter of the cove that she spoke for the first time, asking, in halting French, who they were.

"We're angels," said Tom. "The Heavenly Twins. At your service, mam'selle."

The boat grounded on the shingle and the two young men splashed into the foam and hauled it safe ashore. Then Tom reached over the side, dragged the girl to her feet, heaved her ignominiously across his shoulder and dumped her down beside David. "You look like a drowned cat," he informed her cheerfully.

"Pardon?"

"Are you English?"

She nodded.

"Well, that explains it."

"Explains what?"

"No sane Breton would have risked his neck on the Lanvaux Channel in April in that pea-pod of a boat. The wind blows all ways out there. Where are you from?"

"The First Kingdom."

"No, I mean now. Where did you set out from?"

"Saint Anne."

"Saint Anne?" repeated Tom, turning to David. "Where's that?"

"It's one of the islands," said David. "There is a château on it."

"La Tour," said the girl. "It belongs to my Godfather."

The young men exchanged glances. "You're an aristo?" Tom asked.

The girl shivered and clutched the jacket about her. "Will you take me back? My friends will pay you well for your trouble."

They stared at her and then at one another. Finally David asked in English: "What is your name?"

"Alice."

"Alice who?"

"Alice," she repeated. "Just Alice."

"Well, who's your father?" asked Tom.

"My father's dead."

"Who was he?"

Her lower lip trembled. "Does it matter?"

"No," he said, "not a bit. What matters is getting you into some dry clothes before you catch your death."

"I'm all right," she said. "Oh please take me back to Saint Anne. Please."

He realized she was crying; slow, fat tears were gathering and trickling down her pale cheeks. As he stared at her he saw her tongue slip from the corner of her mouth and lap one away. It was just the sort of totally unpremeditated thing that Witchet might have done and it winged straight as an arrow to his heart. "How far is it to Saint Anne?" he asked David.

"It would take at least an hour in that old tub. Two's more likely."

Tom gnawed at his thumbnail and then glanced up at the sky. "All right," he said. "I'll take you back. In your own boat. We'll tie a reef into her just to be on the safe side. Help me tip her out, Dave."

"Have you gone quite mad?"

"Have I ever been anything else? It's all right. I know what I'm doing."

"But you've still got to get yourself back."

"What of it? I'll sail back in her boat and leave it here. She and her friends can pick it up tomorrow. Does that suit you, my lady?"

"Thank you," she said.

"Then let's get started. And we'll pray that the wind holds steady."

The tide began to turn just as they entered the main channel and the sea crests settled. Tom soon got the feel of the boat and began to relax. "Whereabouts in the First are you from?" he asked.

"New Exeter."

"Are you a citizen?"

"Not really. We live just outside."

"And what are you doing on Saint Anne?"

"I'm staying with my God-father."

"He's the one who owns the château?"

"Yes."

"Should I know him?"

"I don't know. Are you from the First Kingdom too?"

"That's right. From Tallon. Quantock Isle."

"And you live here in Brittany?"

"At Corlay. I'm a student there. So's David."

The girl who had been sitting with her back toward him, gazing ahead, now turned her head and glanced round at him with sudden interest. "You're a Kinsman?"

Tom grinned. "No, not yet."

"I'm Kin."

He was astonished and his expression must have shown it because she sketched the Sign of the Bird over her breast and smiled at him.

It was the first time he had seen her smile and he found the manner in which her lips quirked upward at the corners wholly delightful. "Well, well," he said. "Fancy that. Kin *and* an aristo. It must be a pretty rare combination for the First."

"I never said I was an aristo."

"Ah, but you are though."

"Why do you say that?"

"Well, for one thing only an aristo maid would dare to be seen out in boy's clothes."

"You can't sail a skiff in skirts."

"Oh, I'm not blaming you," he said. "I think the garb suits you."

She turned her head away and some strands of her bright hair, dried now by the sun and winnowed by the wind began to flutter about her ears. "What kind of a Kinsman are you?" she asked.

"Not any kind yet."

"You know what I mean. What will you be?"

"Next month—if I pass my examinations—I'll be a piper."

She swung back to face him again. "Truly?"

"You don't believe me?"

"Of course I do, if you say so."

He stuck out his cloven tongue at her and flicked it apart like a snake's. At that moment a sudden gust of wind made the boat heel sharply. A shower of cold spray cascaded over them both. Tom laughed. "We may have to swim for it yet. I can't see David coming out to rescue the two of us."

It was not long before they were across the main channel and scudding between the wooded islets of the archipelago. "That's Saint Anne straight ahead," said Alice, pointing. "The château's on the south side. You can't see it from here."

"If I put you down on this side can you make your own way back all right?"

"Yes, of course I can."

"And what will you tell your God-father?"

"I won't tell him anything. He'd be furious if he knew I'd been out sailing alone."

"But what about the boat?"

"Oh, I'll get Peter to come with me and collect it to-morrow."

"Who's Peter?"

"My brother."

"Is he Kin too?"

"Not yet."

Tom glanced up at the swelling sail. "How old are you, Alice?"

"Eighteen and a bit. And you?"

"Eighteen next December."

The small waves bubbled against the thrusting hull and

the mast squeaked derisively. "And how came you to be Kin?" he asked.

"I am. Isn't that enough?"

"Did you think you were about to meet the White Bird out there in the channel?"

"I prayed, if that's what you mean."

"Was your prayer answered?"

"It must've been, mustn't it?"

"Then you really do believe in the Bird?"

She stared at him, a faint frown gathering like a shadow between the delicate arches of her eyebrows. "Why do you say that?"

"I just wondered."

"The White Bird brought me here," she murmured. "I know it did."

"And do you know why?"

"No," she said. "Not yet."

The retreating tide had exposed a crescent of yellow sand off the tip of one of the two promontories that formed the northern shore of the island. Tom guided the boat toward it and told the girl to be ready to haul up the centerboard as soon as he gave her the word.

Within minutes the skiff was beached, the sail fluttering like a white flag, and they were both standing on the shore. An unfamiliar shyness seemed to have afflicted them both. She stripped off his jacket and handed it back to him. "I haven't thanked you properly for what you did," she said. "I don't know how to. When I offered you money it was before I knew you were Kin."

"We wouldn't have accepted it anyway," he said, shrugging on the jacket. "How long are you here for?"

"Till the end of May."

"Perhaps we'll meet again."

"Yes," she said.

"Have you ever been to Corlay?"

She shook her head.

"Would you like to?"

"Oh *yes*," she said, her eyes shining. "I'd like to *very* much."

"Nothing simpler," he said. "You come, I'll show you round."

"I'd have to ask my God-father first."

"Bring him too. And your brother. Come to the *donationem*."

"What's that?"

He told her briefly about the ceremony of graduation and then, observing how she was shivering said: "You'd better trot off home quick and get yourself changed before all our efforts are wasted."

They touched hands briefly and he watched her turn and jog away up the beach until she had disappeared from his sight among the hazels and scrub-oaks. He re-launched the skiff, and as he was drawing clear of the shore, he glanced back over his shoulder. He saw a flock of startled pigeons leap into the air above the distant trees, guessed her whereabouts, and raised his arm in salute.

On the evening before the *donationem* David burst in upon Tom with the news that they had both passed their Finals and that Brother Francis had returned and would be presiding in person over the graduation ceremony.

Tom affected indifference but was secretly delighted. "All we have to do now is to make certain he has a good swig of Kinsman Ronceval's elixir," he said. "After that anything will seem a work of pure genius."

David laughed. "By the way, the *dispositionem* have been brought forward to Friday. I suppose that means he'll be in charge of those too. Have you submitted your *suppliance* yet?"

"I spoke to Marwys about it months ago. He was supposed to be having a word with old Paul. I don't know if he did."

"But aren't you going to submit one in writing?"

"Saying what?"

"Well, about staying on as a tutor at the Music School. That's what you want, isn't it?"

"Is it?"

"You haven't changed your mind, have you?"

"I just haven't thought about it, that's all. Here, Dave, I want you to listen to something. Shut the door."

David did so and then stretched himself out on his bed and thatched his fingers into a head rest. Tom took up his pipes, fingered a soft, rippling scale and then with his eyes resting upon David he began to play.

For seven years David had been a willing audience for his friend's music; he had seen Tom's lips threaded with bright blood when he had insisted upon practicing before his tongue was properly healed; he had witnessed each separate painful upward step toward the ultimate pinnacle of mastery; but this time his heart told him he was hearing something altogether outside his previous experience, something mysterious and magical and almost frightening.

All around him the room was becoming curiously insubstantial, the solid stone walls seeming to tremble as though he were viewing them through sunlit water. They faded, becoming ever more faint, until at last they had vanished completely from his perception and he found himself gazing out upon some unknown landscape in which the trees were as red as blood and strange and monstrous creatures moved dimly browsing among the crimson groves. Over everything there hung a sense of wan and brooding melancholy. He became aware of an unfamiliar heaviness in his chest as though each breath he drew were costing him an intolerable effort. At that point the music stopped, the vision slowly faded, and the walls of the room solidified about him once again. He unlaced his stiffened fingers and found that his shirt was drenched with cold sweat and that his skin had crawled into shivering gooseflesh. He sat up and stared across at Tom who was gazing at him curiously. "What was it?" he faltered. "What happened? What did you do?"

"I don't really know," said Tom. "Tell me what you saw."

David shuddered. "A sort of red place. A forest, I think. There were creatures in it. Huge. Like dragons. I've never seen anything like it in my life. Not even in dreams."

Tom held the pipes out to him. "Take a look at those, Dave."

David reached over and took them. "But these aren't yours," he said. "Where did you get them?"

"You don't recognize them?"

David shook his head. "Should I?"

"They're his," said Tom. "The Boy's. The ones the Wizard of Bowness fashioned for him."

David's mouth opened soundlessly and then closed again. "But those are locked up in the reliquary," he whispered. "Along with the Testament."

"They were," said Tom. "I borrowed them this afternoon. I wanted to hear what they sounded like."

David sketched a rapid sign of the Bird over his breast and thrust the instrument back into his friend's hands. "Go and put them back," he whispered urgently. "Quick. Before someone finds out."

"They won't. No one ever looks in there except on Holy Days. Besides I left a set of my own in their place just in case."

"You're *mad*, Tom!"

"The last person to play upon these was my father," mused Tom, stroking his fingers up and down the gleaming barrels. "Did you know that?"

"Who says so?"

"Old Magpie told me. He was there when it happened. It was just before my father was killed."

"I thought Gyre had them."

"Before Gyre died he gave them to Francis to take to my father. I think that really makes them mine by right."

"Of course it doesn't. Anyway, you've got your own."

"They're not the same, Dave. I *know*. *These are tuned for me!*"

"What do you mean?"

Tom's voice became intense, vibrant with suppressed excitement. "The moment I reached inside the reliquary and touched them I felt it—a sort of trembling inside me. Like that time we were caught in the thunderstorm up on the *lande* and had to shelter in the *bergerie*. But it was more than that, Dave. *Much* more. A sort of *rightness*."

"Even so, you can't just *take* them."

"I could," said Tom. "Nothing easier. But I won't."

"Well, go and put them back then."

"Don't worry. I will." He paused momentarily. "Tomorrow."

"Tomorrow? Why not today?"

Tom looked up from the pipes and his eyes seemed to flicker like brilliant green dragonflies. "Because tomorrow I shall be playing them in the *donationem*."

"*You can't do that!*"

"Who says I can't?"

"But they'll *know*, Tom! Marwys and Doctor Paul and the rest of them! They're bound to!"

"What does that matter?"

"It matters to *me!*" said David fiercely.

Tom looked at him with genuine surprise. "What do you mean?"

"I mean you *don't* need to do it! You *don't* have to! You're just saying that. It's a sort of game for you—an interesting experiment to see what happens. Well, that was all right for *me*—but it's not right for *them*. Not for all those folk who'll be there in the Great Hall tomorrow. If you can't see that then you want your head examined. I mean that, Tom. I really do."

There was a long, thoughtful silence. Finally Tom tilted back his head and smiled. "You're right," he said. "I don't need them at all. Not for my *Quartet*, anyway. That'll be played just as I planned it, on my father's pipes."

"And you'll put those back in the Chapel?"

"We'll do it now," said Tom, rising to his feet. "Come on. I'll need you to keep a look out."

Chapter Two

Although the passing years had transformed the color of his short, wiry hair from gray to white they had otherwise been most merciful to the one time Senior Marshal of the Secular Arm of the First Kingdom. The solemn sentence of Maximum Excommunication which Cardinal Constant had passed upon him had left no outward mark, and a lifetime's temperate habits combined with a regime of hard exercise in the field had ensured that he was now in better physical condition than many a man half his age. But the untimely death of his old friend and companion in arms, Robert Earl of Exeter had caught him unprepared, as had the action of Robert's brother, Philip, Duke of Bodmin, who had seen fit to contest the succesion to the throne on the grounds that Robert's eldest son Arthur was a bastard who had been conceived out of wedlock. Philip had taken his case before the Ecclesiastical Court in York and they, seizing a heaven-sent opportunity to sow discord among the enemy, had given his claim their official blessing.

Personal loyalty to Earl Robert had never blinded Richard to the fact that Prince Arthur was in no way likely to prove the kind of strong ruler the Kingdom needed. Delicate from birth, prey to epileptic seizures, adored and pampered by his mother, everything about Arthur seemed to lend credence to Philip's claim. Indeed the Earl Robert himself had more than once toyed with the notion of declaring his second son Peter to be his lawful successor, but fearing the breach which such a declaration would inevitably have opened up between himself and his wife and thus (through her family connections) with the Second Kingdom, he had in the end done nothing.

Immediately after Robert's death Richard, the single most powerful liege man in the Kingdom, had been wooed by both factions. He had temporized by suggesting that Philip might reign as Regent until Peter came of age—a solution which, though indisputably in the best interests of the Kingdom as a whole had, unfortunately, pleased neither party. Lady Margaret had set to work upon the senile old Bishop of New Exeter who, finally yielding to persuasion, had duly crowned and anointed Arthur ruler of the Kingdom in New Exeter cathedral on Midsummer's Day 3034. Admirably concealing his own misgivings Richard had knelt before him and sworn the Oath of Loyalty, while Duke Philip, nothing if not prudent, had taken himself off to Northumberland out of retribution's way. After some muttering and grumbling the First Kingdom had turned over and settled down to sleep once more.

For the better part of two years it had seemed to Richard that his doubts had lacked substance. Urged by his mother Arthur had gone out of his way to seek the Marshal's advice on matters of State and, with one or two notable exceptions, had acted upon it. But the old, easy, familiar relationship based upon mutual respect which had existed between Richard and Arthur's father was gone forever. A new breed of courtier had begun to appear at the castle bringing with them what seemed to Richard to be bizarre forms of dress and outlandish behavior—so much so, indeed, that he had been heard to declare that it was a nice problem to decide which of his Lord's companions were men and which were women. He might have been inclined to ascribe his personal distaste for such frivolities as being due to his age had it not been for the fact that the Lady Alice, and to a lesser extent her brother Peter, seemed equally ill at ease. The constant round of masques, balls and suchlike sophisticated and costly diversions with which Arthur filled his days left his younger brother and sister confused and bewildered and first Alice and then Peter had turned to Richard for guidance.

For the Lord Marshal the situation was delicate. His Oath of Loyalty bound him to Lord Arthur as titular head of the Kingdom but he knew, well enough, that his new master had not forgiven him for advocating a regency as the best solution to the question of the succession. For eighteen months Richard had made a studied point of tactfully refraining from any direct criticism of Arthur in front of his younger brother and sister. The nearest he had come to it was when he had personally intervened to secure for Peter a command in the army, reasoning that the ultimate value to the State of this military experience would outweigh the Court's contention that the Marshal was endeavoring to exercise undue influence over the heir presumptive to the throne. But when Alice had come to him in great distress and told him that Arthur was insisting upon her betrothal to the Duke of Westmorland—a man three times her age and a notorious lecher—Richard finally decided that enough was enough. He had requested a private audience with the Lady Margaret and, using his authority as Alice's God-father as his excuse, had demanded that she forbid her son to countenance so grotesque a match.

Lady Margaret had heard him out and then confessed that any influence she may once have had over her eldest son was already matter for history. "Not only would he refuse me, Richard," she said sadly, "I can assure you that he would also take the greatest pleasure in doing so. All I can suggest is that you approach him yourself. And I pray, for Alice's sake, that he will pay heed to what you say."

The interview with Arthur which followed was to take its rightful place among the more macabre experiences of Richard's life. A believer in the old adage that it pays to strike while the iron is hot the Marshal had gone straight from the Lady Margaret's quarters to the candle-lit State Apartments where he had found his Sovereign Lord and Master engaged with his friends in a masked charade. The performance was based, he was informed, upon the court entertainments of the ancient Roman Emperor Tiberius. This called for a form of costume which appeared to allow more than ample opportunity for the participants to display both their physical attributes and their gymnastic ingenuity.

Richard regarded it all with a cool eye and, during an interval for refreshment, approached Arthur and requested a word with him in private. He was informed in loud tones that the Noble Emperor Tiberius had no secrets from his friends.

"But, my Lord," Richard protested, "what I have to say concerns the Lady Alice."

"So much the better!" cried Arthur. "Our little sister is most dear to all our hearts."

"Then some other time, my Lord. With your permission."

"Which we cordially refuse," returned Arthur. "Speak your piece or hold your peace, my Lord Marshal. The choice is yours."

Glancing round at the smirking, semi-naked sycophants Richard found himself recalling some of the stern audiences he had held with the Earl Robert in this very room and he felt a dark tide of anger rising within him. "Very well, my Lord," he said. "I am here expressly to plead with you to revoke the order of betrothal between the Lady Alice and the Duke of Westmorland."

"Are you indeed? And since when have you been appointed our adviser on domestic policy?"

"Do I need to remind you, my Lord, that your father saw fit to honor me by appointing me Alice's moral guardian?"

Arthur flushed darkly. "Then might we suggest that you use your best authority to inculcate a modicum of obedience in our sister—your willful charge. We now stand *in loco parentis*, do we not?"

"You do, my Lord."

"And we think the match is an admirable one in every possible respect."

"Nay, my Lord. The Duke is both syphilitic and a proven lecher."

This roundly uttered observation brought gasps and muted squeals of shocked delight from the enthralled audience.

Arthur giggled nervously. "You speak from personal experience, no doubt."

"Everyone knows it."

"Very well, Lord Marshal. You have had your say. This audience is at an end."

"No, sire, with your permission it is not. You force my

loyalty and my love for your father and the Lady Alice into open conflict with my sworn vows to you as my leige Lord. I do not think this is either in your own best interests or those of the State. I am confident that you will reconsider your decision and will see fit to release your sister from this most ill-advised match."

As he was delivering himself of these words he observed that Lord Arthur had begun to tremble as though he were afflicted with a sudden palsy. His teeth rattled like dice in a cup and flecks of spittle gathered on his trembling lips. The absurd laurel wreath he was wearing tilted forward over his eyes, and in a sudden violent spasm his spine arched like a bow and he fell backwards on to the stone-flagged floor.

With admirable presence of mind Richard stooped over him, dragged open his rigid jaw and thrust the stems of the wreath between his clenched teeth. As he did so Arthur sprayed a pungent jet of urine over the naked feet of a young woman who was standing nearby. Richard scooped up the pathetic figure into his arms, carried him to a vacant couch and sent for the court physician. Then he strode out and abandoned the Court of Tiberius to its own devices.

Two days later he received a summons from Lady Margaret and, presenting himself before her, he was informed that Lord Arthur, having given the matter his due and earnest consideration, had seen fit to rescind the contract of betrothal between the Lady Alice and the Duke.

"Did he say why?" Richard inquired curiously.

"Oh yes. He is dissatisfied with the proposed terms of the marriage settlement."

Richard nodded. "Any means suffice so long as the end is achieved. Did you hear what happened?"

"I should like to hear your version, Richard."

He recounted what had passed between himself and Arthur and then said: "For some time, my Lady, I have been contemplating a visit to my property in Brittany. For a variety of reasons I think this might be an excellent opportunity to take a holiday. With your permission I intend to invite Alice and Peter to accompany me. I feel the change of scene could well be beneficial to us all."

Lady Margaret nodded. "Take them, dear friend. And take my blessing also."

"And Lord Arthur?"

"Leave Arthur to me, for this, Richard. Between the

two of us I suspect that he will be only too glad to see the backs of all three of you."

Dressed in his familiar sober habit of dark blue leather Richard swung himself easily down from the saddle of his hired horse, glanced up at the sculpted figure of the White Bird of Kinship hovering over the château gatehouse and then called out to the two riders who were accompanying him: "It seems we're late."

A boy of some twelve years trotted forward and ducked his head politely before the visitors. "The ceremony has started, sir," he said, reaching out to take the reins from the rider's hand. "The Hall is already full."

"We misjudged our tide," said the Marshal. "Can we still get in?"

"If you do not mind standing, sir. We can leave your horses here for the moment and I will take you straight to the Hall."

"That's most civil of you."

"You are guests of Corlay, sir, and welcome in true Kinship."

He led the three late-comers through the gate, down the long, paved roadway into the château courtyard and then up the wide steps to the Great Hall where he engaged in a whispered consultation with another youthful steward who was guarding the door. Richard stood aside to allow Alice and her brother to enter first then touched their young guide on the shoulder and, as he turned, slipped a silver coin into his palm and closed his fingers around it. The boy flushed and shook his head in protest. "To buy some feed for the horses, lad," murmured the Marshal and followed the others inside.

Broad shafts of sunshine streaming down like golden buttresses from the high windows filled the Great Hall with mellow light. At the far end in front of the huge fireplace and beneath the lovingly reconstructed minstrels' gallery, a substantial platform had been erected. Seated in a row upon it, robed in white, were the Faculty of the College, and standing in their center, addressing the assembly, was the man who, more than any, was responsible not only for this impressive ceremony, but for the whole astounding phenomenon that the world knew as the Cult of Kinship.

Peering over the multitude of heads that separated him from the dais Richard's keen eyes detected in Brother

Francis's features the lingering evidence of that black night nearly a score of years before when Constant had thought to rid the world for ever of the Apostate and his pernicious heresies. Beneath the frosty gray of the hair which Francis wore combed forward in a monkish fringe, the burned right eyebrow and eyelid were scar-puckered in a manner which made him appear preternaturally shrewd, almost as though he were taking careful aim at you down the shaft of an invisible crossbow. And yet, in spite of this, Richard fancied he could still detect the shadow of a young priest who had once held him in converse in a corridor of the York Falconry while he was awaiting an audience with the Black Bishop. Who could have guessed what that young man would become? For that matter who could have guessed what either of them would become? He caught Alice's glancing eye and smiled at her. How much of a man's life lay in his own shaping: how much was done for him by God, whatever the form you chose to acknowledge Him in? Son of Man; Bird of Kinship; did it really matter so very much? His memory roved back to his meeting in a hunting lodge with a tearful child who was now this beautiful young woman at his side. Who had guided them then? The God whom Constant had denied him, or the Bird which Francis worshipped? There are no gods, there is only God and He is everywhere . . .

Francis concluded his address and raised his arms in ritual blessing. The audience rose. "Let the Blood of the Boy ransom us: let the Bird of Dawning hover over us: grant us the Bliss of Kinship for Eternity." "Amen," responded the multitude, Richard among them, and, as they resumed their seats, the ceremony of the *donationem* began.

The name of a newly fledged Kinsman was read out; a young man rose from the front of the hall, mounted the steps to the dais and knelt before Francis who placed an amulet about his neck. Then, while the youth remained kneeling, one of the Faculty read out a brief description of his *donation* (in this case an illuminated index for a section of the library). There was a tumult of applause; the Kinsman rose, bowed gravely to the Faculty, and then, beaming with relief, scuttled back to his place.

When Tom's turn came Alice reached out and gave her brother's sleeve a surreptitious tug. The Annunciator informed the assembly that this Kinsman's *donation* was a musical composition for four sets of pipes which would be performed as the conclusion to the ceremony. Tom rose to his feet, bowed, received his applause, then mounted the stairs to the minstrels' gallery and vanished up those very same steps by which, long ago, the Magpie had made his escape.

After the last of the Kinsmen had been called the Annunciator informed the audience that, according to custom, the *donations* had been placed on display in the Chapel and that all were welcome to inspect them after the ceremony was concluded. Probationers would be on hand to act as guides. As he was speaking, three pipers, one of whom was Marwys, emerged from the curtained stairway at the rear of the gallery and silently took up their places.

As the Annunciator resumed his seat to a patter of polite applause, Tom himself re-appeared at the entrance. He stood for a few seconds looking out over the sea of expectant faces then, with a faint smile, took his place beside Marwys in the center of the little group and waited for the inevitable coughing to die away. When the Great Hall was utterly silent he gave a barely perceptible nod and raised his father's pipes to his lips.

"I believe there's a master-key, Peter. One to unlock the whole world." Seated upon the dais, gazing out over the heads of the audience and thinking idly of what he would say to the Portuguese Legate who was due to arrive at Corlay within the next day or two, Francis heard those words as clearly as if they had been whispered directly into his ear from the lips of the Boy Himself. He half-turned his head, caught the first notes of Tom's pipes, and thereafter was lost to himself and to the world.

If all music is heard with the ears and great music with the heart then the music of the angels is heard with the soul alone and no two souls ever hear it alike. In the years since it was first performed *The Donation Quartet* has probably been heard by more people than were inhabiting the whole of the earth in the year when it was composed. Since then it has been arranged and re-arranged countless times by countless hands to satisfy the demands of musical *ensembles* of all sorts—even symphony orchestras—until it has become an integral part of the very fabric of Kinship, part of the living myth itself. But none who hear it have ever heard what Francis heard, or David, or Alice, or the Lord Marshal Richard, or indeed any single person who was present in the Great Hall on that sunny afternoon in the second week of May in the year A.D. 3038.

Perhaps the most telling tribute that the *Quartet* has ever received was the absolute silence which greeted the conclusion of its first performance, a silence so profound, so *stunned*, that it must have seemed that even to breathe would have been an act of sacrilege. In the *Eleventh Letter to Brother Matthew*, looking back over an interval of almost seven years, Francis was to class it among the three great spiritual experiences of his life, but even he does not attempt to describe it, taking refuge in the words of an ancient poet:

> *Until, the breath of this corporeal frame*
> *And even the motion of our human blood*
> *Almost suspended, we are laid asleep*
> *In body, and become a living soul:*
> *While with an eye made quiet by the power*
> *Of harmony, and the deep power of joy,*
> *We see into the life of things.*

The notebook containing the draft of the original score of the *Quartet* still lies in the library at Corlay—that very same notebook which Tom once took with him to *L'Index*. It is a curious and, in some ways, strangely revealing document. Scattered here and there among its pages are odd, elusive scribbles, jottings, even a number of caricatures, which seem to have little or no bearing upon those magical ciphers which occupy the stave lines. *"Don't explain— reveal"* *"Learn and forget"* *"Blood and shit grow the best roses"* *"Seek everything—find nothing"* *"P's a fool—to do something for its own sake is pure idiocy"* (this has been crossed out and beside it is an elaborate caricature of Brother Francis with a napkin tied around his neck and a knife and fork clasped in either hand, about to feast upon a large roast chicken labelled "B of K"). There are many more—some of the drawings positively Rabelaisian—but all are indisputably the work of Tom's hand. Needless to say this notebook formed no part of his official *donation*. That came in the shape of a neatly transcribed score and carried the pious dedication: *"To the memory of my father Kinsman Thomas of Norwich, and to all my friends and*

*teachers at Corlay, this composition is dedicated with deep
affection and respect—Thomas of Tallon."*

As soon as she left the Great Hall Alice made straight for
the first Probationer she saw and asked him if he would
seek out Tom and tell him that she was anxious to speak
with him. Overhearing her request Richard at once put
two and two together. "So our trip owes less to fortune
than I had supposed," he observed. "Or do I misconstrue?"

Alice laughed. "I assure you that he doesn't know we're
here, Uncle."

"But he knows *you*, eh?"

She nodded.

"And how did that come about?"

"By accident. We met one day when I was sailing. He
invited me to the *donationem*. He didn't say anything
about his own offering though. I wonder why?"

"He certainly has a remarkable talent for the pipes."

"Oh more than *that*, Uncle! *Much* more!"

Richard smiled. "Aye, well, perhaps so. I'm ignorant in
such matters. And truly it was a joyful sound. How say
you, Peter?"

Alice's brother who was two years her junior but very
much her sibling in looks nodded his head and murmured:
"Hartcombe Forest."

"Eh?" said Richard. "What's that supposed to mean?"

Peter blinked and then frowned. "I was there, Uncle.
I'll swear I was. It was as real to me as you are now. You
know the place, Allie. Where the stream runs through that
glade. Where the shrine is. I can't have dreamed it, can I?"

"I don't know," she said. "Perhaps your soul went back
there seeking for something. I think that happens sometimes."

"It didn't happen to you though."

"No," she said. "What my soul seeks is not in Hartcombe."

"Here comes your piper now," said Richard.

Tom was moving toward them through the throng with
David at his side, but their progress was slowed by all the
people who wished to thank him for what he had given
them. He nodded and smiled and made self-deprecating
gestures and eventually came up to Alice. "I'd no idea you
were here," he said. "'Why didn't you tell me you were
coming?"

"I'll explain later," she murmured. "We heard your music, Tom. That's all that matters."

He gave her a curiously veiled look then smiled and said: "That sounds like real praise. Now are you going to introduce us?"

Alice hastened to do so and the men were bowing to one another when Tom suddenly slapped his hand to his brow with an agonized expression and cried: "Oh *no!* Richard of *Hawkridge!* My Lord Marshal!"

Richard laughed. "At your service, young sir. But why yours particularly?"

"But I come from Tallon, my Lord! On Quantock Isle."

"Tallon? Tallon? Ah, yes. I have it. A fishing vilage, is it not?"

"Just across the water from Blackdown, sir. The most beautiful place in the whole Kingdom."

"She has indeed bred a most gifted son to do her honor," said the Lord Marshal graciously. "We were all much affected by your music."

"You are most kind, sir." Tom spread his hands helplessly and then laughed at Alice. "I really don't know what to say. I had no idea you were . . . Would you like us to show you around, my Lord?"

"Indeed we would," said Richard. "The fame of Corlay has spread far too wide for us to pass it by."

The next hour they spent in exploration of the château and in wandering with other sightseers through the sunlit gardens. Blossom clung like clotted cream to the mossed branches of the apple trees and on the blue mirror of the lake the silvery swans arched their slender necks and kissed their own reflections. A circuitous route brought them finally to the Chapel. As they were about to step inside and view the exhibited *donationem* they met Brother Francis coming out. He noticed Tom at once and came across to congratulate him. As he did so he caught sight of the Lord Marshal. The two men eyed one another doubtfully for a moment then, with a slow grin, Richard said, "We've both come a long way from the York Falconry, eh, Francis?"

"*Richard!*" Francis's ravaged face was a marvelous study in mingled astonishment and delight. He held out his arms wide and the two men embraced like long-lost brothers. "Marvels beget marvels!" he cried. "Sure the White Bird has brought you here to us today of all days!"

"This bird maybe," smiled Richard laying his hand upon Alice's shoulder. "I know of none other."

"You will, you will! Ah, but my heart is strangely moved! Let us leave these children, Richard. Come with me and drink a glass of wine for old times' sake. Sure you cannot deny me. And our wine is most excellent."

"That is true temptation," laughed the Lord Marshal. "Who am I to refuse such an offer? So let us meet at the gatehouse in an hour, Alice. If this vintage is all he claims for it I may need help to gain my saddle."

The two men entered the château and climbed the twisting stairs to the apartment in the Queen's Tower which had once been Jane's but, since the reconstruction, had been allotted to Francis. The rooms were sparsely furnished but not so austere as to be uncomfortable, and the view out across the lake was as beautiful as it had ever been.

With his own hands Francis poured two glasses of white wine and presented one to the Lord Marshal. "May I propose a toast, Richard?"

"That is your privilege, Francis. So? What is it to be?"

"I give you the Seven Kingdoms."

"Aye. Why not? To the Seven Kingdoms."

They touched glasses and drank.

"This wine is indeed excellent," said the Lord Marshal. "I must arrange for some to be shipped across to us. Does it travel?"

"We press only enough for our own needs," said Francis. "But you shall have a cask as a gift. I undertake to deliver it to New Exeter personally."

"How so? Are you planning to visit the First?"

Francis glanced sharply across at his guest. "You have not heard?"

"Heard what?"

"That Philip is preparing to move against Arthur."

Richard stared at him. "Who tells you so?"

"I had it from the Fifth some three weeks back. There is a score of longships ready drawn to Barrow. But sure you must have known of this?"

"Rumors only. I give them little credence. Northumberland would never risk an arm in Philip's cause."

"In Philip's, no. But Northumberland is father-in-law to Anne of Doncaster. As Robert's eldest child Anne has the prior claim till Peter comes of age."

"Then how does that leave Philip?"

"As Regent in Anne's stead."

"Aye, that would bring the wheel full circle," murmured Richard. "You know, had Margaret not been so besotted with her runt, Philip would be Regent now for Peter. 'Twas what I strove for."

"You tell me nothing new, Richard. And now you will be called upon to defend the worse against the bad."

"How if I join forces with Philip?"

"You wish to burn at York? Somehow I've never thought to see you in a martyr's shift."

The Lord Marshal smiled thinly. "Whichever way it blows it'll be an ill wind for most. Not least our Kinsfolk. Have you thought of that?"

Francis refilled their glasses. "There's God's purpose in all things, Richard. The Bird brought you here to us today as surely as the sun rose in the east."

"Is that the answer to my question?"

"It could well be. But I suspect your answer already lies in your own heart. Ask yourself why you broke your solemn oath to Constant at the risk of forfeiting your immortal soul. Blind obedience is no longer enough, Richard. We have passed beyond that. Does a man dying of thirst question the nature of the hand that holds a cup of water to his lips? No one is asking you to deny your God. We do but invite you to step out of his shadow into the light of ours."

"And you think my doing that would scuttle Philip's fleet?"

"No. But the whole Kingdom united in Kinship would prove just as effective. Northumberland champions Philip because he sees in the First a realm weakened by dissension; its ruler a spoiled and pampered invalid; sedition being preached openly from the pulpits. If it were not for the inevitable reckoning at York would not you yourself be tempted by the prospect of a strong Regency?"

"Aye. But with who as Regent?"

"Philip, of course."

Richard laughed. "This wine of yours is stronger than I thought. I could have sworn that you said Philip."

"And so I did. Hark you, Richard. Philip distrusts Northumberland. He fears that once the First is taken (and at what cost?) it will be Anne's husband, Henry of Doncaster, and not himself who will mount the throne in

New Exeter. When Earl Robert broke with York he took his brother with him. That brother knows full well how that will tell against him once the Secular Arm climbs back to power. Offer Philip a feasible alternative which will allow the First to keep its independence and him the Regency and he will grasp it like a drowning man."

"It is easy for you to speak so, Francis. It is not you who will be tried for treason."

"You fear your oath of loyalty to Arthur? As I recall it that did not prevent you from opposing Lady Alice's match with Westmorland."

"You are well informed."

"I have to be, Richard. That is why I can tell you how it stands between Philip and Northumberland. I can also tell you that Arthur has you now pricked out for personal disloyalty."

"A shrewd guess but nothing more."

"We have our ears at court, Richard. Our friends need you with them."

The Lord Marshal walked across to the window, looked out over the sunny lake to the hills beyond and sipped thoughtfully at his wine. "You must have known that I would be here today," he said.

Francis was silent.

"Was it Alice?"

"Does it matter?"

"That lass saved my life once. Did you know that too?"

"Perhaps she is about to do it again."

Richard nodded absently then said: "Are you still in contact with Philip?"

"We are."

"When does he plan to make his move?"

"Some time in June. No date has yet been fixed upon."

"Then tell him he must hold off until we send him word that Arthur has signed a deed of abdication in Peter's favor."

"And how are you going to persuade him to do that?"

"I know not as yet."

"The Bird will lead you to it, Richard."

"And you to the First, eh, Brother?"

"I am sure of it. If you will answer for Arthur, I will answer for the rest."

"Are you telling me that Philip will *declare* for Kinship?"

"If you can unchain him from Northumberland he will."

"But Philip's no more Kin than I am."

"Less, Richard. Far less. But, like you and Robert, he appreciates the strength of unity. The rest will follow as the day the night, and it will not stop at the First."

The Lord Marshal looked at the Apostate with a wholly new respect. "That bird of yours has broad wings," he murmured. "Do you really think they're strong enough to carry you back to York?"

"To York and far beyond," said Francis. "It is but a question of time."

As David had surmised Brother Francis presided over the *disposition* interviews. At these it was decided how the newly fledged Kinsmen were to be deployed. In the early days of the foundation it had simply been a question of dispatching them as independent missionaries to whichever corner of the world was most urgently in need of the Message, but more recent practice had been to allocate them to a curacy where for a year they performed pastoral duties under the guidance of the resident Kinsman. For this they were allowed to submit to the Board a petition known as a *suppliance* in which they set out their reasons for requesting some particular *disposition*. Sometimes the Board acceded to these requests; more often they refused. They never explained their reasons for a refusal.

When it came to Tom's turn to face the Board he bowed, took his place on the lonely seat before the long table and waited, conscious of seven pairs of eyes regarding him curiously. After what seemed an eternity Francis said: "You appear to be the only graduate who has not submitted a *suppliance*, Thomas. May we know why?"

"I forgot, sir."

"And if you had not forgotten, what would yours have said?"

Tom opened his mouth as if to reply, then closed it and shook his head instead.

Francis' unscarred eyebrow lifted. "You have forgotten that also?"

"No, sir."

"Then tell us."

Tom moistened his lips with his forked tongue. "Some months ago I thought I would like to work as a tutor in the Music School. I spoke to Kinsman Marwys about it. He said I should say so in my *suppliance.*"

"But you forgot to do so."

Tom's hesitation was obvious to all. "I—I think I wasn't so sure any more, sir. About being a teacher, I mean. I don't think I've got the patience for it."

"Patience is a matter of self-discipline."

"Yes, sir."

"You think yourself lacking in self-discipline?"

"For teaching. Yes, sir, I do."

"But not otherwise?"

"I don't know, sir."

"Yet on your record here it says that you have been blessed with quite exceptional powers of concentration."

Tom said nothing.

Francis laid down the paper he had consulted. For a count of perhaps ten seconds he was silent. Then, holding Tom as it were steady in his sights he said: "We are all agreed, Thomas, that you have been gifted in a manner which is unique in our experience. If there were any lingering doubts on the matter your *donation* has dispelled them. You do not need me to tell you this but I do it anyway, if only to demonstrate to you that we are not altogether the ignorant old fools you sometimes take us for." He held up a hand to silence Tom's incipient protest. "It is perhaps inevitable that you should, for genius such as you possess in abundance is always impatient with mere talent, however well-intentioned that talent may be, and, alas, we count no wise old Morfedd among our number. What we do have we have shared with you freely: the rest you will have to find for yourself with the Bird's guidance."

He paused, delivered himself of a sound that could almost have been a sigh, and continued: "Until the *donationem* I freely confess that, despite what I have learned of your parentage, I had not seriously entertained the possibility that you might prove to be the Child the Testament has promised us. Nor do I do so now. But if you are He —the Star Born—then you will know as well as I do that nothing I could say to you now would ever divert you from your destiny.

"Which brings me to the immediate question of your *disposition.* Had you submitted a *suppliance* then—for reasons which must be as obvious to you as they are to us—we should certainly have given it every consideration.

And we could, of course, still direct you into the Music School. However, I think that the explanation you have given us for your change of mind is a valid one, and within its somewhat egoistical compass quite refreshingly frank. I have therefore decided to direct you to return to the First Kingdom where you will work for a year in a pastoral capacity under the direction of Kinsman Anthony of Holywell. After that, well, we shall see what we shall see."

Tom bowed and was about to take his leave when, with a lifted finger, Francis motioned him back into his chair. "In view of all that I have said to you, Thomas, and in deference to a long-standing request of your mother's, I am prepared on my own responsibility to make you a loan of those pipes which you"—he paused, and one could almost see the quotation marks dropping into place around the word—"'borrowed' the other day. They are to remain in your personal charge for just so long as you and the Bird require them." He smiled faintly, nodded his head and said: "And now you have our permission to send in the next supplicant."

Tom, his face and ears the color of a cloud at sunset, bowed for the last time and gratefully made his escape.

Chapter Three

At the end of May Tom and David arrived at Tallon for a final long holiday together before they both departed to their separate *dispositions*—Tom to Downscombe on the outskirts of New Exeter and David for a further period of two years' study in the Kinsmen's hospital at Alençon. Tom's worldly possessions, packed into a roped wooden box, were heaved up on to the quayside from the deck of the coaster which had ferried them across the Somersea from Chardport. Sharing the burden between them the two young Kinsmen set off up the steep hill to Kiln Cottage.

Before they were halfway to the top they heard shrill

cries of "Tom! Tom!" and glanced back to see a fair-haired
boy and a young girl scampering after them. They set the
box down on the cobbles and waited for the children who
came panting up and flung themselves upon Tom like
eager puppies. "We were in Uncle Simon's yard," gasped
the boy. "Tammy told us you'd come. Does Auntie know?"

"We've only just this minute stepped off *The Cor-
morant.*"

"I'll run and tell her," said the boy and rushed on up
the hill.

Tom's six year old half-sister Anne plumped herself
down on the box, blew out her cheeks and grinned up at
him. They shared the same cast of features, square chin
and dark curly hair, but her eyes were hazel gray like
Rett's. "Are you a real Kinsman now?" she asked.

"Aye, Mouse. As real as you are."

"Show me."

Tom dipped his hand inside the open neck of his shirt
and pulled out the bronze talisman of the Bird which
Francis had placed around his neck at the *donationem.*

Anne examined it critically and wrinkled up her snub
nose. "What does it do?" she asked.

"It protects me from nosey little girls. Come on. Shift
yourself." He scooped her off her seat, took her small
brown hand in his and lifted one end of the box with the
other. "Have you learned to read yet, Mouse?"

"Of course I have. Well, big letters."

"And what else have you learned?"

"I can whistle. Mike's been teaching me. And I can
spit. I can spit best of all us girls. Look."

Frowning fiercely she pursed her lips and spat out a
neat little white blob a full three paces up the hill ahead
of her.

"Very good," applauded Tom. "Excellent! Have you
ever seen a better six year old girl spitter, Dave?"

"Never," said David.

Anne flushed pink with pride. "Shall I whistle you
something too?"

"Have you got enough breath left?"

"Of course I have. You don't need much breath for
spitting. Listen."

She frowned again, glanced up at him sideways then
suddenly whistled a long, pure, clear note as sweet as a
throstle's and ended it with a truly melodious trill.

"That's really very good," said Tom, genuinely impressed. "You sounded just like a bird."

"What bird? Guess what bird I was."

"A chicken?"

"A *blackbird!*" she scolded, thumping him with her free hand. "Grandad's made me a whistle like the ones he used to make for you."

"He has? Can you play it?"

"A bit. Not many tunes though."

"How is Grandad?"

"He's all right. He's gone to Aisholt in the van today. So's Witchet. Look! There's our Mam!"

Jane had appeared at the top of the hill with Michael beside her. She waved, Ann waved back, and Tom felt as though a second heart had begun to beat in his breast.

Mother and son embraced in the open roadway, she still damp from her labors in the pottery, he with the pale powder of salt from the voyage still dusting his cheek. "Dear heart," she whispered drawing him close. "My own dear piper's son. Welcome home."

"How is it with you, Mother?"

" 'Mother'?" she murmured. "Faith, Tom, I hardly recognize myself by that title. You seem to have sprung into a man overnight."

"He's a *real* Kinsman now," said Anne proudly. "Show her, Tom."

Tom grinned, pulled the talisman from his shirt and proffered it to Jane.

She turned it over in her fingers and nodded. "Yes," she said, "a real Kinsman. Do you know yet where they are sending you?"

"Oh yes," he said, smiling and withholding the information from her like a tantalizing morsel. "Yes, I know."

Her eyes scanned his face, read the smile. "Well?"

"Downscombe. New Exeter."

"You tease me!"

"It's true, Mother. Ask David. I'm to pair with Anthony of Holywell."

"The Healer? But Tom this is *marvelous!* I thought it might be Africa or America."

"You didn't know, then?"

"Know? How could I know?"

"I wondered if maybe you'd got word to Francis somehow."

Jane shook her head and then, suddenly recalling herself, turned to David and gave him a warm kiss of welcome on either cheek. "Forgive me," she said. "I offer you but sorry Kinship, David. But I expect your own mother would understand. Come, bring the box into the house and we will find something to celebrate with."

Witchet and her father returned from Aisholt just in time for supper. Now into his seventieth year the Magpie appeared more than ever bird-like. With his brisk cockscomb of snow-white hair, his bright eye and his quick, darting movements he seemed set fair to achieve his ambition of dancing out a full four-part reel to Tom's piping on his hundredth birthday. "And after that you can chop me up into kindling for the kiln and fire a pot to hold my ashes."

Witchet at fifteen seemed to be hovering undecided betwixt girl and woman. Her hair which in childhood had been as pale as ripe barley was now shaded to a gleaming honey gold and she wore it cropped off at an indifferent shoulder length as though unwilling to acknowledge it. But if she had inherited her coloring chiefly from Alison, it was from the Magpie she had received her gift for shaping things with her hands. Tutored by Jane she had become a highly skilled potter and for the past three years had contributed a fair share to the production from the workshop. The clay "went" for her, and she had besides a knack of catching a likeness of either human or animal that had meant a ready sale for her little figures in the shops of the capital.

The one serious blight on her young life was the fact that since she had come to puberty she had been tormented by fierce headaches which struck without warning and left her ashen-faced and all but witless. The consensus of local opinion was that they amounted to no more than "growing pains" and would pass accordingly, but Alison had insisted on taking her to New Exeter to consult the Kinsman whose fame as a healer had spread far beyond the circles of the Kinsfolk.

Anthony of Holywell had pricked her with silver needles, asked her all manner of questions some of which seemed to have no bearing at all upon the matter and finally had written out a prescription for an infusion of herbs which she was to take whenever she felt an attack coming on. "It will help," he had told Alison, "but I doubt that it will cure them altogether. The cause of the affliction lies hidden somewhere in the blood vessels beneath the bone. It may slip away as she grows into her full womanhood."

They had taken the prescription home, made it up to the Kinsman's directions and, just as he had foretold, the red teeth of the agony were drawn. Witchet gradually lost her terror of those moments when the world seemed to melt at the edges and come flooding in to drown her, and the name of Anthony of Holywell was added to those who featured in her nightly prayers.

When she entered the house and found Tom arrived her delight was truly something to behold. She clasped her hands across her chest, skipped up and down, and then, the excitement having proved more than her body could bear, bolted outside to the privy pursued by the ribald laughter of her brother and young Anne.

Later she took a place opposite Tom across the supper table and hung upon his words as he told of all that had happened to him in the year he had been away. When he began to describe the *huesh* which had drawn him to *L'Index* the spoon she was holding slipped from between her fingers and fell with a clatter on to her plate. "The girl," she whispered. "The girl in the sea."

Tom broke off in the middle of his sentence and stared at her. "What did you say, Witch?"

Witchet had gone deadly pale. Minute beads of perspiration were pricking out across the skin of her forehead. They glittered in the lamplight like specks of gold dust. Her eyes, their pupils sloe dark and unnaturally large, were still fixed upon him, but he knew she was not really seeing him at all.

"What is it, Witch?" he demanded. "Are you all right?"

Recognizing the familiar symptoms, Alison rose from her seat and hurried out into the scullery. In a moment she was back carrying an earthenware cup which she held to her daughter's lips. Witchet swallowed a mouthful and then pushed the cup aside muttering: "No, it's all right. It's not that."

Tom looked from her to Alison and then glanced round at the others. "But she's not *huesh*," he said. "How *can* she know?"

"Know what, lad?" asked the Magpie.

"About Alice."

"Who's Alice?"

"No, wait a minute!" cried David. "First ask her what she meant, Tom."

Tom looked across at Witchet and saw that a faint trace of color had begun to creep back into her cheeks. He smiled at her. "What made you say that, Witch?"

"I—I saw it," she whispered.

"When? Just now?"

"About a month ago. I had one of my headaches."

"But *what* did you see?"

"Someone in the sea. A girl. She was holding on to something."

Tom and David exchanged glances. "Is that all you can tell us?"

"I pulled her in . . ." Witchet's voice trailed off into silence.

"*You* did?"

"She wouldn't let go. I pulled and pulled . . ."

"Aren't you going to tell us what this is all about, lad?" asked the Magpie.

"Just one more thing," said Tom. "Can you remember *when* this happened, Witch? Was it at night?"

"In the afternoon. I was fixing handles in the workshop."

"I remember," said Jane. "I ran and got your medicine for you."

"April the seventeenth?" said David. "Was it Friday, April the seventeeth?"

"It could have been then, yes."

"Was it the *huesh?*" asked Rett.

"No, I don't think so," said Tom. "She seems to have been *with me* somehow. It happened just like she said." And he went on to describe the events which had taken place in the Lanvaux Channel a month and a half before. When he mentioned the name of Richard of Hawkridge there were exclamations of disbelief from all sides.

"It's perfectly true," David assured them. "They all came to the *donationem*. Alice and her brother and the Lord Marshal. She invited us to visit them at La Tour."

"And did you go?" asked Rett.

"No. We got a message from her to say that the Lord Marshal had been called back to the First but that she hoped we'd meet her over here."

"You're joking!"

Tom got up, walked into the room where his box was

lying and returned with a letter which he handed to his step-father.

Rett frowned at it and then passed it across the table to Jane.

"What does it say, Auntie?" asked Michael.

"You might as well read it out, Mother."

Jane tilted the paper to catch the light. *"La Tour, Saint Anne, Sunday,"* she read. *"Dear Thomas and David. I am most sorry to tell you that my God-father has been called back to the First Kingdom on an urgent matter of state business. Peter and I sail with him tomorrow from St. Brieuc. I do not think we shall return to La Tour this year, but if you are visiting Quantock Isle do not fail to let me know so that we can meet again either in New Exeter or perhaps at Downscombe. With thanks once more for the donation. Alice."*

"Downscombe?" said Rett. "Why does she say Downscombe? Does she live there?"

"I wondered about that," said Tom, "until I heard where I was being sent. Alice is Kin."

"Never!"

"Yes, I have heard it so whispered," said Alison. "What is she like, Tom?"

"She's all right."

"That tells me everything! Is she as beautiful as people say she is?"

Tom grinned. "She looked like a drowned pup when we fished her out of the Channel. After she'd dried off a bit she reminded me of old Witch here. Longer legs though. But she was dressed like a lad. Mind you I think it suited her."

"She is *charmante*," said David. "Not proud at all. You would not guess she was an aristo."

"And what about the brother?"

"Peter? We both liked him. He did not say much—he was shy, I think—but when he asked a question it was a sensible question."

"He was on his best behavior," said Tom. "They all were. Even the Lord Marshal. He trotted off for a private booze-up with the Old Man. It seems they knew each other back in the old days. Did you know that, Mother?"

Jane nodded. "I remember Francis speaking about Richard. He used to say he was the only Marshal who had never forgotten he was still a man. I don't know how well they knew each other."

"I rather liked him," said Tom. "I never quite got over who he was though."

"They say he is like a second father to the Lady Alice," said Alison. "He made Lord Arthur break off her betrothal to the Duke of Westmorland."

"Aye," said Rett. "We did hear so. There's little love lost between Richard and the Runt. I swear I wouldn't sleep easy o'nights if I was him."

"If you were who, Uncle?" asked Michael.

"Either of 'em. When great lords fall out the worms are like to feast. For my part I'll not be weeping for the Runt. So long as he's perched on high I'm always keeping a weather eye out for the crows."

"Then it's Philip of Bodmin you should be worrying about, not Lord Arthur," said the Magpie. "Over at Aisholt the word is Duke Philip'll be back afore the corn's cut. The Squire's bailiff was round last week pricking out fealty men."

"Who told you so?"

"Jim Mannock at the Red Lion."

"Jim's an old blabberer. He'll tell you anything he thinks you'll listen to."

"Maybe. But something's afoot. They were up top making over Hurley Beacon last Tuesday and that's not due till August."

"Will you be called to the colors, Uncle?"

"And who'll pull in the mackerel? You, I suppose?"

"But if they call you?"

"Ah, don't be daft. They won't call us."

"You and Simon both owe fealty, don't you?" asked Tom.

"Aye, we do, Tom. To Squire Merridge. We bought the bugger off for a royal apiece last year. He waited till the fish were shoaling, then sent that teg's bum Lawrence round banging on the doors with his pole." Rett parodied the bailiff's pompous accent: " 'The Squah of Merridge commands you to present yourself on Aisholt Green at noon tomorrow with bows and bolts in loyalty to your oath,' then he sticks out his paw for us to buy him off. We reckon he must have cleared ten royal in Tallon alone."

"But if Duke Philip does land?" said Michael. "What'll happen then, Uncle?"

"A heap of poor fools will get their heads broken and the fish will have a holiday."

"Will the Falcons come back?"

"No, they won't come back," said Jane firmly. "They'll never come back again. Lord Richard will see to that. Now tell us all about the *donationem*, Tom. Did it go off well?"

Her son caught the appeal to turn the tide of dark talk and did so willingly.

When supper was over and the children had been dispatched to bed Jane and Tom strolled up into the twilit garden behind the cottage. It was the first moment they had been alone together since his return. They reached the old cherry tree, sat down side by side on the long, knee-high branch which had served three generations as a seat, and gazed out across the wine-dark Somersea to where a solitary star hung low in the sky above the distant coast of the Second Kingdom.

"Do you remember when you played your pipe to me here?" said Jane. "Perched up like a robin on the wall yonder."

"The first time we came to Tallon, you mean?"

"That's right."

"I remember," he said and laughed. "And do you remember rolling all down the back of Thorncombe Barrow? That was the same day."

For a while they exchanged memories like bright tokens of identification and then Tom said: "*Did* you ask the Old Man to send me back to the First?"

"I told you not."

"I know. But I couldn't help wondering. It was something he said."

"Something Francis said?"

"Yes. At the end of my Board, just as I was getting up to go, he beckoned me back and told me that he was going to lend me the Boy's pipes. He said you'd asked him to."

"Francis said that?"

"I can't remember the exact words, but he mentioned you. I thought maybe you'd written to him or something."

"The only time I ever wrote to him was when you first went to Corlay. I didn't think he'd have remembered it."

"What did you say to him?"

"I told him who you were."

"Is that all? You didn't mention the Boy's pipes?"

"I can't remember. I may have done."

"But what would have made you do that?"

She glanced round at him. In the shadows her face gleamed pale as a moth's wing. "It's what your father would have wanted, Tom. It was your birthright. Do you know what I'm talking about?"

"You don't mean the Testament?"

She nodded. "It was Marwys coming out of the blue like he did which made me do it. I'd waited ten years, Tom. Ten long years. I could have written to Francis any time to tell him we were both still alive. I just didn't *want* to believe it—not to *have to* believe it."

"Francis made it pretty clear to me that *he* doesn't believe it."

"Do *you?*"

Tom rocked himself backward and forward until the little hard green cherries pattered like raindrops against the dark leaves of the tree. "Sometimes I do and sometimes I don't," he said. "As I read it it isn't going to matter much one way or the other. One thing's for sure though. I don't believe in miracles. Not Francis's sort, anyway."

"But the Boy . . . ?"

"I know what you're going to say, Mother. People want it to be so and so it is. But that's not the answer. Not for me. And not for the Boy either, whatever people may say. Oh, yes, he realized men must change, but he knew that the change has to come from within yourself—from *in*side not *out*side. That's what *The Lament for the White Bird* is all about. It only *seemed* miraculous because it was so new—so simple. Those people who stood beneath the walls of York suddenly *believed in themselves,* knew that it *could happen!* And so it did. And it can *still* happen! It could happen now, right here, if we really wanted it to, just like it did then. The miracle is already here—in all of us—it's *always* been there. All we've got to do is to keep still for long enough to hear it!"

Jane slipped her arm about his shoulders and drew him close to her. *"Tom, Tom, the Piper's Son,"* she murmured, *"Learned to play when he was young."*

Tom kissed her.

"But the only tune that he could play
Was Over the Hills and Far Away."

Tom laughed. "One tune's enough," he said. "Just so long as it's the right one."

"And which is yours? Over the Hills and Far Away?"

"It makes a call to the heart, doesn't it?" he said. "The truth is, I've reached a sort of crossroads and now I find I can't read what's written on the finger-post. Maybe I should have stayed on at Corlay."

"Why didn't you?"

"Because everyone seemed to be expecting me to."

"Is that all?"

"Oh, it's part of it for sure. But only a part. I think I must be a bit like old Marwys in some ways—always hungry for something new."

"Some thing—or some one?"

"Ah, you may well ask."

"I thought perhaps it might be the Lady Alice. David tells me she is very taken with you."

"With my music maybe. Alice is a nice girl, but she's not for me."

"Because she's who she is?"

"Or because I'm who *I* am."

"Are you going to see her again?"

"I don't know. Maybe. I've promised to take Dave over to Downscombe before he goes back. He wants to meet the Healer. I suppose we could pay our respects to the Lady Alice at the same time."

"At the castle?"

"Well, that's where she lives, isn't it?"

From the trees high up on the hillside an owl screamed and a moment later it was answered by another further away. Jane gave a sudden impulsive shiver and it seemed to Tom as though a bubble of icy air had formed itself around her. "What is it?" he asked.

"Can't you smell it?" she whispered.

"Smell what?"

Again she shivered. "Earth. Cold, damp earth."

"You're imagining it," he said standing up and drawing her to her feet. "Come on, let's go back indoors."

Chapter Four

Kinsman Anthony of Holywell dwelt in a long, low, rambling barn of a house called by the curious name of "Stickles." It overlooked the chattering waters of the river Exe which drained the high uplands of the moor and tumbled eastward in a series of noisy cataracts before being harnessed to drive the wheels of the wool mills in the industrial suburb of Edgecott. Later, broadening out, it changed its color from a peaty brown to a doubtful silver and flowed away south to join the sea below Tiverton. House and river seemed wedded to one another. The sound of hurrying waters was never absent—muted and musical in the hot, dry summers; a thunderous roar in the winter spates—and the light flung upward from the leaping ripples wove a constantly shifting network of reflections across the low ceilings of the raftered rooms.

Tom and David arrived at "Stickles" on a warm hazy afternoon in the second week of June. They found Anthony of Holywell, together with three of his five children, working in the steeply terraced gardens at the back of the house. The Kinsman proved to be a small, round man with a corona of faded gingerish beard framing his open, sunny countenance, and a bald pate which gleamed like an autumn onion in the brassy sunshine. In his right hand he was clasping a curved pruning knife.

As the visitors approached he closed up the knife, dropped it into the pocket of his gardener's smock, tipped his head to one side and thrust out his hands in welcome. "Thomas of Tallon, is it not?" he cried. "Sure I cannot be mistaken."

Tom acknowledged his own identity and shook the proffered hand.

"And how's your sister keeping?"

"Witchet? She's much the better for your treating her.

But she's not my sister. We just grew up together. I'd like you to meet my friend—David of Ronceval."

"Ah. Your Heavenly Twin, eh?" said Anthony, shaking David's hand. "You see we already know all about you both, though in truth I was not expecting you yet awhile. Well met, David. You have come from Tallon today?"

"We left at daybreak," said David, "and caught a crab-boat across to—was it Tolland, Tom?"

Tom nodded.

"And you've legged it up here from there? Have you eaten?"

"We brought some faring with us," said Tom, "and had it up on the hills."

"Then let us rinse away the dust of the high road. Jenny, lass, run in and tell Mother to set out some ale for our guests."

A young girl with flame-colored hair and freckled cheeks skipped away down the steps and vanished into the house through a back entrance. The Kinsman waved an arm up the slope. "Everything grows apace here. We can scarce keep abreast of it. Come, let me show you."

He took them each by an arm and conducted them up the hillside to where a long row of wooden bee-hives was nestling beneath a hazel hedge. Neat brick paths herring-boned the steps of each terrace into tidy beds of herbs, each marked with its own label pokerworked on wood. David, visibly impressed, was soon deep in discussion of herbal technicalities which meant little or nothing to Tom. "You would have done better with him as your second," he said to the Healer. "I fear I'll prove a sorry hand at the simples."

Anthony laughed. "Each to his own calling, Thomas. We need those pipes of yours more than we need another doctor. You bring us an elixir for the soul, or rumor lies."

"You have no piper, then?"

"Oh, aye, we have Kinsfolk who can finger any tune you care to call for and sweet voices in plenty, but we hunger for the magic Marwys spoke of."

"You know Kinsman Marwys?" Tom was unable to conceal his surprise.

"Indeed we do. Some four years back he passed a full month here with us."

"I never knew that."

"No? We missed him sorely when he left. He too has the gift."

"The gift of a pair of restless feet, for sure."

"Aye. That in abundance. He spoke often of you, Thomas."

"I'm flattered to hear it," said Tom. "Marwys is one of the very best. But I believe his true gift lies in shaping."

"Yes, yes. We have a fine example of his skill indoors. You shall see it anon." Anthony stooped, plucked a leaf from a shrub, rubbed it between his finger and thumb and held it to his nose. "Dragonweed," he said, proffering it to them. "Most sovereign against the silver-rash. There was a lot of it about in the mills last year. It's carried in on the fleeces."

They descended to the house and Anthony led them round to a paved arbor overlooking the river. Here his wife Susan, brown-eyed and buxom, was waiting to greet them with a jug of ale. "Your room stands ready for you, Kinsman Thomas," she said. "There is just the bed wants making up."

Tom hastened to explain that he had only called in to pay his respects. He would be taking David back with him to Tallon and then returning by himself to Downscombe at the beginning of September after he had seen his friend off for France.

"But sure you'll both pass a day or two with us now that you're here," she protested.

"Oh, they'll stay, wife, they'll stay," said Anthony. "Tallon can well spare them, and we have much here of interest to a budding surgeon."

So it was settled. Susan bustled off to prepare a room for them both, and they sat back and allowed themselves to become drowsy on the Kinsman's ale while, with a little prompting, he told them the story of how, thirty years before, when he was in the last month of his apprenticeship to an apothecary in Bideford he had attended one of the Old Tale Spinner's "tellings" in the market place and had first heard the story direct from the old man's own lips—

"Once upon a time, far away among the Northern Hills in the Fifth Kingdom there was born a Wondrous Boy . . ."

Bees droned among the wisteria blossom; the river babbled quietly to itself of Come and Gone; fork-tailed swallows dipped and skimmed above the eddies; all transmuting themselves into music somewhere inside Tom's dreaming head, thence to emerge in the far distant future as one of the *Six Songs of Summer*.

He surfaced from his reverie to hear Anthony saying —presumably in answer to a question of David's—"I think what Francis is doing is fleshing out anew the bones of the old Church. No doubt he has to. He needs the organization. Thirty years ago there was nothing like Corlay is to-day. Nobody even dreamed of such a place. All we had was the naked dream of Kinship itself. But that was enough. More than enough. Men and women took fire and burned so brightly with the flame that they set fire to others. Ragged Kinsmen wandered up and down the countryside and preached the Brotherhood of Man. They broke down the old dry stone walls of fear. 'You can change,' was their message. 'The White Bird of Kinship has come to set you free. Behold, your prison door stands open wide! Step out into the sunshine and claim your heritage! The world and everything within it is the birthright of the Kin!' Ah, it was like young wine, I tell you! Golden! Sparkling! And it worked. A miracle truly happened. Instead of the battle trumpets of Jericho, the pipes of peace sounded and all the walls came tumbling down. We heard the song of freedom and our eyes grew clear and bright. We looked at each other and met eyes as bright as our own. How simple the truth was. The whole world is Kin." He reached out, refilled their tankards from the jug and then refilled his own.

"But—?" said Tom. "Do I detect a 'but' hovering around somewhere?"

Anthony smiled. "I'm in my fifty-second year, Thomas," he said. "I'll be fifty-three on the twenty-third day of next month. For twenty-eight years I've ministered and preached the Word here in Downscombe and in the villages round about. It's all of thirty-three years since Susan and I made the long pilgrimage to York. And now people tell me that Portugal will declare for Kinship before the year is out: Poland is tottering on the brink: Italy is sure to follow. Marvels upon the heels of marvels. Where will it all end? Yet you ask me is there not a 'but' somewhere—and you're right. There is. For deep in my heart I can't help feeling that the Faith which Portugal and Poland and Italy will declare for will not be quite the same as that which drew

Susan and me to York all those years ago. That was something different, something simpler, something as sweet and as natural as a flower in the hedgerow. But this new Kinship? What is it exactly? What will it become? A thing of parishes and preferences, of bishoprics and hierarchies and all the rest of it? The old order writ new or a new order? Which is it going to be? Can you tell me?"

Tom extended a finger and coaxed a drop of spilled ale into the symbol of the Bird. "If the Boy had lived," he said, "he would be about as old as you are now, Anthony. Doesn't that strike you as strange?"

"Aye. I suppose it does now you come to mention it. I've never really thought of it before."

"Well, I think it's important," said Tom.

David gave a histrionic groan. "Oh, spare me *that* again!"

"But I'm most interested," said Anthony. "Tell me why you think it important, Thomas."

Tom raised his eyes and met the Healer's squarely. "Because I believe that the Boy's vision was essentially a child's vision," he said.

Anthony blinked at him. "But what else could it have been?"

"Don't misunderstand me," said Tom. "I'm not saying it wasn't true, or divinely inspired, or whatever else you choose to call it. I'm sure it was all of those things—and more. The Boy's death was one of the greatest acts of pure faith this world has ever seen precisely *because* it was an act of perfectly *pure* faith. He believed utterly in an *impersonal* vision. Up there on the walls of York he genuinely *became the whole world*. And he died because no human being born of woman can ever encompass that and live. Had he not died when he did, then sooner or later he would have seen his vision fade away into the light of common day. As it is he lives on as part of his own impossible dream of human perfection; he is trapped within it forever like one of Marwys's marvelous figures. And that is precisely where we all want him to be. Because there he is safe—and so are we."

"And here endeth the Revised Gospel according to Kinsman Thomas of Tallon," David intoned ironically.

"No, not quite," said Tom. "I still haven't answered Anthony's original question. The old order writ new or a

new order? I think the best we dare hope for is that it will
end up being a bit of both."

Late in the evening as their thoughts were beginning to
turn toward bed there came a clattering of hoofs from
the riverside road followed soon after by a loud knocking
on the front door. Susan went out to see who it was. Tom
and David heard the murmur of voices but deemed it im-
polite to eavesdrop. Then a worried looking Susan reappeared and beckoned to her husband.

Left to themselves Tom and David eyed each other
speculatively. Finally Tom rose from his seat, drew aside
the curtain and peered out. Against the reflection from the
river he could just make out the dim silhouettes of two
riderless horses standing in the roadway directly below the
house. One of the animals tossed its head and the jingle of
harness drifted to Tom's ears. He turned to David with a
grin. "This looks like being one of those spiritual rewards
of the doctor's life that you're always talking about—the
midnight call."

There were footsteps in the passage and the door
opened, but only Susan reappeared.

"Is anything the matter?" asked Tom.

She smiled vaguely, her thoughts still far away, and
then she shook her head. "These things happen," she said.

"Does Anthony need any help?" said David. "I'll go with
him willingly."

"No, no," she said. "He'll have all the help he needs to
hand. But it's most kind of you to offer."

"What's it about?" said Tom. "Or shouldn't I ask?"

"I'm sorry, Thomas," she said. "I'm still in a bit of a
tizzy. That one who's come is Robin, Lord Richard's man.
It seems his master was taken sick two days back and now
he's had a sudden turn for the worse."

"Richard?" echoed Tom. "The Lord Marshal?"

"Aye, lad. Richard of Hawkridge. There's fear he may
have taken poison."

Tom stared at her as though unable to believe his ears.
"Poisoned himself! I don't believe it!"

"Nay, you mistake me, Thomas. How the stuff got to be
inside him, no one knows. But that's what Anthony thinks
to it."

They heard the sound of voices in the roadway and then
the clatter of iron-shod hoofs on stones. Susan went to the

window and looked out. The drumming died away into the distance. "That fool should ha' come to us yesterday," she grumbled, "stead of wasting his master's time with the castle leech. All Brynlas is good for is drawing blood. But they're jealous of my man's skills." She twitched the curtain straight. "Had it not been that Lady Alice made him come 'tis like enough the first news we'd have heard would've been the funeral bells from the Minster."

"The Lord Marshal's a man of oak," said David. "It will take more than a spoon of wolfsbane to fell him."

"Let's hope you're right," said Susan. "For it will surely be a black day for Kingdom and Kinsfolk alike should Lord Richard take leave of us."

Tom remembered a remark of Rett's. "Is it true he's quarreled with Lord Arthur?"

"Oh, yes. They've shared some harsh words between them of late. And 'tis common talk that Arthur bears a grudge longer than most men. But I doubt even that one would drop his strongest shield when he's most in need of it. He may be spiteful but he's nobody's fool."

"So you think it's an accident?"

"I know not what to think till Anthony's back. Let's get him cured first and look to unravel the cause afterward."

"Will he be late, do you suppose?" asked David.

"I doubt we'll see him again much before daybreak. And I'll not be waiting up for him."

"Nor I," said Tom, stifling a yawn. "No mark of disrespect to anyone but my head's nodding for a pillow."

They had been asleep for scarcely an hour before the sound of a horse roused them yet again. The Marshal's servant was back, this time with a scrawled list of medicines which Anthony needed urgently. David scrambled into his clothes, hurried downstairs to the room which served the Kinsman as a dispensary and helped Susan to sort them out. While she was parceling them up he asked the man Robin how his master fared.

"He's in a foul way, lad," was the dismal reply. "He's all a gory flux. He vomits up black blood one end and it sluices out of him the other."

"Do you know what's done it? What he's eaten?"

"Nay, I know naught. But for sure 'tis nowt I've fed to him else I'd be lying likewise."

"But doesn't _he_ know?"

"Right now, lad, he knows nothing and he cares even less."

He seized the package and vanished back into the night leaving Susan and David gazing helplessly at one another.

Anthony did not reappear until close to noon the next day and his face and his shaken head told them all they needed to know before ever a word was spoken. He brought with him a metal pot which, despite its lid, still stank abominably. This he deposited in the dispensary and then he stripped himself down to his undershirt, walked out into the river and scrubbed himself from head to foot with handfuls of coarse salt. While he was so engaged there came drifting up the valley the first melancholy chimes of the Minster minute bell, tolling out its grim news to a shocked city.

Changed into fresh clothes and with his hands bleached pale from the acid he had used to scour them, Anthony joined his wife and the two young Kinsmen in the arbor. While he broke his fast on bread and cheese and pickled onions he told them how he had passed the night. "Thirty-six hours before they send for me!" he growled. "All I could do was to ease his going out, poor fellow. Had they thought to summon me when first he sickened, like as not he'd be back on his feet by now. As it was Alice only found it out by accident. Her maid heard tell of it from Brynlas' boy who'd helped to cup him. *Cup him!*" In his anger he brought his knife down so hard upon an onion that bits flew out all ways across the board. "As if he wasn't losing enough blood to drown in! I swear that pious mountebank's in league with Death! Well, maybe I'm too harsh with him. Doubtless he did his best by his own lights. And Richard can't have helped. That's something you'll soon learn, David. Your worst patient's always your healthiest one. Wounds apart, the Marshal never had a day's illness in his life. Not even a toothache."

"And do you know what caused it?" David asked.

The Kinsman shook his head. "I could not question him till just before the end when his mind cleared. For the rest he rambled back and forth 'twixt York and New Exeter and Brittany. I heard him hold converse with Cardinal Constant and the Earl Robert as though in truth they stood there at his bedside. When at last the tannin and valerian doused the fire, his eyes cleared of pain and Alice told him who I was. He whispered thanks to me for all my trouble and murmured how he'd heard reports of my skills. So then I asked him if he could tell me what he'd taken in food or drink that tasted strange to him. He looked up into my face and then across at Alice and I knew by his labored breathing and faint pulse that the end was very close. 'Strange food?' he whispered and I swear I saw him smile as he said it. 'Strange drink? Aye, man. Ye call it Kinship, d'ye not?' He never spoke another word.

"I sent Alice away, stripped off the foul bed and cleaned the body up and told Robin to burn the linen. Then between us we clothed him afresh and laid him out, and all the while Robin weeping like a girl for love of what he'd lost. Nor had I heart to chide him for in truth he wept for both of us. And for young Alice too."

"Aye, the poor lass," murmured Susan. "She'll take it mortal hard. Since the Earl's death Lord Richard's been the world to her."

"What do you suppose he meant when he said 'Kinship'?" asked Tom.

"I know not," said Anthony. "But Alice told me it had been much on his mind throughout his ravings."

"And she didn't know?"

"I did not think to ask her."

"Was arsenic the bane?" said David.

"Or something very like," said Anthony. "Antimony perhaps. I have a stool put by may tell us something. Whatever it was it clawed his insides into tatters. At the end he was passing only blood."

Tom shuddered, seeing clear in his mind's eye the strong, confident man who had stood beside the lake at Corlay and had joked with him about the white birds which floated upon it. "If I was to call at the castle would they let me in to see Alice?"

The Kinsman and his wife looked at him with such obvious surprise that he felt constrained to add: "I met her at Corlay. I would not be going as a stranger."

"Well, they're not over-fond of Kinsmen up there, Thomas," said Anthony. "You might get your heels nipped for your pains."

"And how would I get there?"

"Your quickest way's through the forest," said Susan. "If your heart's truly set on it I'll have our Jenny put you on the path."

"Shall I come with you?" asked David.

Tom shook his head.

Long familiar with his friend's moods and expressions, David pursued the matter no further.

Tom approached the castle from the southwest, striding down that Royal Ride where once, many years before, the Lord Marshal had cantered to a meeting with young Alice. The sky had thickened to an overcast and the air, sultry and oppressive, seemed to fawn upon him. Away to the south above Winford Hill a giant thunderhead hung brooding darkly over the bent backs of the moors. On either side of the Ride the dun-colored trees were as motionless as mourners at a graveside. Even the piping of the birds seemed dispirited as though the news of the Marshal's death had saddened them too.

When he came within sight of the castle he saw that the standards had already been lowered to half-mast though there was no breath of wind to stir them. A dour-faced sergeant at the outer gate asked him his business and then passed him through with a jerk of his head. At the main gate he waited by the postern while a supercilious lackey sauntered off to inquire whether his journey had been in vain.

Inside the guardroom he could hear voices discussing the Marshal's death and arguing as to who was most likely to succeed him. The names put forward as candidates meant nothing to Tom until he heard a voice propose Lord Peter's and he at once pricked up his ears. "There's an old head on young shoulders," said the invisible advocate. "*And* he's served his time with the colors. That's more than you can say for a lot of aristos I could name."

"Aye, 'tis true," said another. "I was in the Third under him at Lynton when we fell foul of Dyffed's raiders. I swear the Old Dog himself (God rest his soul!) couldn't have handled it better. And Peter was but a whelp then."

"He's but a whelp *now*," said a third.

"Nay, man, he's blooded, and the Marshal's taught him many a trick o' war. They did say as how the old Earl was grooming him for the throne when he was—"

"Whisht, Will! D'ye seek to serve Lord Richard's shade in heaven?"

"Aye, well, 'twas but common barracks talk at the time."

"Those times are gone for good, Will. Ye'd best forget 'em."

"Trap shut: eyes 'n' ears open: blade sharp 'n' obey orders," said a new voice. "Who's for a roll at dice?"

"Your bones or mine, Sarge?"

"Cheeky scut!"

At that point the lackey returned and told Tom to follow him. They were the only words he addressed to him during the time it took them to penetrate to the distant section of the castle which housed Lady Alice's private apartments. They passed various little groups of servants who glanced up at their approach and then, perceiving that it was nobody of importance, returned to their whispering. Once Tom heard the sound of a lute being plucked and a man's light tenor voice singing tunefully, and once the sound of distant laughter drifted to his ears along one of the interminable corridors that honeycombed the palace, but his main impressions were of emptiness and a sort of uneasy, prickling apprehension.

At last they came to a wooden staircase which they climbed up to the second floor. Here the lackey signed to him to wait while he tapped with his fingernails upon a paneled door and murmured something into a shuttered spy-hole. Then, as though Tom had already ceased to exist, he sauntered past him and disappeared down the stairs.

The elaborately coiffed head had scarcely vanished from sight before the door edged open and an elderly woman beckoned Tom in. She closed the door behind him, refastened it with a chain and an iron bolt, then preceded him through a small anteroom whose windows allowed him a glimpse of leaded roofs and chimneys. She knocked on another door, opened it, and stood back for him to enter. As the door closed quietly behind him, Lady Alice, dressed in a velvet gown of so dark a shade of blue that it might have passed for black, rose from the window seat and held out her hands to him in greeting.

He stepped forward, took her hands in his, and saw that her eyes were red and swollen from weeping.

"Thomas," she whispered. "Oh, Thomas . . ." and then her pale, drawn face had crumpled beneath a new onslaught of grief.

Moved by an instinctive compassion he put his arms about her and let her head droop forward on to his shoulder while, as though to a hurt child, he murmured: "There,

there . . . it's all right . . . it'll be all right," and rubbed his cheek gently back and forth against the soft golden tresses of her hair.

Gradually, as the fierce, bitter tide of misery slackened, she started to mutter inconsequential scraps of an apology and to fumble with a damp, screwed-up ball of handkerchief. He took it from her, stroked the tears from her cheeks, and led her back to the window seat.

She sat with her eyes closed and her hands lying limp in her lap while she struggled to regain her breath. Her breast shook with huge, quivering gasps which broke up her attempts at coherent speech into a series of oddly disconnected phrases. "Oh please forgive—me I'm so—sorry I didn't—mean to greet you like—like this at all."

"What's yours is mine," said Tom. "That holds as firm for grief as anything, my Lady. I am most truly sorry for what has happened."

"But you didn't love him—love him like I did. He was such a good—such a *good* man, Thomas." And the tears gathered afresh, overflowed, and trickled down her cheeks like warm summer rain.

Tom gazed at her helplessly and then, without saying another word, he quietly unfastened the latch of his knapsack and drew out the Boy's pipes. He closed his eyes, his lips moved in a silent prayer and then, with a sensation akin to that of a swimmer abandoning himself to waters of unknown depth, he set the pipes to his lips and began to play.

Hardly had the first tentative notes floated on to the air than he knew something was happening which was completely alien to his experience. Afterward, in an attempt to describe what happened, he was to say to David: "I felt something absolutely extraordinary—a sort of flowing *inward, into me from outside* of an enormous sweeping tide of pure *power*. I'd never known anything like it in my life. I seemed to grow *huge,* like a giant, until I contained *everything!* And it was all *in* me—*a part of me!* It was mine to do with exactly as *I* wished. And I was *free,* Dave—absolutely, utterly *free!* That was the whole point, the absolute, ultimate key. I, Thomas the Kinsman, had been suddenly gifted with this, as though it had been placed in my hands and someone had said quite simply: 'This is yours, Tom. Do with it what you will.' Just that. No: 'Use this gift only for good' or: 'Use it to celebrate Kinship,' nothing but the gift of the naked power itself. You can't imagine what it was like, that sense of power. Do you remember years ago when we climbed right up on to the roof of the Queen's Tower and I told you that I knew, just for a second, that if I wished I could simply spread my arms and sail out over the hills like a bird? Well, that moment was no more than a tiny glimpse of the country where I now found myself. I was in the land of Truth: there were no secrets from me anywhere; I was its King. I suppose you could say that for the first time in my life I really *understood* what the Boy had known and that all the doors of the world stood wide open before me. And then at that very instant of total awareness, when all I had to do was to step forward across the threshold and claim my Kingdom, something held me back—something so stupid, so silly, so *ordinary* that I know it can't really have been anything of the kind.

"I opened my eyes and I saw that a tear had trickled all the way down Alice's neck and was on the point of disappearing into the dip between her breasts. *And I became that tear!* There's no other way to explain it. I lost myself in it, I drowned in it, I transformed it into silver beads and strung them on a golden thread of song and handed them back to her. I saw her eyes open and grow wide, and her lips open warm and wet. I swear to you I felt the very beating of her own heart like a bird I held cupped in my hands. The wonder she was feeling, *I* felt. I had found the key I sought and it was the very same key that Old Morfedd had first fashioned for the Boy. I knew then what Tom had meant when he told the Tale Spinner: 'I take their thoughts and give them back my own.' Just as you have learned how to heal a wounded body, so I learned then the secret way of healing the wounded heart. And yet I truly believe that it is something I have always half known and have been able to call to my aid without ever knowing what it was I did. Wanting it to happen, wanting it with all of myself, that had been enough. But now I *knew;* I had the *knowledge* of it; I felt it like a spider feels the fly along the web. And, knowing it, I knew at last what it was the Boy had sought for and, in the end, had paid for with his own life's blood."

A bowl of heliotrope and honeysuckle was standing apart on a little table in one corner, its scent lay heavy and swooning on the languid air. Away in the distance thunder muttered mutinously. The room was as still as a deep pool hidden in the green depths of a forest. In the ivy beyond the open casement window an invisible bird sang its plaintive, one-noted song: *weep-weep; weep-weep; weep-weep.* The pipes lay silent across Tom's knees like twin bars of the dark night sky. Without looking at Alice he was conscious of her gaze resting upon him. It was almost as if he could feel her touching his face with her hands.

"Why did you come to me, Thomas?" Her voice as she asked the question was perfectly calm and composed.

"Anthony told me what had happened," he said, raising his eyes to meet hers. "I guessed you had need of me."

"I have been so afraid," she said. "So afraid, Thomas. I have kept the door fast bolted ever since I got back this morning."

"Afraid of what? Your brother?"

She nodded. "Arthur killed Richard," she said. "I *know* he did."

"How do you know?"

"I just do. I feel it. It's like a sort of black shadow—a darkness in him. I think he wants to destroy everything. The Kingdom. Richard. Peter. Me. Everything."

Tom stared at her. "Did Richard say something to you?"

"No," she said. "Not about that."

"But about something else?"

"I know that he went to see my mother. Three days ago. Robin told me."

"Go on."

"That night he was taken sick—like white hot coals inside him, Robin said. And all the next day too. But he wouldn't let Robin send for the doctor. Then he got worse and worse and his mind began to wander and Robin sent for Surgeon Brynlas. That's how I got to hear what had happened. I rode straight to the Falconry and when I saw him I made Robin take a horse and fetch the Healer."

"I know," said Tom. "We were with Anthony when he came."

"Arthur killed him, Thomas. He poisoned him. I don't know how but he did."

"Have you spoken with your mother?"

"They won't let me. When I got back this morning I went straight to see her. There were guards posted outside her door. They told me they had their orders direct from Lord Arthur to let no one in without his authority."

"Where's Peter?"

"Richard sent him off on a tour of the western defenses as soon as we got back from Brittany. He said he expected to be back here by the end of June. He'll come as soon as he hears what's happened."

Tom drew his fingers lightly up and down the barrels of the pipes. "Tell me about Lord Arthur," he said. "Why should he have wished Richard dead?"

"Arthur's sick, Thomas. Sick in his mind. We have known it for years. He quarreled with Richard before we went to Brittany."

"What about?"

"Arthur had pledged me to Lord Westmorland against all my pleading. I turned to Richard for help. He made Arthur cancel the betrothal. I don't know how he did it."

"And for that you think Arthur killed him?"

Alice got up from her place, tiptoed softly across to the door and suddenly pulled it open. The woman who had let Thomas into the apartment was crouched, open-mouthed on the threshold, caught in the very act of eavesdropping.

"Get up, Betty," said Alice wearily, "and tell us who has bought your ears."

"Oh, my Lady, forgive me. I heard the music. I could not help myself."

Alice stared at her and then turned to Tom. "Does she speak true?"

For answer Tom picked up the pipes and said: "Look at me, Betty."

The woman rose slowly to her feet and turned her frightened eyes reluctantly toward him. At the instant they met his own he began to play.

She stood framed in the doorway, rapt in a dream, while the melody of the pipes coiled itself around her entranced soul like a tendril of gossamer. It grew tighter and tighter as the pitch rose even higher, and then it snapped.

"Do you hear me, Betty?" he asked gently.

"Yes, master."

"Then tell us true now, and no harm will come to you. Who sends you to spy upon your mistress?"

" 'Twas Surgeon Brynlas, master," she said simply. "I did not wish to do it. I love my Lady, dearly."

"And what did he tell you to do?"

"I am to tell him of my Lady's dealings with the Kinsfolk."

"For this he pays you?"

"No, master, he pays me nothing. I'm afeared of him."

Tom looked across at Alice. "Maybe we should speak with Master Brynlas," he said. "Perhaps he knows more than he should."

"Brynlas is Arthur's man," she replied.

"His tool perhaps. Was that why Richard would not send for him?" He turned back to Betty. "You will go and seek out Master Brynlas, Betty. You will tell him your Lady has been taken sick. You will make him come with you. You will forget everything else you have heard in this room. It has not happened."

"Yes, master."

"Go to your bedchamber, Alice. I do not want her to see you when I release her."

As soon as the bedroom door had closed Tom raised the pipes and blew three high, clear notes. The last was still vibrating on the air when Betty turned and scuttled back into the ante-room. Tom heard the rattle of the chain, the clatter of the drawn bolt, the slam of the outer door, and then silence. "She's gone," he called. "How long do you suppose it will take her to find him?"

Alice re-entered the room. She closed the bedroom door behind her, stood for a moment with her back to it, then walked across to Tom and gazed down at him. "Are you a mage, Thomas?" she asked childishly.

"And what is a mage?" he replied with a smile.

"One who has the power to enchant others."

He laughed and shook his head. "Before you found Betty you were about to tell me something. Something about Arthur and Richard. What was it?"

She sat down beside him on the window seat, pressed her knuckles to her chin and frowned. "It was something Peter said to me the night before he went away. He'd been much in Richard's company ever since that day we went to Corlay. He came in to take his farewell of me and as he was about to leave he said: "Fear not, Allie, your White Bird shall nest here soon enough." And then he kissed me and went off."

"You think that was something more than a brother's affection?"

"Yes, I do," she said. "Perhaps it was the way he said it. I really felt he meant it. He wasn't just teasing me."

Tom gnawed at his lower lip. "What was the urgent business that called Richard back to the Kingdom? Do you know?"

"There was some talk of Uncle Philip preparing to invade us, but Richard laughed at it. He said Uncle had more sense than to try anything of that kind. He wasn't worried by it."

"But he did come back. Did he go straight to Arthur?"

"I expect so. He would have had to make a report to him. He often did that."

"And how long after you returned from Brittany was Richard taken ill?"

"Murdered," she corrected. "About three weeks."

"Do you not think Arthur would have acted sooner had the quarrel over you been the cause?"

"Yes," she said. "I do not think that was why he did it."

"And yet you're sure he did."

She nodded.

"Well, there's no way further down this path," he said, "unless Master Brynlas can lead us."

"And you can make him?"

"I shall try," said Tom. "With such a stink of corruption in the air he may not prove so hard a window to open."

Chapter Five

Milton Brynlas was a man in whose presence one could scarcely fail to be conscious of the skull beneath the skin and thus, by extension, of the brittle texture of human mortality. Of singularly forbidding aspect, tall and bony almost to the point of emaciation, he dressed invariably in funereal black and favored a close-fitting cap whose pointed peak jutted out like a ship's prow just where his thick dark eyebrows met above his long thin wafer of a nose. His eyes too were black and set so close to one another that a wit in Lord Arthur's entourage had once observed that were it not for the surgeon's nose he would have made a splendid Cyclops.

It was Brynlas' undoubted skill with the knife which had earned him the confidence of the Earl Robert who had seen fit to entrust the well-being of his sickly son to his care. Gradually the doctor had succeeded in gaining a sufficient influence over his charge for those who were less than well disposed toward either to hint darkly at the Black Art. Although such rumors were totally without foundation, Brynlas made no effort to dispel them. He appreciated how much of a doctor's success lies in his reputation.

The Earl's untimely death and Arthur's accession to the throne seemed to have elevated Master Brynlas to that peak of fortune to which, he believed, his talents and his devotion had entitled him. Nevertheless, it took only one attempt at exercising his influence to convince him that he was guilty of a most grievous error of judgment. He discovered that Arthur had no intention of sharing power with anyone. The recollection of that horrendous interview which had concluded with his once docile pupil screaming that he would personally disembowel the surgeon and feed his entrails to the hounds before his own eyes, could still raise a cold sweat of terror on Brynlas' gaunt cheek. At that moment he had learned what it feels like to be the rider of a runaway and to discover that the reins have snapped. Too late to fling himself off, his only hope was to cling on tight and to pray, and he had small faith in the efficacy of either.

As he hastened up the stairs to Lady Alice's apartment the surgeon was a deeply worried man. The nature of the Lord Marshal's death and his own private suspicions as to who was responsible for it made him fearful that the same hand might already have turned against the Lady Alice. Should it prove so then nobody was safe. Obsessed as Lord Arthur was by morbid fancies and gifted with the strength of madness, he would think nothing of dragging the whole kingdom down about his crazy head.

He strode like a spindly mantis at Betty's shoulder and waited while she knocked at the door of her mistress' bedchamber. When there was no audible response he thrust the woman aside, opened the door and went in.

Alice was lying on her back in the tester bed with the covers drawn up to her chin and her eyes closed.

The surgeon hurried forward and stooped over her. "How is it with you, my Lady?"

Alice groaned feebly, and at that moment Brynlas' attention was caught by a slight movement behind the curtain which screened the head of the bed. He glanced up just in time to encounter Tom's eye and to catch the first notes of the pipes.

It was enough. He felt his skull sing as though it were a wine glass being stroked by a wetted fingertip. He fought to close his eyes and turn his head aside, then, finding he could do neither, he promptly lost the desire. At that moment if the surgeon could have been said to be aware of anything it would have been a most strange sensation compounded of relief and gratitude and an almost childlike trust.

The music stopped.

"Can you hear me, Master Brynlas?"

"Indeed I can," was the mild and friendly reply.

"We believe it is your wish to be informed of my Lady's dealings with the Kinsfolk."

"It is my Lord's wish, not mine. He is in great fear of the Kin."

"How so?"

"He believes they threaten him."

"In what way threaten him?"

"They plot to steal his Kingdom."

"He has told you this?"

"Aye. Many a time. It is no rational fear, nor is he rational. Nightly he dreams of birds and has done this month past."

"Did he seek the Lord Marshal's life?"

"Truly I do believe it."

"And did you not help him to his purpose?"

"Not I. Lord Richard's death serves no one but the Kingdom's enemies. 'Twas a mad act bred of a mad fear."

"But fear of *what*, man? Of the Marshal?"

"Of his own brother, too. Lord Richard played to set young Peter on the throne."

Tom stared at him and then down at Alice. "Do you know of this?"

She shook her head.

"So, tell us more, Master Brynlas. How come you are privy to all this?"

"I had it from the Lady Margaret's lips. She showed me the deed of abdication which Lord Richard had drawn up for Arthur's signature. It named Duke Philip Regent till Peter comes of age."

"When was this?"

"On Thursday last. She swore me to secrecy."

"Had Lord Arthur seen it?"

"Not then, I think. I warned her it would drive him to a frenzy, but she knew that at least as well as I. 'Twas then I begged her to have a care lest she draw down his rage upon herself."

Alice thrust herself up from the bed, her face white. "Not our mother," she whispered. "He would not dare!"

"We cannot judge him by ourselves, my Lady," observed Brynlas. "When the Black Spirit takes your brother he knows not right from wrong. I have heard him rail against your mother by the hour."

"He would not harm her though."

"In his right mind, no," said Brynlas. "But when the devils take him he knows not what he does and cares the less."

Alice shivered, and at that precise instant she and Tom both heard the sound of raised voices in the ante-room. Her startled eyes had scarcely turned to his before Betty appeared in the doorway crying: "Oh, my Lady, there's some wild maskers come to bring you to my Lord!"

"Tell them I am unwell."

"I have, my Lady. They will not be denied."

"I'll not go with them."

"Ah, but you must, my pretty lady!" cried a strange squeaky voice, and through the open doorway came prancing as motley a collection of grotesques as it would be possible to imagine. One—either a child or a dwarf—was sporting the gross likeness of a pig's head. Behind him skipped a fox rattling a tambourine, a lion, a rat blowing upon a penny whistle, and a unicorn. Bowing, scraping, and caterwauling they danced up to the end of the bed, and, ignoring Tom and Brynlas, seized hold of Alice by the arms. "To the Handing!" they squealed. "Your Lord and Master waits! Away! Away!" and before anyone had really grasped what was happening Alice was hustled out of the room. She flung an imploring glance backward over her shoulder and then she was gone.

Tom had covered some half dozen paces toward the bedroom door before he bethought himself of the surgeon. "Where do they take her?" he demanded.

"To the Banqueting Hall, I imagine."

"What for?"

"I know not. Some antique frolic or other. Lord Arthur is never short of a bizarre fancy."

"I fear they intend her some mischief."

"Nay, they do but jest."

Betty scuttled into the bedchamber, bobbed the two men a brief curtsy, and snatched up a pair of slippers from beneath the bed "They would take her barefoot, the rogues!" she panted and scurried out again.

Tom looked down at the pipes he was holding and then across at Brynlas who now appeared more than ever like a death's-head in the sickly thunder-light. "I owe you an apology, Master Brynlas," he said. "I supposed you had helped Lord Arthur to dig the Marshal's grave."

A faint flush reddened the surgeon's waxy cheek. "And put my life between a judge's lips?" he murmured. "Lord Richard was far beyond my reach when his man came for me. I did my best by him. His death bell tolls for all of us."

"Then Lord Arthur is truly mad?"

"I do believe it."

"So what can we do?"

"*We?* You speak of princes, man!"

"And princes are not men?"

Brynlas drew in a hissing breath. "I have seen him strike down more than one for saying less than that."

"Do all go in fear of him?"

"All who know him do. Lord Richard was the only man who dared to face him out."

"And for that he died?"

The surgeon's silence was more eloquent than words.

Tom walked across to the window and looked out. He felt empty, drained, as though all the strength which had flooded in to him had leaked silently away and left only a useless husk behind. He no longer even knew why he was where he was. His thoughts were all inconsequential, pictures which flickered like the sheet lightning in the oppressive sky—Francis peering at him one-eyed across the table at the *disposition* Board; Marwys handing a carving to Witchet; the Magpie laughing; odd scraps of *huesh* —like bright beads streaming from a broken necklace they fell, and, falling, lost all meaning. At last only one remained, a solitary, isolated vision of a single tear on Alice's white breast, and with it, hovering like a whispered caption, some words which Francis had once penned in the margin of one of his essays: *Truth can exist for us only in Minute Particulars.*

He closed his eyes, rested his throbbing forehead against the cool glass, and contrived to hold the picture still in his mind's eye. No sooner had he done so than he realized with a kind of sick certitude that *she* was the "Minute Particular" which he had been drawn there to find. It was as if a crack had opened from the top of his mind to the bottom and all her desperate need of him came flooding in. The transformation was almost miraculous. His lassitude fled and he was consumed by a fierce, leaping, flamelike rage. He swung round upon Brynlas. "Take me to that place where she is!"

"Nay, man!" cried the surgeon. "Your twin tongue will be a spur to Arthur's spite. I'll not be party to it!"

"Lead me but to the door. I ask no more. I will not say you did it."

Something in Tom's voice, or in his eye, or in the fading enchantment of the pipes persuaded Brynlas that he would do well to agree. He nodded. "You do not go unwarned," he said. "Follow me."

They descended the stairs, passed down dim, echoing corridors, some of which looked as if they had not felt the touch of a broom for months, and came at last to a small arched door. "What you seek lies through there," murmured the surgeon and he turned and strode back along the passage, his heels clacking on the flagstones.

Tom waited until he was out of sight then pressed his ear against the thick oak panels. He could hear faint sounds coming from the other side but nothing which he could distinguish. An infernal cold seemed to have settled deep into the void of his stomach. He thrust the pipes down inside his shirt till they were lodged firm between his belt and his waist, then, with his heart pounding, he grasped the iron latch ring and quietly twisted it. It turned reluctantly beneath his hand. When he judged the latch to be fully clear of its hasp he leaned his shoulder gently against the door and inched it forward. The hinges squeaked like mice; a thin sliver of yellow light appeared between the panel and the jamb; and a babel of voices and laughter sprang toward him. He sipped his breath, felt the ice in his gut melting into cold water, and applied his eye to the crack.

Brynlas had served him well. He found he was peering out along a lofty arrassed wall from the face of which slender bas-relief pillars rose like the jets of petrified fountains to support the high, arching roof. Directly above his head he could just make out the dark shadow of timbered flooring and he guessed that his door must be one of those which permitted access of some sort to a minstrels' gallery as in the Great Hall at Corlay. From the gusts of laughter and the sporadic applause he assumed that a show of some kind was in progress but as yet he could see nothing of it. He edged the door open a further careful inch, and, to his profound relief, saw that a screen of fretted wood had been positioned between himself and the main body of the hall. It was separated from the outer wall by a gap just wide enough to allow the passage of a human body and while it concealed the door it also effectively blocked his view of what was taking place beyond.

A sudden tumult of laughter gave him the opportunity he needed. He squeezed himself round the edge of the door, darted forward to the wooden screen, and found that he had company. Two men in gray woolen caps and greasy aprons were already crouched there peering out through holes in the wooden tracery. They glanced up as he joined them. One raised a finger as thick as a sausage to his lips, and the other—a lad of no more than sixteen—treated Tom to a slack-lipped grin of complicity. Both men reeked of rancid fat and fried onions. Tom nodded, knelt down beside them and applied his eye to the nearest convenient spy-hole.

There were perhaps a hundred people in the hall which had been set out in the form of a crude amphitheater. Benches had been stacked upon tables and these dragged into a rough semicircle, leaving clear a carpeted area which was serving as a makeshift stage. The dim, yellowish light which filtered down from the high windows was augmented by a score of oil lamps suspended by chains from a wrought-iron wheel immediately above the auditorium. In

the pool of light a juggler in a costume of red and yellow
was weaving a skillful aerial arabesque out of the colored
balls he flung up from the flickering shuttles of his hands.
Liveried servants bearing silver ewers moved back and
forth replenishing the wine cups that were thrust out to
them. "Yon's Master Zigaldo," whispered the man who
knelt at Tom's side. "They do say he's the best ball man in
Christendom. He's wasted on these pricklets."

He spoke with reason. The audience were plainly bored
with the juggler's skills, giggling and chattering among
themselves while he went through his elaborate routine and
never once faulted.

Tom could see no sign anywhere of Lady Alice though
he had soon identified her brother. Lord Arthur was
sprawled back in his cushioned chair in the very center of
the foremost rank of spectators, arrayed in a striking costume of scarlet silk which shimmered like flames whenever he shifted his position. He was in animated converse
with a little group of courtiers, emphasizing his points
with movements of a parchment scroll which he held in
his left hand, and he scarcely deigned to acknowledge
the conclusion of Master Zigaldo's performance.

The juggler was followed by a group of female courtiers
in Greek tunics. To much ribald laughter and ironic applause they performed to a lute accompaniment a dance/
charade presumably devised by themselves. They pranced
about displaying themselves in a series of artistic poses
while the lutanist warbled out the unlikely information
that these were "Nymphs of woods and streams, who, tho'
seldom seen, Brought Great Delight, by Day and Night,
to lovers' Dreams." The high point of the act came when
one of the nymphs inadvertently caught her naked toe
under the edge of one of the carpets and in her headlong
tumble succeeded in displaying almost everything she had
to offer in the way of great delights.

The whole thing was so surpemely inept and fatuous that
Tom was nine parts convinced that his apprehension had
been totally unfounded. But that uneasy tenth part still
kept his eye pressed to the fretted acanthus and his attention concentrated upon the figure of Lord Arthur. As the
prolonged applause for the Nymphs died away he saw
Arthur rise to his feet and unroll his parchment. Having
gestured for silence and cleared his throat he announced:
"And now for your instruction and delight, dear friends,

it is our royal pleasure to present a masque devised by ourselves and dedicated to all those who love white birds and fair maidens. Music there for—Leda and the Swan!"

From a curtained entrance on the far side of the hall there came a wild skirling of bagpipes and into the light burst an extraordinary menagerie of masqued beasts led by those which Tom had seen in Lady Alice's bedchamber. Blowing their whistles and rattling their tambourines they pranced and cavorted all round the hall, leaping, tumbling and somersaulting until they had completed an entire circuit, whereupon they formed themselves up into two ranks and, mopping and mowing, mimed a prodigious welcome.

The curtains were pulled aside and four men dressed from head to foot in hangman's black came in bearing between them a sort of covered litter. They carried it right into the center of the auditorium, set it down, and then retired. No sooner had they vanished than the animals flung their arms into the air and began beating them up and down in unison.

Suddenly, at some silent command, they all fell flat upon the floor and out through the curtains came waddling a most curious and comical figure, presumably intended to represent a swan. It had perhaps some tenuous affinity with a very plump, short-necked duck, being white and feathered and possessing a wooden beak, webbed feet, and a pair of stubby wings which it flapped up and down with commendable vigor, discarding several feathers in the process. It bowed to the audience who applauded it industriously, then, escorted by the animals, it waddled its way toward the covered litter into which it poked its head, apparently investigating whatever was inside.

What it found there obviously excited it in the most remarkable way. It leapt up and down clapping its stubby wings and then began to waddle about the auditorium. As it did so, from a concealed slit low down in the underbelly of its costume, a large, white-painted wooden phallus began to protrude.

The spectators went wild, hooting, whistling, and clapping as if possessed. The swan, delighted at its reception, clowned about making little amorous rushes toward the squealing women in the front rows, and then returned its attention to the litter. Approaching it from the area of the auditorium where Lord Arthur sat grinning broadly, it raised itself on tiptoe, flapped its wings wildly, and emitted a sound not unlike the crow of a triumphant cockerel. It was the signal for the pig, the lion, the tiger and the fox to dart forward and each seize a corner of the cover.

There was a kind of breathy sigh of anticipation from the rapt audience. It died dramatically into utter silence when, in one concerted jerk, the cover was stripped away to reveal the Leda.

Alice lay completely naked, spreadeagled over a long, humped leather pad. A silk scarf had been tied across her mouth; her wrists and ankles were lashed to the frame of the litter; her eyes were closed.

Crouched far forward in his chair, his hands gripping the wooden arms so hard that his knuckles shone bone-white, Lord Arthur cried out: "To it, you feathered fool! Don't keep your lover waiting!"

The swan waddled forward, hopped up on to the end of the litter and began to shuffle slowly up toward its hapless victim. There was an uneasy murmuring among the audience and one foolhardy voice was moved to cry out: "Nay, nay, my Lord, this jest has gone too far!"

It is unlikely that Lord Arthur even heard him. Shrieking: "Behold! your Bird is come for you, my Lady!" he sprang forward into the auditorium and advanced crabwise upon the litter as though intent upon assisting personally in the grisly violation which his sick mind had devised. He was within an arm's length of Alice when a wriggling serpent of pure white light ripped the sky into shreds and splintered the hushed air with startled screams. It was followed almost instantaneously by such a roar of thunder that the sound of piping was almost drowned.

But nothing could have drowned it entirely. The mad rage that boiled over in Tom was something which the man who had devised those pipes could scarce have dreamt of. The wild invocation swirled up like a twisting column of dark smoke, like no music ever heard before, and the air was suddenly alive with great swathes of sweeping shadow and the rush of monstrous feathered wings. Something dark and terrible had been loosed into that great hall, something which swooped down and beat blackly against the minds which the piper sought to destroy, filling them with such a nameless dread that they ran this way and that clutching at their bent heads and crashing blindly against each other in their frenzy to escape. And when they fell to the floor the screaming did not stop even though their mouths were closed for the terror had come to roost inside their own heads.

White and shaking Tom stumbled down into the body of the hall and approached the litter. With trembling fingers he tore loose the gag from Alice's mouth and then, snatching a knife from the belt of one of the men who lay upon the floor he attacked the bonds that held her. As soon as she was free he pulled her clear, tore a cloak from someone's back and having swaddled her in it drew her over to a chair. The air about them was thick with the fetid stench of terror but the roar of the avenging wings was gone and only the growling of the thunder and rush of rain remained.

Blind as moles the courtiers blundered and scrabbled about among the tangle of chairs and fallen benches. Some moaned, and when they touched one another they whimpered and shrank away. Only Lord Arthur, forsaken of all reason, smiled foolishly as he sat upon the carpet hugging himself and babbling about a great bird of thunder which was come to pluck his enemies' eyes out.

Gradually the uncontrollable shivering which had afflicted Tom began to abate and his breath to come easier to him. He looked around at the carnage and was amazed at what he saw. He did not doubt that he had the power to heal these broken people and restore them to their wits but as yet he lacked the will to do it. The volcanic violence of his blind and terrible rage had left him numb and he suspected that it might not all be spent. Even his pity for Alice, though genuine enough, was curiously ambivalent, as if some part of him insisted on blaming her for having shown him the deep core of primitive darkness which lay within himself. So he sat silently beside her and could not as yet bring himself to touch her again.

By and by some of the servants came into the hall. Tom overheard them whispering to each other and he called out to them to go and tell Lady Alice's woman to bring some clothes for her mistress.

They approached him fearfully and one said, "Lord bless us, young sir. What mischief's here?"

"They conjured up the devil," muttered Tom. "Go now. Make haste. Do as I say."

The man crossed himself, tiptoed around the dribbling

idiot who was his Sovereign Lord and Master, and hurried out.

By the time Betty appeared with a cloak, a gown and some slippers, Alice was beginning to emerge from her state of shock. But she could not take her haunted eyes off Arthur and cringed away whenever his nodding head came lolling toward her. Tom wondered what had passed between them before she had been shackled to the litter but he dared not ask. "Who is the Steward of the Household, Betty?"

" 'Tis Sir Robert Bailey, sir."

"Do you see him here?"

She paused in her buttoning-up of Alice, darted a frightened glance around the room and shook her head.

"Do you know where he might be?"

"In his own quarters, I daresay."

"Leave Lady Alice and go fetch him here. I'll finish that."

She opened her mouth as if to protest then caught his eye and nodded. "What am I to tell him, sir?"

"Tell him his Master has need of him," said Tom, and leaning over Alice's bare back he drew the bodice of the gown about her, made fast another button and whispered in her ear: "Fear not, sweet maid. He cannot hurt you now. His mind is dead."

Beneath his fingertips he felt her quivering like a lutestring overstrained and the black mad rage stirred once again in the depths like something hungry and untamed stretching itself. He closed his eyes and touched her naked neck with his lips until the fury sank back and settled and was still once more. But he was certain now where the Bird of Darkness had its dwelling place and what its wings and claws were made of.

"I will go and fetch Kinsman Anthony," he murmured. "Betty shall take you back to your room."

Alice shook her head. "No," she whispered, and it was the first intelligible word she had spoken. "No. You must not leave me."

Steward Bailey had seen service under the old Earl, and in his time had witnessed many curious sights, but never anything to compare with that which greeted his eyes when he strode into the Banqueting Hall. At first he assumed they were all blind drunk, but then he caught sight of Lady Alice and her companion and he made his way toward them. In so doing he came across Lord Arthur and stood rooted in astonishment. "S-sire?" he stuttered. "Are you ill?"

Tom rose to his feet. "He is mad," he said flatly. "He has lost his wits."

"And who are you, sir?"

"Kinsman Thomas of Tallon."

Steward Bailey looked down at the sorry figure at his feet, then round at all the others. "What ails them all, Thomas?" he said. "Are they bewitched?"

"Aye. Maybe," replied Tom. "Why don't you ask them?"

The Steward glanced at him sharply, unable to figure out the tone of his voice, then perceiving one he knew, he stepped in among the wrack of stunned bodies crying: "John, man! What ails you? Don't you know me?"

Tom observed the Steward curiously for a moment then said: "It is not for me to say so, Sir Steward, but I think you would be best advised to take your future orders from Lady Alice and her mother. Lord Arthur is now Lord in name only."

"But what happened, man? How came they thus?"

"I doubt you would believe me if I told you."

"Why so?"

"They conjured up the devil."

"Is't true?"

"Aye. True enough."

"I have heard him speak of it often," muttered the Steward. "But I never thought . . ."

Tom laid his hand upon Alice's arm and whispered something in her ear.

"Sir Robert," she said. "Will you please escort my brother to his chamber?"

"I will, my Lady."

Again Tom whispered.

"Leave the others be and make certain all the doors are shut."

"But my Lady, is that wise?"

"Those are my orders, Sir Robert."

"Very good, my Lady."

The Steward returned to Lord Arthur's side and succeeded in coaxing him to his feet. Supporting him by an arm about his waist he half-led, half-carried him out. As she watched them vanish through the curtains Alice shuddered violently and burst into tears.

"Betty will take you back to your room now," said Tom gently. "I will join you there presently."

She looked at him imploringly and shook her head. Her eyes glittered like stars in water.

"Trust me for this, Alice. You must."

"You promise you will come?"

"I promise, sweet Lady."

He laid her cloak about her shoulders and walked beside her to the door.

As Alice and Betty reached the foot of the stairs which led up to her apartment, they both heard, faint and far in the distance, the honey-sweet healing melody of the pipes.

The sun was setting as Anthony and David rode up to the castle gates along a driveway which the recent storm had left patched with puddles of liquid gold. Long streamers of light shot through the tissue of melting cloud and gilded all the tops of the high westward moors and the still dripping trees of Hartcombe Forest. The rain rinsed air was as soft and milk-sweet as a baby's breath.

The same lackey who earlier had conducted Tom to Lady Alice's apartment was waiting for them by the postern, but this time he was all groveling civility as he led them to her door.

Betty opened to them, curtsied, and ushered them in. "My Lady and the young Kinsman attend upon the Lady Margaret," she informed them. "They will be here presently," and she called out to the lackey who was still hovering in the background: "Go you at once and tell my Mistress that the Kinsmen are arrived."

She closed the outer door and led them through into the sitting-room which was now overflowing with the delicate, rose pink light flooding in from the west.

"How is it with your mistress, Betty?" inquired Anthony. "Is she well?"

"Aye, sir. Thanks to the young master she is much recovered."

"Has she been sick then?"

"Oh, sir, she has been most sorely abused, poor lady."

"The message said nothing of this," said David. "In what manner abused?"

"In truth I know not all the shameful story, sir. But they were most cruel and wicked with her, poor thing. Most cruel and wicked."

"How so?"

"They would make evil sport of her, sir. The masked devils came for her. It was the Lord Arthur's wish they said. I only know the part of it. But I have seen the black marks on her where no marks ought to be."

David looked across at Anthony, his eyes full of doubts and questions which he did not know how to frame.

Anthony said: "But all is now well, you say?"

Betty nodded.

"Then let us give thanks to the Bird for that."

Betty recollected her duties. "There is wine or cordial to hand, sir, if you wish it."

"Thank you, Betty. A glass of wine would suit us very well."

She went out of the room to fetch it and David said: "What think you?"

Anthony shook his head. "I know not what to think till Tom arrives."

"But her own brother . . . ?"

"We have only *her* word for that."

"But *would* he?"

"Truly he has a most sorry reputation," said Anthony. "But such a thing I could not hang on any man by hearsay alone."

They had drunk one cup of wine apiece and were halfway through their second when they heard footsteps in the anteroom and Tom's voice saying: ". . . until your brother comes." Then the door opened and Alice entered the room with Tom at her shoulder. She ran to Anthony and embraced him. "Dear, dear friend," she sighed. "Now truly I begin to live again."

David saw the signs of strain lying like a shadow across Tom's face and moved across to his side. "What have you been up to?" he murmured. "We've been hearing some wild tales. Is she all right?"

"Alice will live," said Tom with the faintest hint of a wry smile. "But we're both a deal older and wiser than when you saw us last." He took the half-empty wine cup from his friend's hand, lifted it to his lips and drained it in a single gulp.

David fetched the silver jug and re-filled the cup. "We

found the nature of that bane they used," he said. " 'Twas as I thought—white arsenic."

Tom blinked as if for a second he could not imagine what his friend was talking about. Then his face cleared. "Aye, poor Lord Richard," he responded. "Sure it seems a lifetime ago. But it was not Brynlas did it, Dave. That we know for sure."

"Who then?"

Before Tom could offer his opinion on the matter Anthony said: "What's this she tells me, Thomas? Lord Arthur abdicates? In Peter's favor?"

"Aye, it's true enough," said Tom. "The deed is signed in a fashion—and suitably witnessed. Duke Philip stands as Regent till Peter comes of age."

"How is this possible?"

"It was the Lord Marshal's purchase. It seems he bought it with his life."

"We know 'twas arsenic killed him," said Anthony.

"So David tells me. The Lady Margaret fears that she was used by Arthur on the evening when Lord Richard called to see her."

"How so?"

"A man of Arthur's brought a gift from him—a peace-offering as she thought—a dish of sugared fruits. She tasted one but found it bitter and spat it out. She thinks that Richard might have eaten one or two. When she heard that he was taken sick she remembered what had happened and asked for the sweets to be brought to her, but there was no sign of them anywhere. She sent word at once to Arthur and within an hour a guard had been posted at her door. No doubt they'd still be there if we hadn't released her."

"We?" said David. "Who's we?"

"Alice and me and Steward Bailey."

"And what of Lord Arthur?"

"Ah," said Tom, turning to the window. "That's something only he could tell you. But my Lord Arthur does not seem to speak much now."

"You talk riddles," said David. "Are we not to know what has happened?"

Betty came quietly into the room carrying a lighted lamp which she set down upon a table. At once the evening glow withdrew to the casements where it fingered Tom's pale face with a soft flush of color. His eyes appeared to be fixed in rapt contemplation of some point in the remote distance over the hills and far away, and Alice, seeing him thus, went over to him. She laid her hand upon his arm and murmured: "It is best we tell them now, Tom, or it will live on in us for ever."

"So tell them then," he said. "For my part I'm easy either way."

Chapter Six

A longship painted red, blue and white, and dressed over-all in a joyous carnival of bunting, sailed into Bodmin harbor on the twenty-ninth day of July having first made landfall on the outer islands of Redruth and St. Austell. Among the many flags that fluttered so bravely from her rigging was one which depicted a white bird hovering against a background of azure blue.

Duke Philip's homecoming had been most thoroughly prepared; nothing foreseeable had been left to chance. The civic dignitaries of Bodmin were all assembled on the quay-side to kiss their Lord's hand and to wish him the long life and prosperity which, they hoped, would ensure that their gold chains of office remained shiny and their money bags full. The Duke acknowledged their homage gracefully and accepted the token key to the Citadel which he raised aloft for all to see before returning it to the Lord Mayor. The Captain of the Civil Guard led his troop in three rousing loyal cheers and the city gave itself over to holiday.

For a week thereafter Philip and his lady held open court in Bodmin Castle. Busy as foraging bees the messen-gers and envoys came and went, and early in the morning of the sixth of August one brought the letter for which Philip had been waiting. It was brief and to the point. Lord Peter, Heir Apparent to the Realm of the First King-dom, embraced his Uncle, Duke Philip of Bodmin, and looked to him for his wise help and guidance in the diffi-cult and arduous years that lay ahead. In evidence of this

he enclosed two tokens: the sign of the White Bird of Kinship and his father's ring. Should Duke Philip see fit to
accept the Honorable Office of Regent then these were
the twin loyalties which he must be prepared to avow in
public in the capital on Saint Bartholomew's Day.

"I see Lord Richard's hand in this," observed Philip to
his wife. "The Apostate surely knew what he was about
and we did well to heed him. So, my chuck, you'd best
get that"—he indicated the small gold crucifix which hung
about her neck—"a speedy pair of wings or keep it hid in
public."

Compared with some of Francis' international triumphs the
Public Declaration for Kinship of the First Kingdom was
a comparatively minor affair, but it was none the less
sweet for that. The official ceremony was held in the open
air on the steps of the Minster and it was Brother Francis
in person who took the wooden bowl of salt water, dipped
his finger, and drew upon the foreheads of Duke Philip,
Lord Peter and the Lady Margaret the sign of the winged
Bird with which the Old Tale Spinner had once reclaimed
the lost soul of Falcon Gyre on the shore of a distant
northern sea.

The obligatory *Lament for the White Bird* was played
not by Tom but by Kinsman Marwys who had traveled
with Francis from Corlay. The one person who had done
as much as anyone alive to bring this day about was missing from the festivities and no one seemed to have the
slightest idea where he was, though both David and Jane
had their suspicions. They, together with Rett, Alison and
the two younger children formed part of the vast concourse
which filled the whole of the Minster Square. Witchet, who
was unwell, had stayed behind in Tallon with the Magpie.

At the very moment when Francis was raising his arms
preparatory to calling upon the White Bird of Kinship to
spread its wide protecting wings over the First Kingdom,
Kinsman Thomas was lying by the side of Alice in a
brackened dell deep in Hartcombe Forest and was most
busily and skillfully employing his curious tongue for purposes far other than those for which it had been intended.
Nor was he conscious of the slightest twinge of either
guilt or remorse as he did so. As for his partner her immediate world had contracted to the confines of her own
slender frame only for her to discover a whole new uni-

verse of exquisite sensation encompassed within it. She did not doubt that Francis's White Bird hovered over them both.

Whether Tom had seduced Alice or Alice, Tom, was something neither of them bothered their heads about. They were being swept along on a foaming tidal wave which they both knew held more in it of hunger than of love. But that hunger was a glory in its own right and assuaging it was doing more to heal invisible wounds than either could have dreamed of. So, for a while at least, eternity lay in their lips and eyes, bliss in their brows bent, and in due course Tom would recollect it all in tranquility and the world would find itself the richer.

When, temporarily sated, they lay back and gazed up at the slow summer clouds drifting overhead, he was suddenly moved to ask her how it was that she had come to be floating in the channel of Lanvaux.

"I don't know," she said.

"But there must have been a moment when you decided to go there," he persisted. "When you committed yourself. Before you even set out maybe."

She turned her head and studied his face, frowning faintly just as he remembered having once seen her frown when he was sailing her back to Saint Anne. Finally she said: "Why are you asking me this?"

"I'll tell *you* if you tell *me*," he said. "What made you go out alone?"

"But I often sailed on my own."

"You said Lord Richard would be furious if he knew you'd done it."

"I said that?"

"Or something like it. Wasn't it true?"

"I was supposed to take someone with me. But not in the same boat. That's all I meant."

"So you're telling me there wasn't really any particular moment when you just sort of felt you had to sail into the channel?"

"No, I don't think so. If there was I've forgotten it."

"You realize that if you *hadn't* done it we wouldn't be here now?"

"We might."

"I don't think so. I think it *had* to happen the way it did. Shall I tell you why?"

"I wish you would."

"It's quite simple really. I knew you were going to be out there."

Alice was silent for a long, thoughtful moment. "How could you have known?" she said at last. "I didn't even know myself."

"I'd seen it happening in a *huesh*—a sort of day-dream. A kind of vision, if you like. David and I had already been to *L'Index* twice before it actually happened. We were waiting for it. For *you*. You can ask him if you don't believe me."

"A vision?" she repeated tonelessly. "What sort of a vision?"

"Well, I didn't know it was going to be *you*," said Tom. "It was just a *huesh* of a girl floating in the water. That's why we were able to get out to you so quickly."

"You aren't just making this up, are you?"

"I swear I'm not. All I'm trying to do is find out if you had anything to do with it. I want to find out how this thing works. You see, I think there must have been a moment when you pictured yourself out sailing alone in the Lanvaux. You must have imagined yourself doing it. Before it happened, I mean."

"How long before?"

"I don't know exactly. A month. Three weeks."

Alice became very still, so still indeed that Tom turned his own head until he was looking directly into her eyes. Like breath fading from a mirror he saw the mist of doubt slowly begin to clear. Her face became touched by an expression of childlike wonder. "Yes," she murmured. "I'd forgotten all about it . . ."

He waited for her to go on but she seemed to have lost her way.

"What had you forgotten?"

"It was the night when Richard went to see Arthur about my betrothal. I had a dream . . ."

"Go on."

"About . . . about drowning." She shivered. "It was horrible. A nightmare. I wish you hadn't reminded me."

He lifted his hand and laid it on her bare breast. "Was it in Lanvaux it happened?"

"I don't know where it was. But it wasn't that." Her eyes were fixed on him with a kind of helpless horror. "It was *them*," she whispered. "Those animals. The rat and the pig. *They* were drowning me. *That was my dream!*" and she panted and shuddered with the recollected terror of it all.

He took her into his arms and cherished her and soothed away the grisly remnants of the horror until at last the shadows melted from the backs of her eyes and her mouth opened again warm and hungry for his. And then, when he was wholly absorbed in her, lavishing himself upon her, lost to the world, his mind was suddenly rent by such a wail of anguish that his soul fainted within him.

"What is it?" she gasped, jerking back her head. "What's the matter?"

"Witchet," he whispered. "Something's happening to her. She's calling me."

He scrambled to his knees and began groping for his clothes, but she could see from his blind face that he was listening to something which could have existed only inside his own head, for she could hear no sound other than his wild breathing. It was as though in the twinkling of an eye she herself had completely ceased to exist for him, had become invisible, vanished. But his utter desolation pierced to her heart like the thrust of a sharp spear. She felt his anguish through him, and, in that single moment, learned something of the true nature of her feelings for him.

They reached the castle stables just as the homeward-bound procession was wending its way back from the ceremony and the Minster bells were flinging out the joyful tidings across the brightly bannered city streets to the encircling moors. Most of the horses had been pressed into service for the procession and Alice ordered a groom to saddle up the best that was left. While this was being done she tried to discover the source of Tom's fears but he either would not or could not tell her more than she already knew which was that Witchet was calling him to her side. "You must try to find David," he said. "Tell him to tell the others where I've gone. I'd do it myself but I know there isn't time. I may too late as it is."

"When do you think you'll be back?"

He shook his head. "I don't know. Soon, I hope."

The groom led out the snorting horse. Tom shouldered his knapsack and swung himself up into the saddle. "I'll head straight for Tolland," he said. "Just pray I can find a boat."

Alice nodded, laid her hand lightly upon his knee and

formed her lips into a silent kiss. Their eyes met in a brief, naked glance and then he kicked his heels into the horse's flanks and clattered away. She watched him till he passed out of her sight but he did not once look back.

Just after three in the afternoon, gray as a ghost from the dust of the long, hot ride, he cantered down the valley into the little coastal hamlet of Tolland. The tide was on the ebb and golden sandspits were already beginning to glisten in the channel. Five miles out the gray-blue hills of Quantock quivered in the afternoon haze. A few boats were drawn up in the little harbor, but apart from an ancient graybeard and a young boy who was mending a net, the quayside was deserted. Tom rode right up to them, swung himself down from the sweating horse and asked if there was anyone who could ferry him across to Tallon.

The old man shook his head. "Bob Foley woulda done it but he's away in New Exeter. Ain't none other. 'Sides she's dropping fast now," and he indicated the harbor with an upward jerk of his head, underlining his observation by spitting into the rapidly sinking waters.

"Will *you* take me?" asked Tom.

The old man stared at him and then began to shake with laughter. "Lord bless us, young master!" he wheezed. "It's nigh more'n I can do to pull this 'ere needle, let alone an oar. I've not been afloat this five year past."

"Do you have a boat?"

"Not no more I don't. I used to run a proper beauty but I sold her to Parson when the old back took bad. That's her down there. The *Sea Witch*."

"Would the parson lend it to me?"

"Not he." The old man chuckled. "He's tighter'n a tick. 'Sides you'd have to go t' New Exeter to ask him. He's away off there today alonger all the rest of 'em. Just me 'n' the lad left."

Tom looked down at the boat and as he did so he became conscious that the boy's eyes were fixed upon him. He turned to him. "Will *you* come with me? I need someone who knows these waters."

The boy darted a swift glance at the old man who said: "Dick, boy, you'll not quit my side without I say so. If he's in such a mighty lather to get to Tallon, let him ride to Monksilver an' tek the ferry."

"There isn't time for that," said Tom. "Will you pilot me, Dick?"

"In *Sea Witch?*" said the boy.

"Aye, *Sea Witch* it is."

"What'll we say to Parson?"

"Leave parson to me. Hark ye, Grandad. This fine horse is yours against my return. And there'll be a royal waiting for the lad the moment I set foot ashore in Tallon."

The old man peered up at the horse with a speculative bloodshot eye and Tom could almost hear him totting up its value, in gold coin. "Come, Dick," he said, "aboard with you or I fear we may not make it across the bar."

Tugged by the strong ebb tide they were soon well clear of the harbor and the *Sea Witch* with all sail set was heeling sweetly to the quartering breeze. The boy looked back and laughed. "I'd ha' come wi' ye for nowt, Kinsman," he said. "I'd had more'n my fill o' the netting."

"I'll find someone in Tallon will help you sail her back," said Tom. "I have to stay there."

"I need none," said the boy proudly. "Grandad knows I've sailed right o'er to Blackdown on my own more'n once. 'Twas for that he let me go wi' ye."

The breeze held true for the half hour it took them to cross the channel but by then the tide had fallen too low for them to enter Tallon harbor. Tom handed the boy a gold piece and some silver. "Look after the horse till I come for it, Dick," he said. "The Bird will wing you safe back home." With that he lowered himself over the side into the waist deep water, turned the boat and thrust it out. Then, praying with all his heart that the two hours he had gained would prove enough, he waded to the shore through the small stumbling waves.

Tallon was almost as drowsy as Tolland had been, though a few curious watchers peeped from the windows to see who it was running past up the hill and were moved to wonder idly what could be lending such speed to the young Kinsman's flying heels. He reached the outer gate, thrust it open and pelted up the flagstoned path to the cottage yelling Witchet's name at the top of his voice.

The Magpie met him at the kitchen door and Tom could scarcely summon up breath enough to ask him what had happened.

The old man shook his head. "You're too late, Tom, lad," he said. "She's been gone this full hour past."

"Gone?" panted Tom. "Gone where? What d'you mean?"

The Magpie stared at him with eyes from which all the color seemed to have been bleached away. "She's dead, boy," he said dully. "Our Witchet's dead."

Tom thrust out his hands and gripped the old man fiercely by the shoulders. "It's not true!" he gasped. *"I know it, Magpie!"*

"Nay, boy, I swear to you there's neither breath nor pulse left in her. Think you I'd lie?"

Tom rocked back on his heels as though he had been punched and then he shook his head stubbornly. "She called to me, Magpie. And she's calling to me still. Where is she?"

"Upstairs. Lying on her cot. But there's nothing we can do for her, Tom. She's far beyond life's reaching."

But Tom was already halfway across the room, headed for the stairs. The Magpie watched him, and guessing that the *huesh* had drawn him felt a sudden surge of wholly irrational hope. It lasted just until he glanced down at the scrap of looking-glass which he still held clutched in his hand and recalled the long hour since he had last seen it misted by his daughter's breath.

With his hand on the latch of Witchet's door Tom paused, and with his eyes closed he dredged through the deep and secret recesses of his innermost mind for the whisper of her voice. Faint and far away he heard it still, plaintive as a bird chiding its mate back to an abandoned nest. Holding it cupped most gently within him he thumbed down the latch and stepped over the threshold into the shadowy little room.

She lay as though in a deep sleep, her face so pale that the veins showed up like a delicate azure tracery under the translucent skin at her temples. So much of his own past life was lying there that his heart ached to look upon it. And somehow he must reach her before she slipped away and was lost forever in the land of eternal shadow. He laid his hand gently upon her forehead and it was as cold as a winter's stone. He knew then where he would have to go to seek her and the sudden fear of where she might lead him all but stopped his own heart in mid-beat. And yet he could not deny the claim of her absolute trust in him. *If ever I'm lost promise me you'll come and find me. Promise me. Promise me.* "Aye, dear Witch," he whispered, "I shall come. Do you but follow me." He bent down and touched her cold lips with his own, then straightening up, he lifted the satchel from his shoulder, tugged the straps undone and dipped his hand inside.

There was neither moon nor stars, nor dawn, nor dusk, nor any time of day, only a dim grayness and a chill wind which blew from nowhere to nowhere carrying with it wild, distant sounds which might have been the cries of birds or the branches of unseen trees fretting one against the other. And there was too, ever present, the far-off sound of the sea which is the whisper of eternal regret. Once the wind stilled for a moment and he heard a sound of heavy breathing in the darkness somewhere behind him and then the noise of an invisible creature lapping at an unseen pool and he dared not turn his head. By and by he came to a place where the shadows clustered even more thickly and here he saw the signs of many prints leading to it and none leading away. He stood still and listened and heard from somewhere deep within that darkness a noise of rustling and flapping and he knew at last for sure where he was come and his heart grew small and faint within him. The thread of his resolution, drawn out finer than an eyelash, passed beyond his own willing, lost all meaning, became absurd, a thing of the Star Born, not of himself at all. *Nothing I could say to you now would ever divert you from your destiny.* So all his life this moment had been waiting for him just as the Boy's death had waited for him and that other death when the mad priest's bolt had torn the soul from his father's breast. High above his head, invisible, a flock of birds was passing over, twittering *promise me: promise me . . .* Gone in a rush of whispering wings, like a dream. Well, so be it. He stepped forward into the darkness.

The Magpie stood at the foot of the cottage stairs and listened to the sound of the piping. It touched a spring of grief within him that had lain untapped since he was a child and the tears ran down his cheeks unheeded. He heard the piping falter and grow faint as though the boy was wandering off, and he crept silently up to the little landing and tiptoed to the door of his daughter's room, unsure whether he could still hear the music or only fancied that he did. At last, unable to restrain himself, he softly raised the latch and opened the door. He heard the sound of a chill wind blowing, the far-off murmur of the sea, and the melancholy cries of unknown birds, but all else was as a shifting smoke before his eyes, and the mellow sunlight from the window on the landing would not cross that strange, shadowy threshold. Nor, for all his courage, dared he step across it.

He stood as still as if he had been nailed to the spot and felt the cold come sliding into his bones like an October sea-mist. A smell of freshly turned damp earth hung upon the air. How long he stood there he could never tell, sometimes he thought it had been a minute only, at others he thought an hour or more; but at last he heard the sound of the piping again and it seemed to thaw the blood in his veins so that he was able to reach out and draw the door shut. He heard the music growing louder and he felt a crazy hope tug at his heart, but he dared not risk a hand again upon the latch. Yet there was something about this music that set his chilled soul twirling like an aspen leaf and even when the melody ceased his spirit still went on dancing, light as a bubble on a stream.

He heard Tom's voice saying something which he could not quite make out, followed by the sound of a dear, familiar laugh, and then he discovered the use of his own voice again. "Tom! Tom lad! Is it all right?"

There was a moment of silence, then more laughter, and the door was pulled open from within. The Magpie found himself peering into Tom's deathly white face and saw that one cheek was scratched from eye to chin as if by briers or raking nails. Behind him Witchet was sitting on the edge of the bed with the bright sunshine streaming in upon her. His voice broke. "Ah, my own sweet lass," he whispered, "and is it really you?"

"Who else should I be?"

He moved over the threshold treading as carefully as if he expected the floorboards to give way beneath him, and then he took her hands into his and felt all the leaping warmth of her young life. And her hands too he touched wonderingly as if he feared that they might melt away like snow.

"How strange you are, Dad," she said. "What's come over you?"

"You feel all right, my love? Tell me true now."

"She's fine," said Tom. "Aren't you, Witch?"

The old man put his arms around her and hugged her

to him and buried his face in her hair. "Aye, aye," he murmured. " 'Tis as you say. I do but know what I saw."

"So you shall tell none of it for my sake, Magpie," said Tom. "That do I charge you with."

"Who are you, boy? Dost thou know thyself?"

"He's Tom," said Witchet. "My Tom. And wherever he goes then I shall go there too."

Tom laughed. "Have a care, Witch, or one of these days I may be holding you to that."

"You could not hold me *from* it if you tried," she retorted.

Chapter Seven

Two days after the Ceremony of Declaration Francis and Marwys crossed over to Quantock for a brief visit to Jane. They hired two hack ponies from the cross-eyed innkeeper in Bicknoller and ambled their way southward down the long, white road to Tallon. When they reached the crest of Lydeard Hill and beheld the Isle of Blackdown lying like a plump patchwork cushion out in the sunlit Somersea Francis reined up his pony and allowed his memory to roll back the long tapestry of the years. He found it still just as bright and clear in his mind's eye as that day twenty years before when he had first stepped ashore in Chardport and made his way over the hills to Broadbury.

"What are you thinking of?" asked Marwys with a smile.

"Of Time, Marwys. Only Time. The most foolish thought of all, for there is no end to it."

"Not of Jane?"

"Oh, Jane's a part of it, and so is Alison, and that strange man they call the Magpie. And you and I both, and many another too. Old Constant, Elise, Richard—the list is endless."

"Are you not forgetting Tom?"

Francis looked down at his pony cropping the dusty

roadside grasses. "I do not forget him," he said, "but I cannot hold him in my mind's eye as I do the others. He shifts about and will not stay steady in one place."

"A wandering star."

"I know not what he is."

Marwys looked at him but said nothing.

Francis made a noise that lay part way between a sniff and a sigh. "Oh, I know what *you* would have him be."

"He *is* Jane's son, remember."

"And she The Bride of Time, eh?"

"You will not have it so, will you, Francis? I've often wondered why."

"Because, my friend, I have long since learned the danger of reading a symbol as a literal truth. A plant must be allowed to find its own way to the light, not one of our devising."

"Yet it was you gave him the Boy's pipes."

"Not I," said Francis with a faint smile. "The Bird did that. I could not help myself."

Marwys stared at him, wondering if he had misheard.

"Oh, yes," said Francis simply. "It was an act of pure impulse. Besides, I guessed that he would cheerfully steal them and then who knows where they might have ended up? This way there's still a chance we'll get them back."

Marwys laughed. "Only a chance?"

"You rate it higher?"

"I read the Testament differently from you, Francis. When first I walked this road I came to find the Child."

"And you found Tom instead."

"All that tells me is that you are no musician and that you discount what Alice told us."

Francis studied his companion thoughtfully then turned in his saddle and looked out across the Tolland channel to the far western horizon. "Well, if you prove right," he said, "his way lies there." He pivoted around till he was facing due east. "Mine here."

"Into the Second Kingdom?"

"And the Third and Fourth and all the rest of them. You heard what Philip said. They're all ripe for the plucking."

"Then your heart is still set firm on York?"

The Apostate's dark eyes seemed to flicker. "York," he murmured. "Did you hear that they have discovered where the Boy's body lies hid?"

"Hid? Did not Constant destroy it?"

"No doubt he died thinking so, but we have just learned that it was spirited away to Kentmere. We will see it enshrined beneath the High Altar yet."

"At the Cardinal's side? They'll prove uneasy bedfellows."

Francis pulled up his pony's head. "Not they, Marwys," he said. "This time it is Constant's turn to move over."

David and Tom spent their last night together lying on makeshift beds in the pottery, their own having been surrendered to the distinguished guests. It had been arranged that, in the morning, David would return to New Exeter by way of Tolland where he would collect Tom's horse. From the capital he was to accompany Francis and Marwys south to Buckfast where a ship was already waiting to take them back to Brittany. From Corlay David would travel on to his own home and thence to his ordained *disposition* in Alençon.

The realization that this was the last time they would be together had driven all thought of sleep from their minds.

"You were very quiet tonight," said David. "What tied the double tongue?"

"I find the Old Man a bit inhibiting at the best of times. Besides, I wanted to listen."

"It must have been strange hearing all that about your father."

"I knew a lot of it already. But not the Carver part. That was all new."

"Your mother never told you?"

"Not a word. Nor Magpie either. But then Mother never talks to me of the *huesh*."

"Why not?"

"She's frightened of it, I think. Or of something."

"Of you, maybe."

"Me? That's really crazy!"

"I don't see why. At times you scare *me*. Over Lord Arthur for instance."

Tom was silent.

"You know what I mean, don't you?"

"You weren't there when it happened."

"I'm very glad I wasn't."

"I could have killed him, Dave. I could have killed them all. I *know* it."

"Why didn't you?"

"Because it wasn't *me* doing it. It was something *in me* which got loose. For a moment I was as mad as he was. I *knew* what drove him—I recognized it *in myself!* I wanted to destroy *him* just as much as he wanted to destroy *her*. That's why I can't go back and try to heal him. I wouldn't dare. I couldn't trust myself."

"But you didn't finish him off. Not completely. Why not?"

"Because if I had I think I'd have finished myself off too. As it was it was touch and go."

"The Bird saved you."

Tom snorted. "Aye, but which Bird? The one I know or the one you believe in?"

"The one you believe in too."

"Do I? You know, Dave, I really envy you. You know just where you're going and you know why you're going there. Me, I'm altogether lost. I don't think I know *what* I believe in any more."

"Rubbish!"

"It's true. I think I've lost faith in Kinship. Sitting there tonight listening to the Old Man talking was like listening to someone speaking in a language I didn't *understand* any more. Francis *knows,* and he knows that he knows. All I can see is questions crowding on top of other questions and no answers I can *believe in* anywhere."

"Are you just saying this, or do you mean it?"

"And I thought you knew me!"

"That's just it, Tom. I *do* know you. And I think something's happened to you. Something you haven't told me about. Is it Alice?"

"I don't know. Maybe. Perhaps it started with her."

"Are you in love with her?"

"No."

"But you're lovers?"

"Ah, that most subtle of distinctions. Yes, of course we are."

"But that's not what we're talking about, is it?"

"No," Tom agreed. "It's not."

"Well? Are you going to tell me?"

"I don't know if I can. I don't know *how to.* But this is what I *think* happened—more or less." And he told David about Witchet's "death" from the moment of that first imperious summons to the Magpie's final entry.

David listened in absorbed silence until the recitation was concluded, then he said: "And Witch remembers nothing?"

"Nothing at all. For her it's as though it had never happened."

"Yet there—in that place you say you went—she recognized you?"

"Of course. That's why she followed me back."

"And this place—this dark place—where was it?"

"Oh, I know that well enough," said Tom. "It was in me. And it still is. I think Witch was sent to show it to me, to make me acknowledge it. After all I'm the one who's going to have to live with it. I've even given it a name. I call it the lair of The Black Bird. How sick can you get?"

"You're not sick, Tom."

"You think not? Well, what *do* you think?"

"Are you sure you want my opinion?"

"If I didn't I wouldn't be asking."

"Very well," said David. "I think you're overwrought—troubled in your mind. Most deeply troubled. I think you've been trying to hide from yourself in Alice and now you've realized that you may well end up hurting her nearly as much as her own brother did. *I think it was you who called out to Witchet at the very moment when it first dawned on you what you might be doing to Alice.* I think you chose Witch because you needed help desperately and she was the only one you knew you could count on to trust you absolutely—the one who would simply pledge her own soul for you if you asked her. She helped you to face up to something about yourself which you already suspected but had not dared to acknowledge—what I can only call the dark side of that huge sense of power and freedom you felt when you first went to the castle and played the pipes to Alice. I think you *were* given that power, you used it, and you discovered that it wasn't altogether what you'd thought it was. You thought it was power without responsibility. But power without responsibility is madness. It's what Lord Arthur had. And whatever else you may be, Tom, you're not Arthur."

A three-quarter moon was sailing serenely among the stars like a glittering galleon. Its beams slanted in through the window of the pottery and silvered a row of jugs which stood ready for firing. Tom counted them and found there were fourteen. "When you go back tomorrow," he said, "I'll give you a letter to take to Alice. Will you make sure that she gets it?"

"Of course I will."

"Don't you want to know what I'll say in it?"

"Can't I guess?"

"Yes, I expect you can." Tom sighed. "Ah, but I'll miss you, Dave. I swear to you that if it wasn't for the fact that I can't stand the sight of sick people I'd be there in Alençon with you faster than a Falcon's bolt."

"So much for Anthony, eh?"

"Just so. I'll have to tell Francis tomorrow."

"Tell him what?"

"That I'm not taking up the Downscombe *disposition.*"

"You're *not?* And when did you decide that?"

"About a minute ago."

David laughed. "You really are impossible, Tom! Are you going back to Corlay?"

"I don't suppose so. I doubt they'd have me anyway."

"What will you do?"

"I just don't know—yet. I'll think of something."

"This isn't because of what I said just now, is it?"

"You flatter yourself, friend. All you did was help me to make up my mind. I'm most grateful to you. Truly I am. I know I'd make a rotten Kinsman."

"That's absolute nonsense!"

"No, it's not. I think I've known it for months really. I just didn't want to face up to it. Somehow I'm going to have to make my own way—find my own answers. I'm not turning my back on Kinship, Dave. How could I? It would be like turning my back on myself. But I've got to prove its truths on my own pulses, not just take them second hand. We'll both meet up again somewhere, further along the road."

"But which road is it to be?"

"How do I know until I've traveled it? Anyway, does it matter? So long as we do meet?"

"No," said David. "You're right. In the end that's really all that matters."

Tom told Francis of his decision just as they were about to take their leave of each other. If Francis was surprised he concealed it admirably. Marwys even went so far as to smile, almost as if he had been expecting something of this kind all along. Tom felt his gesture had fallen more than a little flat and attempted some sort of mumbled apology. Francis waved it aside. "You have served the Cause well enough, Thomas," he said. "You take our blessing with you. You know there will always be a welcome for you at Corlay." He sketched the Sign of the Bird over him.

Tom unlooped the talisman from around his neck and handed it to Marwys. "Give Doctor Paul my regards," he said. "Tell him he was right about the counterpoint. He'll know what I mean."

"I'll see he gets the message."

Tom shook their hands. They climbed into their saddles, and to a chorus of well-wishes for a safe journey departed for Bicknoller.

David left an hour later. Tom and Witchet ferried him across to Tolland where they re-possessed the horse. In a day of farewells, Tom's leave-taking of his friend was the one that gave him the deepest pang. He was close to tears as they embraced and he muttered: "You have the letter safe?"

"Next to my heart."

"You'll write to me?"

"Aye, when I can find the time. And you?"

"Likewise."

David kissed Witchet. "Look after him for us, Witch. In spite of what Francis may think, we still need him."

He swung himself up into the saddle and smiled down at them. "The White Bird shall protect you both. *Au revoir, chers amis.*" With a final salute he kicked his heels into the horse's flanks and galloped away up the valley.

As they were sailing back to Tallon Tom said: "Have you ever fancied seeing the big wide world, Witch?"

"What do you mean?"

"Well, have you?"

"By myself, or with you?"

"With me, naturally."

She frowned. "What would we do?"

"Travel around. See places—people. You know."

"Yes, but how would we *live?*"

"Easy. I'd play the pipes. You could sing and go round with the hat."

"Are you serious?"

"Well, I've got to do *something*, and I don't see myself settling down in Tallon as a fisherman for the rest of my life."

"But what about Alice?"

"Ah," he said. "So you know about her, do you?"

"Well, I guessed. It wasn't very difficult."

"It doesn't sound the sort of life for Lady Alice, does it?"

Witchet gave him one of her long, searching looks, but made no comment.

"Well, it was just a thought," he said. "Forget it."

"Is that why you're giving up Kinship, Tom? To get away from Alice?"

"What on earth gave you that idea? Anyway, I'm not 'giving up Kinship'—I'm just giving up being a Kinsman."

"You know what I mean."

"Oh, how do I know, Witch? I'm all at sea. Hopelessly adrift. I'm just playing it by ear."

"But you know I'd go with you if you wanted me to. You didn't have to *ask* me."

"No, that's not good enough. It would have to be because *you* wanted to. It wouldn't work any other way. Not for me."

"Can I think about it?"

"Perhaps we'd *both* better think about it."

That afternoon Tom went into the pottery and said to Jane: "Which is more important to you, that pot or your own son?"

"What is it, my love?"

"I need to talk with you, Mother. But not here. Will you come for a walk with me?"

Jane got up from the wheel, rinsed her hands and dragged off her smock. "Where shall we go?"

"Somewhere we can be alone. How about along the cliffs?"

"Yes, why not? I haven't been out there for ages."

She took his hand in hers and they set off along the track which wound over the hillside above the village before rambling off northward skirting the coast. A soft summer breeze was wafting in off the sea and the sunlit gulls rode the invisible wave of air which billowed up from the cliff face. "I wondered if you were going to go straight back to New Exeter with David," she said. "I'm glad you didn't."

"What was it like seeing Francis again after all these years?"

"Strange. There was always that fire in him but now it burns as the frost burns. I was surprised he came."

"Marwys must have talked him into it."

"No. I asked Marwys that. He said Francis really wanted to come."

"And did it all happen at Corlay just like he said it did?"

"The killing, you mean? I'm sure of it. Poor Francis. I couldn't take my eyes off his scars. I tried not to look but my eyes just seemed to wander back on their own."

"You needn't worry. The Old Man must be used to it by now."

"Well, he may be, but I'm not."

By and by they came to a narrow valley down which a meager threadlet of a stream trickled out into a tiny cove. Elder bushes and hazels grew there in profusion and a faint scent of wild peppermint perfumed the dim, green tunnel of laced branches which shaded the rivulet. Tom thrust his way among the bushes and emerged into a small sunlit clearing, completely hidden from all prying eyes. "When Witch and I were small this used to be one of our secret places," he said. "I wonder if Mouse and Mike know about it."

He sat down on the sun-warmed grass, reached up for Jane's hand and drew her down beside him. "Why haven't you asked me why I'm no longer a Kinsman?"

Jane smiled. "Why are you no longer a Kinsman?"

"No, that's cheating," he protested. "I asked you first."

"Because," she said, and then shook her head.

"Because what?"

"Because, I suppose, I've never ever really thought of you as being one."

"You never told me that!"

"There didn't seem to be any point in telling you. After all I could have been wrong. I often am."

"Then what *do* you see me as?"

"A musician. Perhaps a great one. Marwys thinks so too. He said your *Quartet* would still live when Corlay had been forgotten."

"Marwys really said that?"

Jane nodded.

"What else did he say?"

"He said he didn't understand you, but that he didn't let it worry him."

"That's just like old Marwys! He didn't say anything about my going back to Corlay?"

"I gathered he thinks you've outgrown it."

Tom appeared to consider this. "He's right," he said at last. "I've been keeping half a toe in that door in case I needed it. But it wouldn't work. I'd probably end up strangling old Paul in his own beard or something equally awful."

"Do you know what you're going to do?"

"No. I really don't. That's what I want you to tell me."

For the first time a gleam of alarm seemed to shiver far down in the depths of Jane's gray eyes. "What do you mean?" she said. "How could I tell you what I don't know myself?"

He turned until he was gazing directly into her troubled face. "I want you to read me, Mother," he said calmly. "Like you once read my father and found the spirit you called 'Carver.'"

"Oh, no, Tom!" she cried. "No, that's impossible! I never do it now! Please, my love, don't ask me!"

"But I *am* asking you," he insisted. "I have to *know*, Mother!"

"Know? Know what?"

"Who I am."

She would not meet his eyes. She twisted her head aside and started to rise to her feet, but he held her fast by the arm and said: "Whatever it is you're afraid of, running away from it won't help either of us. I tell you I'm lost, Mother. I'm scared sick of what's been happening to me and you're the only one who can help me. *You must do it!*"

"Why must I?"

"Because if you don't I fear I'll sink so deep you'll never find me again. And when I do, as like as not I'll drag Witch down with me."

"What are you talking about?"

"Magpie didn't tell you?"

"Tell me what?"

"Why I came rushing back here when you were all over at New Exeter."

Jane shook her head.

"Then read it for yourself, Mother, for I'll tell you nothing more."

"You don't know what you're saying, my love. It's not like that."

"So tell me what it *is* like?"

Jane freed her arm gently from beneath his hand and with her fingertips stroked his tumbled hair lightly back from his forehead. "I would become *you*," she murmured. "I would *be* you. I would know all your secrets; everything you've ever done that you're ashamed of; all the little meannesses, the spites, the wounds, the sorrows, everything. Nothing could be hidden. Nothing. You couldn't just show me a part of you."

"And that's what you're afraid of? Knowing that sort of truth about me?"

"No," she said. "Not that sort of truth."

"What then?"

"Dear heart," sighed Jane. "When you were a tiny baby I did once read you. I didn't really mean to, it just happened by accident. Babies are still so much a part of their mothers when they're little. So close. Closer even than lovers."

"Well?"

"You were so small then, all hot and fevered, and I thought to soothe you. It seemed a natural enough thing for any mother to want to do. But when I opened my mind to yours I found things there which couldn't have been part of you at all—things *you* could never have known about or seen."

"Go on," he whispered urgently. "What sort of things?"

"At the time I thought they might have been the Boy's memories. I don't know. It was only for a second or two."

"*The Boy's?* Are you sure?"

"Of course I'm not *sure*. How could I be? Only the Boy Himself could be sure of that."

"But why didn't you tell me this before, Mother?" he cried. "It might have made so much difference!"

"Would it? Really?"

"Mother, you *must* read me! I'm begging you to! You can't *know* how important it is to me until you've seen what I've seen. Please. I need your help so much."

Jane gazed into his desperately pleading face and felt her heart melting in the heat of his fierce need for her.

She shivered violently. "Very well," she murmured. "Lie down and put your head here in my lap."

He looked up into her lovely, troubled face, dark against the bright canopy of the August sky, and smiled up at her reassuringly. "Maybe we'll find old Carver's ghost again," he said. "Wouldn't that be something?"

"Just shut your eyes, my love, and go to sleep."

"Really asleep?"

"Yes, if you can. It'll make things easier for me."

He closed his eyes obediently and at once found himself recalling the last time his head had lain in Alice's lap. He wondered uneasily what his mother would make of that. Then his breathing grew regular and gentle, the beat of his heart seemed to slow until it merged with the soft surge of the surf creaming in along the shore, and he drifted off into nowhere.

It was a willed act of total abnegation, of absolute submission, to allow yourself to sink down, depth below depth, into another human mind; to permit its naked memories to become your own, to let them print themselves upon you, be absorbed in you, and so become an integral part of you. You took them all or none. Bright flickering lightning flashes of past passion; dark glooming shapes of cloudy threat; visions which implored like cries in the night; thus did her own child's past go drifting through Jane's marveling mind.

Further and ever further down she sank to where his memories of early childhood seemed to condense like morning dew upon spring flowers, unbelievably sweet and sad, perfumed with a child's unconsidered love, intense beyond bearing. So she became that girl again through her own son's remembrance of her. All was so clear, so limpid that she seemed to float light as a butterfly among the blossoms sipping the delicious nectar pearled within them. Why had she denied herself this wonder for so long? You are my son, my own first born. What is it you fear, my love? Surely this is all . . . But soft. Still the downward drift continues. Still she is sinking, lighter than a scrap of evening thistledown, quiet as a breath, down into the ever-deepening shadows . . .

Ah, no! No! I want no more part of this! Too late. Too late. Her alarmed spirit flutters in an air too thin for its weak wings to hold it. The last frail tissues of his infant recollections are melting in the void. She feels the ache of an unimaginably ancient cold and sees a sift of alien stars across an unknown firmament. Night without end. And yet how beautiful it is. Beauty beyond all earthly dreams, beyond all human knowing. Is this star-webbed emptiness your heritage, my love? Child of my own heart's blood? It is no part of me. Fathomless, silent, it waits as it has waited since the dawn of Time, for ages beyond number, till one shall come on silver wings to touch its frozen beauty into life . . .

The vision fades. Is gone. Light as a soaring spark her soul flies up. I know now who you are, know too that I have always known. You are my son, my own dear son, Child of the Bride of Time, who for his birthright shall claim the secrets of the very stars themselves.

A tear like a liquid diamond fell and splashed Tom's cheek. He opened his eyes and found himself gazing straight up into hers. "What is it? What's the matter, Mother? What did you find?"

Her lips trembled but the words remained locked within her.

"You're crying!"

"It happens," she sighed. "It often used to happen so," and leaning down she kissed him tenderly upon the forehead. "Marwys is right," she whispered sadly. "I think I always knew it too."

Tom drew in a breath so deep it seemed as if it would never end. "Not the Boy, then?"

She shook her head. "Those memories are gone. Perhaps they were never there. You are the only one, my love. Old Morfedd's Star-Born. The Child of the Bride of Time."

For a long time Tom lay there without moving, his eyes closed tight. At last he drew in another huge breath, rolled over and sat up. "The lost singer of the Song of Songs," he muttered, "found by the Wayward Wanderer. How *could* that old man have known?" He gave a harsh bark of laughter that had not the slightest trace of humor in it. "And I thought that surrendering my calling was my *own* idea! I'm trapped like a fly in a web."

"But which of us is not, my love? Who is truly free?"

"How can you *accept* that, Mother? I feel like some idiot puppet dangling on the Wizard's string!"

"Yet you accept the *huesh.*"

"I accept it only because it's always been there. But one day I shall turn my back on it just to see what happens."

Jane reached out, caught him by the shoulders and drew his head back against her breast. "Tom, Tom, the Piper's Son," she murmured. "Are you still looking for that finger-post at the crossroads?"

"You saw that too, did you?"

"I saw many things."

He twisted his head and looked up at her. "And was Witch there?"

"Of course."

"And Alice?"

She smiled. "Oh, yes, I saw Alice."

"Well?"

She shook her head. "Alice is a song to you. Surely you know that."

"Ah, you are so right," he said. "But how sweet a song. She is like wine, Mother. My head reels just to think of her."

"When you speak like that it is with your father's voice. How soon do you return to New Exeter?"

"You know that too?"

"I know *you*. You will not leave her to grieve. You cannot. *That* is the web you are caught in, my love. So you will go to her and ease her aching heart with your music as once, long ago, you eased mine."

"And then what?"

"Then?" Jane raised her head. She saw two primrose yellow butterflies come floating across the little clearing and watched them as, in their own oddly arbitrary but purposeful way they wobbled up and vanished over the hazel bushes that hid the muttering sea. "Then will you not go to seek out your destiny over the hills and far away?"

A glimmer of frost lay in the shadowed places beneath the trees where the pale October sunlight had not yet warmed, but the forest path was dry and the drifted leaves crunched and rustled underfoot as Tom and Witchet came swinging down the hill toward New Barnstaple. Twice they paused, once to gather handfuls of young mushrooms, and once to watch two gray squirrels performing aerial acrobatics high in the branches overhead. When they came to a place where the path forked Tom said: "Left or right?"

"That one," said Witchet who could never tell one hand from the other unless she took time off to think about it.

"Then it looks like a sea voyage for us, Witch. How much have we got?"

"Six royal, three quarters, and seven pence," she replied promptly.

"A fortune! Enough for Spain anyway. *Olel Habla Espagnol?*"

"What?"

"I think it means 'Do you speak Spanish?' "

"But I can't *sing* in Spanish!"

"Oh, they won't care. Anyway you'll soon pick it up. And just think of those oranges Marwys told us about. Can't you see them hanging there like golden lanterns in the trees? They all play guitars in Spain, Witch. And they dance—like this." He flung his arms into the air, snapped his fingers, and pranced about kicking up the leaves into a fiery snowstorm.

Witchet laughed. "But what if there isn't a boat for Spain?"

"Well, we'll go somewhere else. Ireland. America. Who cares?"

"On six royal?"

"We'll work our passage."

"You're crazy, Tom. Really you are."

"So what does that make you? Come on, lass. We're missing our tide. I swear I can smell those oranges already!" Catching hold of her by the hand he sprinted away with her down the path which she had chosen.

Like a trail of silver bubbles the sound of their laughter lingered on the frosty air long after they had passed out of sight.